"I don't kill without reason." His look contemptuous. "And you may be Selene's only hope."

I glanced at Rill while trying not to move, then back at him. "Who is Selene?"

"Selene is this planet," he said. "A planet whose females have been increasingly born sterile."

"Would we," I said, swallowing hard, "be of more use alive or dead?"

The Selene
Experiment

Seized, substituted and sentenced... **to die!**

The Selene
Experiment

Wendy C. Giffen

Wendy C Giffen

wendycgiffen@gmail.com
www.wendycgiffen.com

ISBN 13: 978-0-9878279-3-7
ISBN: 0987827936

Printed in 10/13pt Minion Pro
Cover design by Martin Driscoll

Published by
SANDYS · HEATH & BALCHIN
PUBLISHING HOUSE LIMITED
Salt Spring Island, BC, Canada

This book is
lovingly dedicated to
Andrew.

Chapter One

I had no premonition to warn me, not even an uneasy feeling. The evening was humid, with a rich, earthy smell rising from the dense border of flowers and shrubs.

One moment, I was putting chlorine pucks into the swimming pool skimmer, thinking about my children and their families arriving in a few days, and the next I was fighting desperately to free myself from a web of thin filaments that wrapped around me, sticking fast to my skin and relentlessly tightening. I remember thinking that all my loving preparations for the weekend were for nothing.

Terror, pain, and excruciating heat.

Those were my last memories. I don't talk about them now—but it's much harder to keep them out of my dreams.

I am told the experience caused deep shock and that I was suffering extreme withdrawal symptoms.

Later, before my vision was restored, there was a patient voice that repeated endless words. My mind desperately grabbed at them. When I was passive and didn't strain to understand, they took form in my mind and stayed there.

Gradually, I began to glimpse things that seemed almost normal—not just the hands, but sunshine and a table with shadows across it. I soon became aware that the smaller hands belonged to me. They didn't look like my hands, but I followed the line of the arms up to my shoulders. They weren't my shoulders either, but when one of the hands came up to touch it, I felt it.

It seemed odd that big problems didn't worry me—like not knowing where I was or what had happened to me—while little things such as not being able to recognize the food I ate did bother me. I wondered vaguely if it was fattening!

Slowly, my senses gained strength. I heard things further away ... some kind of bird outside the window, an exchanged greeting as footsteps passed my room. The plain yellow walls of my room came into view, along with the room itself: a window with slots in the top and bottom for the air to circulate, a triangle of legs supporting the bed, and bright white sheets that were warm to the touch.

I could smell the air scented with the lingering aroma of a savory food. I felt the texture of the low, molded table with its hot, sunny patches. Yet what really troubled me was that, although the chairs and table were easily recognizable, they had an alien quality, just like the room and the food.

It was both familiar and different. So was I. The smoothness of my skin and the long silkiness of my hair were different—and even in my strangely passive state, I was aware that I wasn't behaving normally ... not even my kind of normally!

I began to sense a routine governing my life. The faces grew into people and came at different times. A man came in the mornings and was impatient with my slowness. He would tug at my hair in annoyance when he brushed it, making me yelp. He slapped me. I didn't cry out again.

I didn't like doing things for him. I wouldn't lift the shapes, and I pretended I didn't understand when he wanted me to repeat words. After a time, he didn't bother with me. He would just walk up and down, looking at something from his sash pocket and talking to himself.

The woman would come later, carrying food. She seemed encouraged when I did things for myself, like the first time I came to the table to eat without being told or the first time I took the lid off my dish by myself. Later, she would press a small panel in the wall, and part of it would slide back to reveal a cleansing room. It was she who cared for me as if I were a child. Perhaps if she had been the one to teach me, things would have been very different. I have been told that if my return to normalcy had been noticed, I would never have escaped. Indeed, I would almost certainly have had a fatal accident.

After the meal, she would read to me and point at the pictures. Unless we had some project, like pushing bright beads into soft clay tablets to form patterns, I was put to bed. I was often in bed by late afternoon and left there till the following morning.

Nobody came to check on me. I suppose I must have slept a lot, or laid there, or maybe they just didn't care! I began trying to see the faces of friends and neighbors in the textured paper ceiling that sometimes moved in the breeze. One curve and splattered shadow on the ceiling looked like the reflection of our willow in the still water of the pool.

Then came the time I got up and began to examine the room, gently touching each thing, stroking or pressing it. It was when I bent down to sniff the fragrant air coming through the slots in the window that I first saw my reflection.

I may have been young at heart, but it had been the body of a grandmother that had put the pucks in the skimmer of the pool … yet it was the reflection of a young woman who looked back at me from the window. Perhaps I should have been more surprised than I was, but I think that my hands had prepared me for the change, although I had never wondered at their youthfulness.

For the first time, I didn't passively accept the situation. I asked myself which was the reality: the woman in the reflection, or the dream of the past? Was it possible that both could be real?

A movement outside drew my eyes to the vista beyond. A white sun shone in a hazy sky of pale lavender. Just below me, a sward of mossy green was surrounded on three sides by a building of functional right angles forming a U. On the fourth side, opposite my window, the lawn stopped at a river's edge, where a profusion of unrecognizable and heavy flowers moved in a breeze. There were stone steps going down into the water, and across the river, dense and unfamiliar greenery stretched to the horizon.

The movement drew my eyes again, and I found myself looking at a blue colored bird clinging to a spiny plant growing up the wall.

Pulling a shelled seed from the stem, it held it firmly in one clawed foot and cracked the seed open with its short, strong beak and dug out the soft fleshy part. It turned its head and regarded me for a moment before hopping out of sight into the foliage.

I stood there, aware of the smooth, warm floor beneath my bare feet. I was aware of my hands on the cool glass and that I had been holding my breath. I exhaled slowly. Where I came from, only birds of prey had eyes on the front of their head … and none of them glowed!

I returned to bed and lay there, trying to block out the dawning realization that this wasn't the world I had lived on, and I wasn't the woman I had been.

I don't know how long my semi-aware and totally passive state lasted, but I do know that my return to a fully conscious state a day or two later was abrupt and mercifully timed. Again, I was in bed. My kindly attendant was bending over me and patting my hand. I looked up into her pale yellow eyes and saw they were full of pity.

As I looked, they filled with tears, and abruptly she pulled her hand away and said, "It is well that you don't understand!" She turned stiffly and went to the door without a backward look. As the door slowly closed behind her, I heard someone speaking as they approached.

"Cheer up, Mogan, the dummies won't need anyone to tend them after tomorrow …" I couldn't hear the last part of the man's sentence as he strode past.

"Is there no hope? Couldn't they reconsider?" Mogan's voice rose shrilly. "They're doing no harm, and there are only three of them left!"

The door sighed shut, and the reply was too fast and too muffled for me to understand. The footsteps receded, and in the silence that followed, I became aware that I had listened to and understood a foreign language I was beginning to think in. Then, lying in the narrow bed, I felt myself start to go rigid with shock. My heart pounded loudly in my ears as I fought against the terror swelling inside me.

Swinging my feet to the floor, I sat there shaking. I tried to reject the knowledge that leapt to my mind. They had been talking about me! Three dummies, he'd said, and I was one of them. After tomorrow, we'd never need looking after again!

Suddenly and clearly, I knew that I was going to be sick. I stumbled desperately to the wall and palmed the plaque that opened the cleansing room door ...

Afterward, I carefully cleaned the indentation in the counter and put everything back in its place. If I was to escape, they must see nothing abnormal about my room or myself.

I had no desire to step forward and introduce myself and explain things. If a harmless simpleton could be disposed of because of its nuisance value, a sane alien—and I was sure I was both—would be dispatched with indecent haste.

I was not aware that anyone checked on me in the afternoons or at night, but I decided to take no chances. Back in bed, I smoothed the sheets over me as Mogan had left them and lay staring at the ceiling, turning over in my mind all the information about my environment that I had so far.

Judging from the sounds I'd heard beyond the door, there must be a corridor there. If there were other rooms off it, they were not in use as the footsteps came and went with no pause until they were at my door and I had heard no other doors opening or closing except at the far ends of the hall where the footsteps started and ended. That suggested our corridor had a door at each end that opened into another corridor.

I frowned. I sometimes heard a door opening, a few footsteps and voices, then a door shutting and silence. I considered the implications and decided the other two might have rooms at each end of the corridor just this side of the main access doors.

I knew, or could guess, nothing about the building beyond the passage. I could see from the window that the building was large. It was absurd to think I could wander about it unnoticed until I found an exit. On the other hand, there was a river at the end of the lawn. I didn't like the idea. If there wasn't something nasty in the river, there was sure to be something even worse on the other side. I had an unpleasant feeling that alien planets, and I had come to accept that I was on one, had alien animals with nasty alien eating habits!

Abruptly, the door opened. I didn't move. The moment the man's face came into view, I feared him. My instinct was not fooled by the blandness of his flabby face, for his slightly bulging eyes betrayed a sick pleasure and anticipation, blended with a revulsion of myself. The soft, full mouth was pursed in a way both stubborn and cruel. His grey tunic and pink hose contrasted with the woman's long green shift.

Behind his short, dumpy figure stood Mogan, her lean and weathered countenance looking rather sick. I was grateful that shock had rendered my expression witless.

"You may rest assured, Mogan, that your obstructive attitude has been noted." His voice was hard, with no vestige of compassion.

"You must do as you think right, sir, but as I have explained, I'm sure they are more aware than they seem." Her voice rose in distress. "It's bad enough to reduce them when they've committed no crime. To allow their last moments to be ones of terror is inexcusable." She wrung her work-worn hands, an ineffectual gesture that brought a sneer to the man's lips.

"Your concern for them is touching, Mogan," he snapped, "though rather misplaced. "Had they recovered, their end would have been more inexcusable."

"But, sir, the whole plan ..."

The man moved toward the bed, ignoring her. "Get the creature sitting up, then give it this." He held out a small medicine cup half-filled with a bluish liquid. Mogan slid her arm gently under my shoulders and raised me to a sitting position.

"Will this be enough?" she asked anxiously. Coming no nearer to the bed than he had to, he put the cup into Mogan's hand.

"More than enough. It'll still be asleep when they come tomorrow." He sounded angry, but I couldn't see his face as Mogan was bending over me and putting the mixture to my lips. I had no intention of swallowing the mixture, but Mogan must have had considerable experience with recalcitrant patients, for with a quick movement my nose was pinched shut and my head tipped back and the bitter dose was down my throat.

Had Mogan been allowed to linger as her tender heart desired, my future would have been hours long. Impatiently, he motioned her through the door and shut it decisively behind them.

I leapt from the bed and frantically palmed at the bathroom door plaque. It responded with agonizing slowness. Leaning over the smooth green hollow in the counter, I pushed my finger down my throat and gagged. Trying again, I held it there and succeeded in bring up both the mixture and the remainder of my dinner.

I was clammy and shaking. Carefully, I put my hands beneath the hole above the hollow, and the water came gushing out. I drank as much as I could, then once again pushed my finger down my throat and retched. Wearily, I repeated the process until I was sure my stomach was empty. I rinsed my mouth, wiped my face, and drank some more cold water to ease my tender throat.

As I leaned back against the smooth, cool wall, I thanked the powers that be for having been given an oral medication and not an injection.

I remained in the cool green room until the shaking left my limbs, and although still clammy, I decided it was safer to return to the bed to make my plans. The bed faced the door, and I slipped quickly between the warm sheets and resumed the position they had left me in, shutting my eyes in case Mogan returned.

I felt a hysterical desire to laugh. I remembered as a small girl I used to do exactly the same thing when I heard my mother's footsteps coming up the stairs to my bedroom when I was supposed to be asleep and not reading. I remembered feeling guilty, frightened, and excited all at the same time. I remembered the strain of looking relaxed. Things hadn't changed much—only now I didn't feel guilty.

My knowledge of what lay beyond the room was pitiful, but so were the choices open to me. I would have to enter the corridor, if only to find the other two! Even in my newly rational state of mind, it never occurred to me to attempt an escape without them. That they may have been drugged filled me with dismay.

I could see time was passing by the growing length of the table's shadow on the floor. A rough plan formed in my mind, with some alternatives for when things went wrong, which I was sure they would as the variables far exceeded any known facts. As the pale twilight increased to the point of low visibility, I reassured myself that from the lack of sound in my part of the building, the day was ending as usual.

This wing always had an empty feeling at dusk, which was intensified by the muted sounds of life and movement coming from across the lawn and the occasional gleam of light from between imperfectly closed shutters.

Having decided there was nothing within the room that would help as a disguise, I swung nervously to my feet and went straight to the door. With my ear against it, I listened, holding my breath.

I pulled the handle toward me as Mogan did, and the door opened inward. Peering down the passage, I wondered if institutions were universal. Except that there seemed to be light without lighting, I could almost have been looking down a passage in my own local hospital. I half expected a uniformed nurse to appear and assure me that I was just having a bad dream and that she would get me a pill.

But this wasn't my local hospital. Behind one of these doors could be someone who wanted to kill me.

There were two doors on the opposite side of the corridor, and on my side there were several doors at regular intervals. I had never heard anyone stop along this passage except at my door, but the two doors across the way drew me like Pandora's box.

"Nothing ventured ..." I thought. My bare feet made no noise as I hurriedly crossed the hall to the nearest door. I pulled at the handle and nothing happened. So I pushed, and it opened easily inward. I gazed in by the light from the hall. The room was nearly bare. Against the wall near the door was a small table and chair. Lying on the table was a pile of printed forms waiting to be filled in.

The only other thing in the room was a waist-high rectangular table. One of the short ends was attached to the smooth white wall by a large metal pivot. Where it attached there was an empty niche in the wall, about three and a half feet wide by three feet high and two feet deep. The table had an unusual surface, as slick as wet ice but not cold to the touch, and the end farthest from the wall pivot seemed capable of rising.

There was nothing here that could be of any use to me. I closed the door and moved on. The next room was more fruitful. I brushed against the wall when entering, and bright lights came on. When I turned from closing the door, the first thing I saw was a pale green, full-length coverall like the one Mogan wore. It hung from a peg against the wall.

The room appeared to be a cross between a lab and a pharmacy. Along the wall, rows of square bottles with unreadable labels squatted on narrow shelves. Some contents looked familiar, like the bright yellow powder that proved to be sulfur. As I checked them, I noticed that none had screw lids, just plastic or glass stoppers. I lifted the stopper from a large bottle of clear liquid and blinked as ammonia fumes brought tears to my eyes. As I replaced the stopper, my fingers lingered thoughtfully on the bottle.

If one could just spray it, I thought it might slow down an attacker, human or animal. Looking around for inspiration, I realized wryly that the only sprays I knew of were cans—and heaven knew how they worked—and spray perfume bottles, of which this room suffered a considerable lack.

A large yellow canister stood clipped to the wall, reminiscent of a fire extinguisher. My attempts to remove it from its wall clip were in vain, which was perhaps just as well since it was quite heavy and my continual repositioning had placed my foot beneath it. I wasn't entirely sorry to leave it and return to the rows of bottles.

After poring over them, I stooped and opened the cupboards beneath the countertop. Here, as I had hoped, I found empty bottles of various sizes. There were also weird kinds of test tubes, syringes, and several other half-familiar things. Unfortunately, there was nothing in which to carry several bottles so I confined myself to six small vials and one larger one, all of which could fit easily into the placket pockets of the pale green coverall.

Carefully, I poured liquids and powders from previously selected bottles into the vials, and it was then I noticed the faint dust rings where they had stood. I regarded them with interest. It was reassuring to have my earlier deductions confirmed … the room hadn't been used for some days.

I didn't take off my blue shift, which I knew to be shorter than the coverall, but I attempted to put the green gown over mine. It took me a little while to find the concealed fastenings, but I found them easy to use once I had. It was quite a good fit really, though a trifle shorter than Mogan's.

Slipping the vials into my pockets, I was reaching for the door before I realized that my disguise was far from complete. Nurses or attendants with bare feet and loose, hip-length hair were unlikely to be the norm.

A ruthless search of the room failed to provide shoes, rubber bands, or scissors. "Oh well, what can't be cured," I muttered as I again went back to the door and listened.

Back in the corridor, I decided to investigate the door at the right end of the corridor first, although I don't know why. I sped silently down the hall to the last orange door.

My approach to the door was very quiet, and so the opening of the door took the occupant by surprise. Her face was a mask of frozen fear as her great black eyes stared at me. Her body was frozen in the act of knotting a sheet.

Chapter Two

"Need a hand?" I said, grinning reassuringly. "Not that I think the window's the best way of course, but perhaps you know more than I do. That wouldn't be hard."

She just swallowed. She didn't move or say anything, she just stared at me ... and swallowed again.

I had shut the door behind me as I entered, so now I came and sat on her bed and looked her over carefully. She looked Asian, but she might not have been from Earth—and even if she was, it was unlikely she spoke English.

"Do you speak English?" I asked, feeling ridiculous. I wondered if I should try "Parlez-vous Français?" or "Sprechen sie Deutsch?" It wasn't as if my French or German were even passable!

Then, haltingly, I spoke in my new language.

"I am not from here," I said. "They want to ..." I paused, searching for the word, "reduce me. So I am going to run away. Are you going too?"

The girl dropped back on to the bed, burying her lovely face in her slender hands, her long blue-black hair falling forward. She wept silently for a few moments, shaking badly. Soon she grew calmer and straightened up and looked at me.

"I go," she replied, and then more boldly, "I going."

I pointed to the window, which looked out over the same courtyard as mine.

"Why the window?" I asked.

She struggled for a word; obviously, we could both describe things in our own languages, but in our new language, many words were missing or slow to come.

"Doorway bad," she announced at last. She pointed to the wall nearest the end of the corridor. "They walking at night, not many, but regular."

A night watchman? A guard? Perhaps medical staff on duty making the rounds? No, not staff, because none came in to check on us at night.

"I guess it's out the window then," I said. I reached for the sheet. Even tied together, the two sheets would never reach the ground—it would be best to tear them into strips and make a rope. Holding one short end in both hands, I gave a hard jerk to start the tear. All my tugging was in vain; the fabric would not rip. I looked up to see the girl watching my efforts.

"Don't worry, I have sheets too, and the other one must as well."

"The other?" She darted anxious looks around the darkening room. Her vocabulary was worse than mine, and although she had understood enough to realize that her life was in danger, it seemed could not grasp the fact that others besides us were kept here.

"Yes, there is one other. I haven't found her yet, but I know where she is if she hasn't been ... reduced. I will bring her and the sheets." I got up slowly, watching her. She seemed terrified. Jumping up, she grabbed my arm.

"Just us! We go now!" Her fear made her ugly, and her grip was so tight it hurt. I pointed to the sheets and spoke slowly for her.

"These sheets aren't long enough. We need more sheets. I'll get the sheets." She seemed relieved and released my arm, nodding.

"Yes, sheet, more sheet."

I listened at the door before opening it. As I sped up the permanently bright corridor, I could understand her fears, although several things about her puzzled me.

At the far end of the corridor, I paused at the door before opening it. I heard nothing. I didn't want to see a dead body, but I couldn't leave without knowing.

I pushed firmly, and the door opened into the darkened room. The first thing I noticed was that the occupant was humanoid and alive, and the second was that she was going to kill me.

I had never liked hard ball games, but if my grudging assistance had done little to improve my brother's batting, it had at least taught me to duck rather than to step back, and it was this instinct that saved my life.

Rill—for she told me that was her name—assured me later that any upright evasive movement would have been doomed to failure. Of a clever and inventive race, she had adapted the beads, lacings, and net bags of our therapy courses into a deadly weapon, like a cross between a sandbag and the *bolas* of South America. If not killed outright, I would have been unconscious long enough for her to finish the job.

But I ducked instinctively, and it went over my head, struck the wall of the passage beyond, and fell to the floor.

She crouched to spring even as it missed me, but she didn't follow through. We both just crouched there in the light from the doorway looking at each other.

Slowly, she straightened. "You are not one of them," she stated.

"No," I said weakly as I rose. "There's you, me, and another girl down the corridor. We're all that's left."

"I thought I was the last, he told her I was," she said.

"Well," I said, pointing to the sheets across the darkened room, "the other girl is waiting, and we could use your sheets."

"Is that what you came for?" she asked, looking straight at me.

"No, I've got sheets of my own. I knew there were three of us, but not if you were still alive. I couldn't leave without knowing, you see." I rather thought she did because she smiled a lovely smile, the sort that makes you feel special and warm.

"Yes, well," I muttered, embarrassed. "We'd better be going then." Grabbing the sheets from her bed, I went out into the bright corridor and waited for her. Carefully, she closed the door, and picking up her innocent-looking weapon, we turned and silently sped down the passage.

Recent events had shaken me a bit, so I opened the door to the brunette's room carefully. She glared past me at my lean companion, and then held her hand out for the sheets in my hand.

The other girl came from behind me, and in the light from the doorway, they soon had the two new sheets tied to the others, a light heap on the darkness of the floor.

Rill closed the door, indicating the light might be seen from outside. Signaling for our help, she moved the bed to the window and crouched down to tie one end of the sheets to one of bed's three legs.

I stepped across to peer out the window. The lights on the left of the square glowed through hangings or around closed shutters. On the right, a beam of light from a ground floor window lay across the lawn. I touched Rill's shoulder and pointed to the light.

"Should we crawl beneath the window? It's high enough from the ground. Or wait till it's turned off?"

Rill looked thoughtful. "We might make a noise if we crawl under it … best wait, but out there."

It was then I realized what a fool I was. I had never really examined the window. Now I understood that the adjustable air slots at the top and bottom of the window were there because the window didn't open! Fear and hopelessness overwhelmed me for a moment. The other two noticed, even in the gloom. The girl reached past Rill and grabbed my shoulder.

"What is it?" she hissed.

"The window," I said, pointing, "it won't open." The girl moaned and began to rock back and forth.

I looked at Rill. "She says someone checks this corridor every so often at night."

"The walking came when you with her," the girl wailed softly.

Rill looked thoughtful. "This building is in silence, and only the corridors have light."

I nodded—the grass beyond our window was in darkness.

"We will have to go through the building," she concluded. "I can kill if it comes to that." She picked up her weapon, and her teeth gleamed in the darkness.

I touched the other girl as she rocked in despair. "Come on, we'll be all right." She moaned softly again and continued rocking. Rill and I exchanged glances.

"Look, my name is Rowhan, what's yours?" I tried to speak calmly as the moments fled past. She stopped rocking and looked at me; trivialities, she could cope with.

"Loona," she muttered.

"And I'm Rill," put in our companion, "and this," she added, "is a door, and we're leaving by it."

Rill opened the door and gestured for us to hurry. "The passage light will be seen through the window," she hissed as we hurried past.

The door closed behind us, and in the corridor we looked at each other. Both Rill, tall and lithe with short, curly auburn hair, and Loona, pale and petite with her long, straight black hair, wore pale blue shifts. They must have seen me as a slender strawberry-blonde in my attendant's long, pale green coverall. We would never pass as hospital staff, but there was not much we could do about it.

"Best of luck," I thought as I turned to the main passage door. It opened in the same way as the others, and in a moment we were looking into a large, airy stairwell leading downward. It was brightly lit, and on the other side, facing away from the square, it had windows at about waist height that stared into the night.

I pointed to the windows. Silently, we dropped to our knees and crawled to the stairs, slithering down on our stomachs. The floor below us had an identical landing, and the stairs continued down. So did we.

The third floor down was the last. Two doors opened from the landing, one into an identical corridor as the ones above, the other out into the night—but it was on the wrong side, away from the square and the river.

I don't know how long the arguments were hissed back and forth. Moments seemed like ages. We knew nothing about this other side of the building and could be caught at once, while Rill knew that people sometimes entered the lawn-swept square from the corner beneath her room.

We only had one chance, and the consequences of being captured would be death. I think if Loona had insisted on separating or going outside, Rill would have knocked her out and dumped her in an empty room. Somehow, even in the short time we had known her, I became convinced she was capable of dealing ruthlessly and competently with fools.

Scowling, Loona gave in, and we entered the deserted corridor and softly made our way to the door at the far end. So far, we hadn't heard any noise, but as we approached the door, we could hear muffled noises from the building's left wing. Rill eased the door open a crack.

A blast of sound met us. The small foyer was empty except for racks of cloaks and wraps on the opposite wall. Various footwear waited beneath them. After the silence of our days and nights, the door on the left seemed to almost vibrate with laughter, the click of dishes and glasses, and something faintly musical. The one to the right was still and silent.

I touched Rill and pointed to the footwear. She nodded. We sped across the room and each scooped up the stoutest pair that looked about our size, and grabbing serviceable garments from the rack, we veered right toward the door to the square. Then we saw Loona still crouched, panic-stricken, in the doorway behind us.

I grabbed her as a loud burst of laughter from the other door sent fear pounding through my veins, and Rill swept up another pair of boots and a cloak.

Carefully closing the door behind us and sinking into the intense darkness outside, Rill turned and forced the leather onto Loona's feet. I swiftly covered her light shift with the cloak, while Rill covered herself. With each of us holding one of Loona's hands, we sprinted across the lawn, dragging the petrified girl through the deepening gloom to the opposite side of the square, where we crouched against the wall in a deeper darkness. We were only a little way away from an open and lighted window.

We had hardly caught our breath when someone sighed within the room, and there was an accompanying creak of furniture as if someone had stretched. Then the scrape of a chair being pushed back. Moments later, an arm stretched through the window to close the metal shutters, and the window closed. A few heartbeats later, we saw the light seeping around the shutters go out. Rill made us wait a few minutes lest the person return for something. Then, still clutching Loona and keeping to the deeper shadows, we hurried down the lawn toward the river.

We passed the nodding, heavily scented blooms and went down the stone steps to the water's edge, where I stooped to make a bundle of my cloak and shoes in preparation for the swim across the river. Loona pulled my sleeve and pointed into the darkness to the left.

"Here I've seen ..." she stopped, desperately trying to think of the word.

"A boat?" I supplied, but I didn't wait for a reply. I moved along the wide steps toward the left, where I could just make out a restraining wall along the river bank. A weed-draped rope dangled from a ring set into the wall. After a little pulling of the slimy line, a long and shallow boat appeared out of the watery darkness.

Rill had quickly guessed what I was looking for, and as the small boat came into view, she pulled it alongside the steps. Loona stepped in as I struggled with the reluctant line in the dark. Rill held the boat until, with a successful grunt, I was able to release it and scramble into our craft. With a nimble leap, she joined us as we floated away from the steps and began to drift down the river.

The boat was low in the water, and a few inches of rain sloshed around in the bottom. Our feet were instantly soaked, as was the bottom of my coverall, but my cloak and shoes were safely on my lap. Rill had not put her shoes on yet. We cared not at all for these minor discomforts as we watched the lighted buildings slip away from us. The muted noises grew fainter until the occasional gurgling of the black river beneath our hull was the only sound we heard.

The boat turned lazy circles in the dark. The darkness was humid, containing the rank scent of river vegetation, muddy water, and the almost overpowering smell of the densely growing plants. Every now and then, an elusive breeze carrying the scent of unseen blossoms, warm and heady, would caress us like the memory of a lover's kiss.

The sable sky above us glowed with myriad stars. There were other sounds now, besides the river, the night breezes stirring the leaves, and the occasional scrape of unseen reeds along the hull. We heard small rustlings of birds in the deeper blackness of the unfamiliar trees crowding the water's edge. The occasional night bird twittered, and we heard the plop of disturbed water. Many long minutes passed before I realized what sounds were missing—and what things.

There was no whine of winged insects homing in on a meal, no irritated slapping sounds from their victims, and I had not yet identified the localized rustlings made by small animals nor noticed anything like swooping bats wheeling hungrily in the darkness.

"Rill, there aren't any … buzz." I made gestures in the dark as Mogan hadn't shown me any pictures of insects. She nodded.

"Not many animals either," she replied.

"Many? I haven't heard any!" I exclaimed.

"Oh yes, I heard something small entering the water, and another thing in the reeds, but so little sign of animal life is very odd." She spoke softly, for sound carries over water.

"Morgan showed pictures of animals," Loona said. "Birds, small things," she added vaguely.

"I don't remember that," I said, "but I haven't been normal … for very long."

"I haven't either," agreed Rill, "but I did notice that I wasn't my normal self sometime ago, but then I sort of slept again."

"Actually," I said, then I paused uncomfortably. "I looked rather older before all this, and—"

Rill laughed softly. "I've definitely improved. I was an old brown creature, the ruler of all my … family." In the darkness, she stroked her arm appreciatively. "Now I'm very pretty again, but there are none of my men to see me!"

Loona sniffed her disbelief in the darkness. "I always pretty, I just as pretty as I am," she announced smugly. "My people not thinking you beautiful, they like my white skin and black hair, they like small and slender. You tall and brown, you hair short!"

But even her rudeness couldn't disturb our newfound camaraderie. The silence lengthened as we lounged in quiet contemplation.

"Where did you come from, Loona?" I asked as I felt around for something to bail with. My feet were getting prune-like and cold.

"Suwon in Gyeonggi," she managed.

It meant nothing to me. "Can you remember the name of the planet you lived on?" I asked hopefully.

She said something that sounded vaguely Chinese, but I didn't recognize it. Then she added, "But on *Star Trek* they called it Earth." She sounded rather forlorn.

"Good, that's where I come from too," I said, pleased. I turned to Rill's shape in the darkness as I scooped up water from the bottom of the boat with a container that had bobbed against my foot. "Where do you come from, Rill?"

"Not that place," she said. She leaned forward and signaled for Loona not to trail her fingers in the water.

I tried again. "The people from our planet have many names for it. We might not have used yours, talk about where you lived. Were you by the sea?" I finished the sentence hesitantly, only half remembering the picture Mogan had shown me and the word she had used for "sea."

Rill's voice was contemptuous in the inky shadows as we passed beneath a denser mass of foliage. "By the sea? Are you a mad one? The sea animals would eat even such as my people."

Not Earth, I guessed. "In the mountains perhaps?"

"The forks of Dehall that straddle our ball would kill any coming so close," Rill said.

"Definitely not Earth," I concluded.

Just then the boat bumped into something, and we were jolted in our places. Rill raised a stick she had earlier broken off a tree. She pushed it into the dark water from where she sat in the bow. "Just the edge of some ground," she supplied in a few moments. "Shall we get off here? It could be an island or the river bank."

"Well, I'd rather not," I replied unenthusiastically. "I'd like to keep floating until daylight, so that I can see where we are, and so I'll know I'm as far from that place as possible."

Loona was fervent in her agreement, and Rill was quite happy to continue, but she pointed out that we had no notion of what the river would do, nor when we would touch bank again.

I thought of rapids, and waterfalls, and even of being taken out to sea, but I judged the river to be too wide and slow for the first two, and the smells were all wrong for the last. I explained my feelings to Rill, who agreed, but she added that one never really knew with rivers. I made a mental note not to visit her planet.

I didn't share my fears that upon finding us gone and the boat missing, the river would be the first place they searched. Getting away from it with the very first light should be a priority. I would save that for later, if Rill didn't mention it first. Having finished the bailing, I settled back in my seat.

"Do either of you know how we got here, or why?" I asked. "And why, having got us, are they trying to kill us?"

"No," Rill said promptly, leaving me to guess that she had been thinking about it too. "We are from different planets, you and I were older evidently, and Loona was younger. The only thing we have in common is that we are females, and as there are so few of us, even that may be of no significance."

"Why do you think we look so much younger? I look like I did at university!" I had used the English phrase for it, and imagining their looks of inquiry in the darkness, I added, "That's a place of learning for adults."

"Well, I don't see that food needs to be young, and they had plenty of time to eat us, so we weren't changed for food," commented Rill.

"I not like this talk! I not food!" wailed Loona softly.

"Well, whatever the reason was, we don't seem to have been a success, or they wouldn't have decided to kill us. I got the impression from something Mogan said that there was a plan we were meant to recover, but from what the man said, we would still have been killed. I just don't understand it." I paused, but they made no comment. "I have no idea how I got here. I was outside by our pool. What about you?"

"I was overseeing the gathering of medicinal herbs," Rill said. "Suddenly, one of the girls cried out. Before I could do more than glance up, sticky, tight bands were around my body. I could barely breath. I don't remember anything after that, not for a long time." Rill spoke calmly in the darkness.

Loona whimpered. "I coming home with girlfriends. Much shopping, good deals … then much screaming. I see big shadow on ground, and then I squeezed very much. Not remember more," she said sadly.

I had the oddest feeling she was mourning the lost purchases.

The night passed peacefully enough, almost without incident. Only once had Loona suggested trying to land so she could do what she had to do, but after Rill's reaction, I'd have done it in my pants, had I any, rather than make the same request.

Once, well into the night, I awakened Rill to point out a faint glow low in the sky to the west. "A city," I exclaimed softly. She stared for a minute, then she shook her head.

"No, a place of sickness," she said, looking worried.

"What do you mean?" I asked.

She seemed to hesitate. "The color of the light and it's feel, it's a place you get sick if you go near ... your hair falls out, men and women stop having babies, you die." She gripped my arm to emphasize her words. "It's bad. I hope the river doesn't go anywhere near it." She did not sleep until the glow retreated far behind us and sank below the foliage that concealed our river.

Chapter Three

The movement of light and shadow across my face awakened me. I had not intended to sleep, but after pillowing my head in my arms like a child, I had dozed off. The morning light filtered through the canopy of fronds above me and moved restlessly over my features as if trying to recognize me.

I jerked upright as my fears of the night before resurfaced. Something was different. Then I breathed deeply, savoring the salty tang in the air. We must be near the sea! Rill was still asleep, curled up on the low seat in the bow, but Loona was not in the boat.

Rill woke at my touch, looking quickly around to assess our predicament. "We are safe for the moment," I assured her. "I just wanted to … you know. I'll be back in a few moments. I think Loona has gone for the same reason."

She looked up sharply, then nodded. "Not in the river," she cautioned. "We'll probably have to drink it."

The bank was steep, but the vegetation was thick and sturdy enough to make good handholds. In a few moments, I was at the top and turning downstream. The bushes, growing in large thickets ahead, seemed like the rhododendrons of home. They were heavy with blossoms but also sweet smelling. They looked suitably dense, and I made my way toward them. As I pushed through the outer branches, soft petals drifted down, bringing back sweet memories of another time and place. Perhaps that was why I failed to notice the steep slope at my feet.

Instinctively rolling into a ball to protect my face, I bounced through the bushes as I tumbled down the slope.

A large clump of springy yellow grass brought me to a halt, and as I cautiously uncurled, I found myself on a stretch of loose black sand. Similar tussocks of wiry grass stretched into the distance in both directions, holding the dunes back from the sea. Lounging against a clump of grass, with dawn's lavender sky and the blue sea at his back, was a singularly amused male who looked to be in perfect health and disastrously bright. I wasn't happy.

"The ladies of Rath are permitted more liberty than their looks should allow," he smiled.

"Hmm," I murmured, getting to my feet and clutching the cloak around me. "Sorry," I added, "must go."

He rose laughingly to his feet. "I protest, sweet lady, I have been alone these many hours and would enjoy your company!" He held out his hand encouragingly.

"The novelty of solitude wore off, did it?" I couldn't help my reply—he didn't seem the sort who would have to spend his time alone if he didn't chose it. His hair was dark and wavy, and although tall, he was the solid, muscular type. His face wasn't really handsome in spite of a nice straight nose and large amber eyes; it was too strong, even a bit rugged. At the moment, his intelligent eyes were creased with amusement, not suspicion.

"Is not a Warlord obliged to do his best?" he teased.

"But so often, or so willingly?" I hazarded, guessing that he was attractive to females, and then turned to mount the bank. His laughter acknowledged a hit, and I hoped I would reach the top before he thought to ask questions of me, but the sandy soil betrayed me, and I barely managed to keep my feet as I slid down again.

"Here," he said, catching and steadying me. "Hold on to me, though why you choose not to use the path I can't imagine." Then he smiled. "Ah, out without permission?"

"Hmm, yes." I nodded. "Just pretend you haven't seen me," I added for good measure.

"Very well, though it tempts me to visit Rath after all. They should be more careful of their possessions." His glance lingered on my neck as he smiled.

"Oh, no one minds about me, really," I reassured him. "I'm no one special."

The laughter left his face, and a stony look possessed it.

"Are we then," his said in a hard voice, "so overburdened with breedable females that even one can be considered expendable?"

I stared blankly at him. Before I could try to answer, his eyes had taken in my crumpled condition, my badly fitting shoes, and lastly, the hospital coverall peeping between the edges of the cloak.

"What is this?" he breathed. Then he slowly walked around me. Stepping back in front of me, he asked mildly, "Do you know who I am?"

"No." I faced him squarely, knowing I couldn't bluff this one. He nodded and thoughtfully rubbed his chin.

"I am Ragul," he said, watching me. "Two hours ago on Deneb, while I lingered over a working breakfast, I received a very polite but evasive request by the Supreme Council to state my whereabouts and my activities for the last twelve hours. 'Odd,' I thought. So after telling them, I escaped to this quiet little beach to think about it further."

There was a long silence. I stared back at him with despair choking me, and I fingered the still unbroken vials beneath my cloak.

"I was puzzled," he explained, "but not now I think." He turned and strode to the clump of grass he had lain against and picked up a canvas roll I had not noticed. Coming back to me, he gestured for me to sit, and without waiting for me to comply, he sat down and opened the bag. Now was the time to throw acid into his helpless eyes, then kill him as he stumbled around.

But I couldn't. Instead, I sank meekly to the sand in front of him. At the sight of the rolls and the bottle, and the delicious smell coming from his newly opened thermos, my mouth watered. He handed me a stuffed roll and a brimming cup before saying anything more.

"How many of you are there at the hospital?" he asked, watching me eat hungrily.

"None now," I said somewhat thickly, wondering how I could slip some of the food into my clothes for the others should I be lucky enough to escape.

"Did they die naturally?" he asked, almost casually.

"I don't know, I just know they were going to kill us." I started to reach for the drink he held out.

"Us?" he queried.

"Hmm." I'd messed up again. I wasn't usually this dim.

"Listen, little one, I'm probably the only person on this world who can, or would, save you. But I must know the truth." He took my wrist and gently shook it to emphasize his words. "They told us you were all defects and were dying one by one."

"I don't know about the others," I said, "but we were the last three, and they were going to kill us, so we escaped. How normal would you like us?"

"That's normal enough." He gave a twisted smile. "The other two. Where are they?"

I don't know what instinct made me throw my left arm up protectively—perhaps a shadow flicking across the sand—but my action saved Ragul's life. It also broke my arm. The speed and weight of the colored balls in their bags were lethal, and they were so silent I could hear the snap of the bone.

I didn't see Ragul move. My eyes were shut tight, with tears trying to squeeze out. I cradled my arm, rocking silently and blindly.

I heard their progress in the bushes above me. I heard the movements stop, the grunts, the murmur of his voice. I heard their clumsy steps approaching, and then their stumbling slide down the slope.

In the silence, I knew they were watching me, so I opened my eyes and blinked back into focus. Rill was in an arm lock.

"A friend of yours?" he asked, holding her tightly.

"I doubt she still thinks so," I replied. "I may be wrong, Rill, but I think he may well be a stroke of good fortune for us, and besides, how do we get home without help?"

"Home?" he said. He released Rill and took a quick step to the side, an action that seemed to please her.

"If you know of us, you know this isn't our … planet," I said, watching him.

"No, of course it isn't, but at the moment it's impossible to leave." He moved toward the canvas bag, and carefully not turning his back on Rill, he removed food from it, as well as a cloth. "You can eat while I tend to your friend's arm," he said to Rill. Going to the base of the slope, he selected straight sticks from those scattered about, and breaking them to size, he came back to me.

Rill ate in silence while he tore the cloth into strips and put the makeshift splint on my arm as I clenched my teeth and tried not to whimper. Wiping her mouth on her cloak, she watched him put the remains of the cloth into the bag.

"Very neatly done," she commented. "Are you a ... soldier?"

"Yes. All Warlords are." He picked up a piece of fruit and bit into it as he lay back against a large clump of grass.

She nodded. "Why haven't you killed us? It would be easy; you are armed." Her glance indicated the lethal-looking object hanging from his belt, which I hadn't even noticed.

"I don't kill without reason." His lip curled slightly. "And you may be Selene's only hope."

I glanced at Rill while trying not to move, then back at him. "Who is Selene?"

"Selene is this planet," he said. "A planet whose females have been increasingly born sterile, due to eggs that fail to mature.

"Would we," I said, swallowing hard, "be of more use alive or dead?"

He had a nice lopsided smile. "Alive," he replied. "We've done all the genetic experimenting we can, with little success, although Moran might have succeeded."

"Well," I said as brightly as I could with a pounding arm, "with all the will in the world, I don't see what two or three women could do, even if they were fertile."

"No, of course not. Not themselves, but if they proved fertile and acceptable," he smiled, "and I can see little reason to doubt the latter, at least our planet will have hope."

I looked at Rill in puzzlement, pain blurring my understanding of what he was saying. But Rill just looked at him. "Who brought us here?" she asked softly.

"I did, as well as a few others." He was calm, but he watched Rill carefully. "We captured a Natog ship and found you still alive on it. From my understanding of their maps, you were are probably from the planet Garlan."

"We call it Dejan," she corrected him.

"Yes? We have a very short space history, but our enemy's map notations mark it down as a very hostile environment."

"We survive," commented Rill.

I shifted slightly to ease my arm. "If you brought us here, enthusiastic acceptance of you might be a little premature, don't you think?"

"I didn't bring you here to die!" He looked at the sun, which was still low but climbing the pale morning sky, and said, "However, we shall all die if you are caught here." Rising to his feet, he looked at Rill. "I can take you all to safety, but you must find your friend and get back here swiftly."

Rill nodded slowly and, having come to a decision, she rose quickly and left.

"Is the other one like her?" He watched her disappear into the bushes.

"No," I mumbled. I was in increasing pain and longed to burst into tears. I also felt ridiculous at feeling a little resentful of his interest in Rill. I didn't know the man, and because of him I might never see my grandchildren again.

But he had turned back and was smiling at me. "Thank the Eggs of Nerta for that! No," he added as I opened my mouth to protest, "an intelligent lady no doubt, and probably a good friend, but one of her is quite enough."

I thought he would probably change his mind after having to spend time with Loona, but then men are different … she might be his type.

Dropping to my side, he looked into my pinched little face. "I haven't thanked you yet, have I?"

"Oh, there's no need," I said, flushing a little, but I did not pretend ignorance of what he meant. "It was just instinct."

"I can see you don't wish to be thanked," he said after a moment, "and perhaps you regret your swift action, but believe me … none of you would last long without me. I can see now why the council was so interested in my whereabouts."

I wanted to deny any regret, but in truth, if my initial action had not been instinctive, then fear of Rill's anger and my own doubts would have slowed my response enough so it would have been too late.

"How do we get away from here?" I asked.

"All in good time," he smiled. "If I told you, you might attempt it without me."

I clenched my teeth as the pain in my arm increased, and I was glad to sit in silence listening to the waves tugging ineffectually at the sand, to the wind, and just occasionally, to the sound of a bird. It was all I could cope with.

I was almost sorry to hear movement above us in the bushes, followed by Loona's grumbles and panting.

Ragul rose to his feet and pulled a small flat box from his tunic. Putting it near to his mouth, he murmured something into it and then turned his glance out to sea. Near us, rising out of the waves, was a small craft, similar to the shuttle on Earth. It moved up to the water's edge, but stopped at another murmured command into the box.

Turning to where Rill had paused at the top of the bank, he urged them to hurry. "We mustn't be found here or leave any trace of this craft," he said, stooping to pick up the remains of the meal and thrusting them into the bag. He helped the other two into the craft before he came back to where I had struggled to my feet.

He didn't ask—he just swung me up into his arms and carried me easily across to the hatch and carefully placed me in the nearest seat. He stepped over me and settled himself in the next seat, fiddled with knobs and switches that closed the hatch, and as silently as it had come we sank below the water again. I was surprised at the lack of noise—helicopters and small planes at home always seemed so noisy.

"I submerged the boat and weighed it down," said Rill. "I thought it would be good if they did not know how far we got or which way we went."

"Boat?" asked Ragul, glancing back in surprise, but no one enlightened him.

"Why we are not fly away?" came Loona's anxious whisper.

"I expect we will when we are out at sea." I glanced at Ragul for confirmation. He nodded, but kept his eyes on a small screen that had graduated green lines moving toward the front of the screen. He manipulated the instruments before him with intent concentration as the lines on the monitor twisted and turned. Soon they became fewer, and then the screen was blank except for occasional dots that swarmed into view and quickly left.

Besides the occasional whine or click from the monitor, there was only a soft humming in the enclosed space. The lighting was dim, but I had seen there were about six seats behind us. Rill and Loona were in the nearest. At the back, webbing enclosed an empty storage space, and there seemed to be a sealed hatch in one side.

The heavily padded seats were black, with webbing straps to secure the passengers. Everything else seemed white, even the windows along each side. There was a warm plastic smell that was faintly comforting in its familiarity, and when at last our craft rose from the water into a brilliant, pale blue sky, the white window shields retracted and gave us our first real view of Selene.

Chapter Four

The sea stretched beneath us, glinting and moving as our seas do in a patchwork of turquoise and blues. Where the sea and sky met, a mist blurred the divide. The haze softened the blue-white sun's searching light.

Before us was a scattering of islands that on our approach grew to a respectable size. They were overgrown with lush vegetation. The rampant greenery had been subdued a bit on one island, and there was a smattering of simple buildings around a lawn. They were overhung with trees, making them scarcely visible from the air.

As we sank quickly toward the buildings, two men strolled out from the shade of a thatched roof that was supported by shell-covered pillars. They paused to watch, shielding their eyes against the sun. The ground rose up swiftly to meet us, but the landing was surprisingly gentle. Hardly had the humming stopped before the men came over to the machine and gestured their willingness to push the craft into the open building in front of us. Ragul grinned and gestured back.

I was surprised the two men could move her, loaded as she was, and I realized that her construction was even more different from our craft than I had thought. As we rolled quietly into the building, its shadow engulfed us. I shivered.

Ragul looked at us. "These men are my friends. They'll want you alive as much as I do." It was all he had time to say before opening the hatch on his side.

I liked the look of the older man at once. His dark hair was graying, but his stance was soldierly, and the lines in his tanned face denoted patience and humor, as well as strength of character. His smiled greeting to Ragul changed to puzzlement as his eyes passed over the three young women in the craft.

The younger man was as tall as Ragul, more handsome, and not nearly as astute as his companion. He grinned and said, "You have the luck of the lords! Can we share, or will you seal your walls against us?"

Ragul frowned. "Have a care, Torren, you speak of ladies." His voice was sharp, and Torren's jaw literally dropped.

"Ladies?" he gasped.

"Ragul, what is this?" The older man looked anxious.

"More than Torren at least has guessed, Degal," Ragul replied, holding the older man's eyes. "Back lad, so we can get out."

Torren stepped back instantly. Ragul pressed a button, and the hatch on my side opened. He got out his side and, coming around to my side, lifted me out gently. My arm hurt dreadfully as I stood there, and I felt very shaky. I lifted my chin and stared at him. "Good girl," he murmured, then he turned to help Loona and Rill down.

"Degal," he said, turning to the older man, "we can talk below, but this one needs medical attention."

The man nodded and, giving us a slight bow, turned and led the way out of the building. I don't remember that walk very well, only long, steep, and narrow descending steps ending in massively thick doors, and Ragul's strong arm around me.

There was a bright room where I lay for a while as they tended my arm. But the drink they gave me made me feel very relaxed and peaceful, so I didn't pay much attention. I awoke in the same room some time later, but now I was on a hover-bed with a light covering. The lights had been subdued.

I sat up, cradling my arm, and swung my feet to the ground carefully in case the hover-bed moved. There was no sign of Rill or Loona, but a mumble of voices came from the next room. Cautiously, I stood up and made my way to the door. The discussion stopped as I opened it, and I found three pairs of eyes looking at me.

There was no sign of Rill or Loona, but Ragul smiled and rose from the stout arm of a curious seat, seemingly made from tight bundles of plant fibers, to greet me.

"You look better. Come, let me introduce you to my friends. This fellow here is Degal." He clapped the older man on the shoulder. "A fine soldier and a good friend." Degal bowed slightly, but his face remained serious. "And this is Torren, my cousin and an officer of the second wing." Torren bowed and smiled briefly, but he too looked far from happy.

"So you have told them?" I said, trying to resist the feeling that I was an alien mutant.

"A little, yes, but not your name," Ragul gently reminded me.

"Oh, yes, of course, we didn't really get time for introductions, did we?" I agreed. "It's Rowhan."

"Rowhan, how nice, does it mean anything?"

"Yes, I think so. My mother said it meant 'greatly beloved.'" I would have gone on, but suddenly my throat got stuck, and my eyes got prickly, and I tried to forget that no one loved me any more. Oddly enough, it was Degal who guessed the cause of my sudden silence. He came forward and, taking my hand, led me to a dark brown, fibrous chair and gruffly suggested that some food would soon make me feel more the thing.

Torren quickly volunteered to rustle up something, but warned me that it was just bachelor stuff, he wasn't up to anything fancy!

Ragul sat back and smiled at me. Degal broke the silence by asking if I knew what had happened to me. I squirmed a little on the matting of my chair, but it was surprisingly comfortable.

"Well, I remember being captured, and there are some odd and terrifying memories floating around my mind that came afterward. But really," I said, "I think I've been in shock and have only recently emerged from it." I paused to remember the last few days. "It's only been the last two or three days that I've been fully myself." I added, "Although I was semi-aware for about two or three weeks."

Degal nodded, "Can you remember your past?"

"Perfectly." I felt slightly irritated.

"Would you indulge me by doing some little tests?"

"Not at all, if you will do some for me." Degal looked startled. "After all," I continued, "the intelligence and sympathetic responses of the inhabitants of this planet observed to date have not been high. They have, in fact, been decidedly low."

Ragul chuckled as Degal's astonished look swung around to him. "I told you you'd get backed into a chamber with no seals," he teased his friend.

I felt oddly pleased that Ragul said I was brighter than his friends had thought. At this point, Torren reappeared with a hovering trolley laden with steaming bowls and cups, piles of fruits I remembered from the institute, their version of rolls, and a delicious savory green paste.

Rill and Loona came in after him—Rill with a stuffed roll in one hand and a steaming cup in the other. Loona looked nervously about until Ragul offered her one of the fiber chairs. Refusing an offered seat, Rill lounged over to me and hunkered down on the floor, stretching her long legs out and leaning back against my chair. She no longer wore her shift, and the green tunic over the long skirt suited her.

"Beats dying," she murmured before taking another long drink. I laughed. I couldn't help it; I really liked Rill.

"Only if someone else does the cooking," I demurred, "and the dishes." Rill spluttered and choked on her roll before asking, somewhat thickly, if my cooking was really that bad.

Loona glared across the room at us. "I not know what you two find laugh about. I not like people try kill me. I not like this ball. I want go home!" She voiced the eternal cry of mankind.

"Well, that's not possible now," stated Ragul, "and perhaps not ever."

"Why not?" wailed Loona.

"Yes, why not?" asked Rill more reasonably, reaching for a steaming stew of vegetables.

Degal exchanged looks with Ragul, who turned to us with a gesture of male resignation.

"Your home is Selene, whether you will it or not," he said quietly. "We have only three remaining hyper-space vessels, three out of the five that went to seek out the ships that carried you." His eyes avoided Degal, whose face tightened with remembered grief. "The loss was terrible, but no more than expected. By many, it was deemed our only chance." He looked at Degal. "If the experiment proves successful, their sacrifice will not have been in vain."

"I think I have heard that somewhere before," I said sadly.

Ragul looked at me sharply, and then he nodded. "I expect all planets have asked the ultimate sacrifice at one time or another."

"So often and of so many," I added, thinking of our endless wars.

Torren's face flushed as he exclaimed, "Well, desperate or not, it was a fantastic effort! Leaving only localized spacecraft to protect Selene, they searched the most likely areas of space, hoping to find and capture a Natog vessel with a particular cargo: people like us, and fully processed. The surviving three ships returned to Selene bringing you and the others."

"No, they didn't," said Rill, putting down her mug.

Degal looked startled. "Yes, they did, dear lady."

"Then where did we get these new bodies?" I put in, and Rill nodded.

"From your own pasts." We all looked at Ragul.

"From what we understand, the Natog have eradicated all disease on their planets, resulting in a vast population and no natural immunity," Ragul said. "Since they were forced out into the galaxy for food, they devised a way of sterilizing living organic matter in an ingenious way."

Degal took over, "The DNA of each victim is read. The most consistent and accurate are processed into a virus, which doesn't take them long. Then the subject is put in an isolation unit and injected with the virus. It rampages throughout the subject, altering all compatible cells and destroying the others. When all the cells have been infected and forced to produce corrected cells, the subject is heated up and the virus dies, leaving the subject in perfect mature health. Then the 'food' can be processed or kept alive."

"That's horrible! But why did you do it? Why did you want us?" I asked.

Ragul sighed. "I'd best tell you something of this planet and our problems, since they are now yours." He selected a warty fruit and carefully began to pare it with a small curved knife as if he was trying to decide how or where to start. "We didn't evolve here. About five hundred passes ago our ancestors were brought here hurriedly. Our old world was endangered by an ancient star that was about to go supernova too near to it. This planet, which we have called Selene, had no native insects, fishes, or animals. In fact, many of the plants you see are not native either, having descended from those brought by evacuees, especially the brightly flowering ones and the fruits and vegetables. The people, flora, and fauna thrived and spread."

He finished peeling the fruit and continued. "The plan, we believe, was to evacuate all the most brilliant people, then equipment and vast amounts of stored knowledge, and then the rest of the people." Ragul hesitated. "It was a pity the gene pool wasn't larger."

"Especially for those left behind," I added sweetly.

"Quite." The awkward silence lasted only a moment. "Our ship returned to the old world, and nothing … just silence."

Rill got up and went over to the trolley and selected a fruit as Ragul continued.

"We weren't even left with star charts, they were on the ship. We had no idea of what was in space around us, nor had we the capability to find out. Our ancestors' only comfort was that most of the bureaucrats who had planned the whole bungled affair seemed, through a clerical error, to have received the wrong kind of fuel and so blew up on launch!"

Everyone seemed to derive considerable satisfaction from this, and I deduced that petty bureaucracy was a galactic problem.

"Time was desperately short when Selene was discovered," Ragul went on. "There was little or no time for in-depth studies on Selene before we arrived. They were not to know that our women were very sensitive to the amount of radiation present here. The difference between here and our old world is so slight … but alas, it's enough."

"How many people were brought here?" I asked. Having seen some results of continual interbreeding in isolated rural communities, I was interested.

"Nearly a million, the richest people and their families, those with power or beauty. Some very intelligent people, and even a few families with useful skills," Degal commented dryly.

"A million! In one trip? That must have been a huge ship! But genetically, that should have been plenty, what went wrong?" Gratefully, I accepted another roll from Rill.

"Nothing at first. After a hundred or so fruitful turns, we had nearly seventy-three million people here. Large families, no problems. But not long after that, they began to notice an increasing tendency toward smaller families. At first, it was thought to have an economic cause, but studies began to show that young couples were eager to have large families so they could subdue more land, grow more food, and so have plenty to spare for centers of learning." Ragul caught my puzzled look.

"All education is free of course," he explained, "but with no wealth behind the Centers of Learning, especially the higher ones, they were unable to support many students, so the parents sent food to the Centers to be used or sold, to feed, house, and educate their children."

"Of course, that's a very simplified explanation," Ragul admitted, "but it's basically correct. Anyway, it seemed that despite their hopes, the families were becoming smaller. After a further six or seven decades, the population peaked at 195 million, of which about one hundred million were too old to breed. The family unit continued its downward trend, many women achieving only one pregnancy, and that often male."

Ragul was pacing the floor now as Degal nodded in agreement with the story. The older man turned to us.

"Some twenty years later, as the breedable population continued to drop, there arose a more prolific family, a woman called Nerta." It was Ragal's turn to nod as Degal continued. "She seemed abundantly unaffected by the slight rise in radiation that had occurred since our arrival on the planet. She offered her eggs to the Malton Center, about a thousand in all.

"Even in those days, Malton had skill in those matters. They took half the eggs and fertilized them with female sperm, split them many times and placed them in infertile women. It worked, about four thousand female babies were born, all of who proved very fertile. But Malton warned that the effect might wear off after a few generations, and the chance of many Nertas evolving were remote."

Ragal took up the tale again. "So Malton started a campaign to collect all unused eggs from women dying prematurely or physically unable to use their eggs etc. They also collected all the female sperm they could. All these, and the other half of Nerta's eggs, were stored at Malton." He sounded bitter.

Degal nodded grimly and said, "And then the Natog came."

"The Natog?" Rill's brows lifted.

"The baddies," I guessed.

A grim smile twisted Ragul's face briefly. "Yes, the baddies. They are they ones who took you from your planet. They live on Netal and possibly another planet." He paused. "A lot of them live there. Too many in fact. They had run out of food, resources, and space, and they had to import the first two in large quantities. They are primarily carnivores, so they harvest planets for protein lifeforms and mine the asteroids for ores, etc. By the time they found Selene, some one hundred and twenty turns after Nerta, we had crawled back to one hundred and thirty-one million of breedable age, but were barely holding at that."

Torren cut in, gesturing occasionally as he spoke. "We were spread out and living on the surface. We had no spacecraft. No armed forces either, as there had been no need. We had no predators or enemies."

Rill nodded, watching the three men intently. "They wiped the floor with you, didn't they?"

"Yes," snapped Degal, frowning at the memory. "I remember my grandfather telling me tales his grandfather told him when he was a boy. So many were lost."

"So," I guessed, "you went underground, developed an army and some weapons, and eventually crawled back to the surface."

"Well, we never really left the surface, we couldn't, but every hold and city is almost half beneath the surface, with massive sealed doors the Natog can't breach in time," Degal explained.

"In time?" I prompted, looking at the three men: Torren lounged in his molded orange chair; Degal sat erect in another with his legs stretched out before him, one leg crossed over the other; and Ragul leaned against a sturdy rack of draws with the fruit seemingly forgotten in his hand.

"You didn't think we'd just sit back, did you? We developed a weapon that could destroy them on the ground. In fact, it is the basis of our space fleet," Ragul responded. "If we can kill them on or near the ground, we have their spacecraft."

"Are all your spaceships theirs?" I asked in surprise.

"Almost all," Ragul affirmed.

"Ragul," interrupted Degal, "we haven't much time."

"Agreed." Ragul nodded and continued as he laid the fruit down. "Among their first targets was the city of Malton. It was our oldest city, and its power source had been brought with us. We don't know what happened exactly. The Natog don't have advanced ballistics, they want live food, but there was a minor explosion somewhere in the restricted area. There was a build-up in the power source ... perhaps in the panic, no one noticed. Malton, the center, and all the stored eggs, sperm, and knowledge ceased to exist."

Degal leaned forward. "And so did our hopes of survival, for the apocalypse that vaporized Malton caused a more distant craft to crash." He shook his head sadly. "It was full of victims from another planet, a few were still alive and unprocessed. Before they died, they dealt Selene its worst blow. An unprocessed female carried a virus that affected the DNA of our unborn females. It permanently retards the growth of eggs."

I shook my head at Torren's silent offer of more food as Ragul took up the story.

"Obviously, some families were more susceptible than others," Ragul said, "and sometimes females can carry the genetic fault for generations without being affected by it, but slowly and surely, our numbers decrease, even though the disease was eradicated. Indeed, two hundred turns after the double disaster, we have barely twenty million of breedable age. Ninety-five million are either too old, too young, or sterile. Of the twenty million, only six are females. If sterility by radiation doesn't get us, the genetic fault will. Or the Natog ... but that's the least likely." Ragul looked grim. "That's why we need you. To see if your kind is immune and viable."

Straightening to his full height, Ragul stretched, and then continued. "Once we had space flight again, and some understanding of the charts we had captured, we began to hope that somewhere in these teeming and hostile galaxies, we might find compatible races to help us."

Degal dissented gruffly. "Not we ... your stepfather and a handful of hot-head friends! Most of Selene was dead against it, and they still are!"

"But not when the second wing opened the sterile holds of a captured Natog vessel ten turns ago," Ragul bit out.

"No, well, there seemed hope then." Degal turned to us. "They were all dead, of course, always had been since the Supreme Council ruled that full decontamination was of prime importance, even in the sterile holds. That was after some of ours were found processed, but still alive for a little while. But these ones ... they were so like us." Degal looked up at Ragul. "It was a last desperate hope really." He looked very tired.

"Can't you use the Natog virus on your own females to undo the problem?" I asked, trying not to look shocked.

There was a grim silence. Ragul broke it. "From having recovered living Selenese from Natog craft, we know that our brain cells respond badly to the virus. The victims die within hours without life support."

"How did you know we wouldn't?" I demanded, fearing the worst.

"We didn't. We could only hope, since obviously many of the Natog's other victims do survive." Ragul's eyes were hard as they met mine.

"We were traumatized, weren't we?" I made it a statement.

Degal looked uncomfortable. Ragul stood firm. "What the hell else could we do?"

Torren added awkwardly, "We didn't need another wild virus on Selene, so we couldn't even feed you until you were processed."

"Why," I asked, "didn't the others survive? We came out of shock, why didn't they? Or did they?"

"Some were not ... viable." Torren's voice shook slightly.

"We are not the only race to suffer the brain cell problem, it seems, and others were quite insane by the time we reached Selene. Some were merely ... absent." Ragul looked grim.

"Of the sixty-one females in the surviving vessels, seven were dead, eight were vegetables, and the rest seemed to range from imbecilic to insane," Torren said.

"So forty-six might have been … findable," Loona said. I'd forgotten she was there. "Where those from?" she asked in a hard little voice. I didn't blame her. I felt a little hard myself.

"All of those came from either your planet, or Rill's." Degal rubbed his nose thoughtfully. "Two good planets it seems, but only," he added to Ragul, "if they survive."

"How did the others die?" I insisted.

"We were told you died naturally. We haven't seen any of you since the landing," Ragul replied.

"That's not good enough," I stated.

"No," said Rill.

"No," agreed Ragul. "We don't know the answers yet. But we will." Turning to Degal, he nodded. "Now we have to supply these three with backgrounds and identities, no easy thing on our world," he added to us.

"It would be if we marked them as sterile," suggested Torren.

"I think their condition would become noticeable," Regal commented dryly.

"What condition?" I snapped. Rill just grinned.

"Would you rather breed and live, or remain untouched and die when they catch you?" There was no compromise in Ragul's voice.

My arm was hurting again, and I clutched it, not answering. For the answer was not as obvious as he seemed to think.

"While it is understandable that you would rather select a mate on your own, this is not the time to do so. Perhaps for your next child," he added more gently.

"You really don't understand, do you?" I said. "You are so focused on your problems that you haven't the slightest doubt that others will see all this as you do. Oddly enough, there are worse things than death, and no, I am not talking about forced couplings." Degal tried to speak, but I ignored him. Speaking quietly as I stared at my hand cradling my arm, I continued, "Only when we have had a child are we totally vulnerable, totally at your mercy." I looked up. "Only then can we no longer choose death." As shock registered on their faces, I added, "Women will endure anything to protect their children. Oh no, Ragul, Warlord, I am very far from making the decision you seem to think so obvious!"

Into the stunned silence, Loona suddenly spoke.

"One of you three? I think YOU very well," she said, fluttering her eyelashes at Ragul. I'm not sure she understood half of what had been said, but obviously she had grasped the bits that were important to her.

"Rill?" I raised an enquiring eyebrow as she looked my way.

She just shrugged and smiled wryly back at me. The jury was still out.

"Do we have the choosing?" Loona breathed, watching Ragul.

"Hmmm, no," he replied. His friends looked at him in surprise.

"Well, who do you choosing?" cooed Loona.

Torren looked embarrassed. "Well, Ragul's will have to speak the language very well," he supplied.

"Just so," agreed Ragul solemnly, "and—"

A buzzer sounded, and everyone jumped. Ragul warned us to silence and moved to press a button on a console on the far side of the room. The screen was turned away from us, but I saw the screen reflected in the objects on the shelves behind him.

"Councilor Ragul, Warlord, and Lord Holder, greetings," came a youthful but formal voice from the console.

"It's Jorgal, isn't it?" Ragul peered at the screen. The boy sounded flushed with pride at being noticed. "Yes, sir. There is an alert, and wing second Torren is recalled, sir." The young officer added, "He said he would be with you, sir."

"Indeed, he is." Ragul smiled and waved Torren to come across. We kept silent. Ragul moved back to allow Torren access to the console.

"Yes, Jorgal, I heard. Where and when?"

Consulting a paper somewhere below the screen, Jorgal looked up. "South Isle, at nine segments, local time, sir."

"South Isle be damned," groaned Torren. "That's two time zones away. All right, orders received and acknowledged." He touched a button, and the communication dissolved.

Ragul gripped his shoulder. "There is nothing else for it, lad. You'll have to go."

Torren nodded. "I know, it's just that …" He fell silent.

"I know," Ragul said, smiling.

They left the room together, concocting a story that would release Torren from his duties in the wing if Ragul had urgent need of him. Degal looked uneasily at us. "Well, I agree with Torren. Loona, you don't speak well enough to be Ragul's mate." His voice was kind and rather gruff. "He's too much in the limelight. Though we will do all that's possible to keep the three of you from view, of course."

Loona's eyes snapped angrily. "If not meeting ones, I good as them." She pointed stiffly at us.

Before Degal could reply, Ragul reentered the room. "No, Loona, you are far too pretty to risk." He smiled down at her. "I wouldn't hear of you being exposed to anything more than you have to."

He looked up at Degal. I thought I could detect a little pleading in his expression.

Degal cleared his throat. "Ah, no, of course not. It would be my honor, yes, great honor to take and hold the Lady Loona."

Loona looked flattered, but undecided. "I choosing next time?" She gazed up at Ragul, unaware or uncaring of the insult to Degal.

"Yes, of course, within reason," Ragul hedged as he pinned a smile to his lips.

"Oh, in that … well." She put her fingers on Degal's honest arm and smiled up at him. "Yes, Degal, I pleased."

After thanking her, Degal looked at Ragul. "It's best they don't know each other's identities, isn't it? In case one's caught?" Ragul nodded in agreement. "Then with your permission, I'll take my Lady Loona to … er, before anyone misses me."

"Excellent choice … you-know-who can stand guard." Ragul grinned at his friend.

Degal stepped forward to clasp his hand in a firm grip. "Take care, lad." Turning quickly away, he guided a reluctant Loona from the room.

"An ill-sorted pair," I murmured to Rill when they were out of earshot.

"None would agree more than Degal," she said, grinning.

Ragul had moved over to a large screen on the wall. He was inserting disks into slots on the wall beneath it during our exchange so I was surprised when he asked, "Do either of you wish to soothe his brow?"

I looked startled. "Would you let either of us go with him?"

"No." Ragul looked down at me. "But it would be interesting to know who wished to, would it not?"

Rill rose from her place on the floor. "I liked him. Let's get on with the plans."

It seemed that our names could be altered to similar ones used on this planet. Mine could become Rowanna, and Rill's could be Rilla. During the next two hours, we learned our supposed genetic lines, who had taken and held our mothers, and our siblings, if any.

We got a quick geographic survey of the main land masses and the main cities, and then we had a short visual tour of life in a town, at least that's what we got out of it. I think it was some kind of orientation thing for rural students, showing them things like how food was dispersed from the central storehouses beneath the ground to which nearly all food was taken, the transport available, and how to get course supplies.

I was almost dazed with facts when Ragul leaned forward and dissolved the picture. "That's enough. You'll never be able to absorb any more in this sitting. And now," he said, reaching down for my good hand.

I know I gasped and flinched back in my chair, but before I could say anything, he smiled and repeated, "And now for another dose for that arm of yours." His eyes brimmed with amusement, and Rill laughed at my flashing eyes and loss of color.

"Yes, of course," I said in a voice cool with what dignity I could muster. I rose and followed him into the room where I had first awakened.

He closed the door firmly behind us and motioned me into a black fibrous chair beside some electronic gadgetry. He was gentle, and the tingling in my arm was rather pleasant. We said nothing during the minutes he worked on my arm.

Then he turned it off and sat back. "Another day or two and that arm will be as good as new." I looked up in astonishment. "So," he continued, "you needn't leap two clegs in the air every time I look at you … until then. By the courage of Marta, woman, why do you find me so distasteful?" He gave me a puzzled glare.

"Ragul, I don't know what the customs are here, but I really need to let you know my bottom line." He looked totally bewildered. "I mean by that the point beyond which I will not compromise." His look grew more guarded.

I looked down at my hands while I tried to find the words to explain my decision. I had a horrid feeling he wouldn't understand. "Ragul," I began again, "I have had a long life, and I have come to have different values than when I was very young. If I have to make the choice you demand right now, then it is death." A moment of silence filled the room. "I won't try to get you to understand, because whether you do or not doesn't really matter. It is sufficient that you have my assurances that it has nothing to do with you." I sighed. "Children, matings, they are hard enough when there is love and shared hopes and dreams … this, what you suggest, is just too hard for me to take on in cold blood."

His look was inscrutable. Then he got up and looked down at me. "It is not I who would kill you, Lady Rowanna, but those who seek you. Even now, others are risking their lives to protect you, for the hope you bring to this planet. I will give you some time, but I do not know how much we have."

He leaned forward and, gently raising my chin with his finger, made me look up at him. "Be assured, my dear lady, my blood at least shall not be cold." And he bent and kissed my lips.

Chapter Five

I shivered. The shuttle-car felt cold and damp after its night in the hanger. We had risen early on our second morning on the island to be ready to lift into the predawn sky. There had been a quick session on the electrotherapy unit while Rill had rummaged for food for a stand-up breakfast. Ragul had been careful to remove all evidence of our presence, in case it was searched.

Rill and I were in the back part of the craft, sitting in the padded black seats, but ready to drop to the floor and hide beneath a blanket at Ragul's command.

He had removed a little gadget from the side of the distance counter before we started the flight. It was a precaution picked up by many service men, and one he had used the night he had found us. With no distance recording and no flight record, no one tended to ask where you had been.

A pale blue-white sun showed above the rim of the sea, and for a while it shone directly into the windows, causing us to squint as we stared at the world below us. A casual scattering of islands curved away to the west. The shallow water that lay between them broke the deep blue of the sea into a thousand different hues, all glittering in the morning sun.

Rill didn't speak much. She would touch my arm and point down at things, like the white-sailed fishing fleet—at least that's what it looked like.

We had slept in different rooms, and the thought had crossed my mind that she may have chosen not to be alone, but her face invited no confidences, and part of me knew anyway. Rill was strong and pragmatic.

Before long, Ragul's warning came back to us, and we dived for the floor and wriggled under the dark blanket, laying as flat as we could. The air was soon warm and stuffy under the covering, and I raised the blanket an inch from the floor.

I could hear the random crackle of sound from the front, an occasional short conversation with other air traffic we passed.

Then we began the gradual curve and descent he had warned us about. The long, tight sleeves of my overdress felt itchy, and my tunic had crept up to bunch around my hips.

"Rill?" I whispered into the heavy, stale air.

"Hmm?"

"Do you think we'll make it?"

"Probably."

I nodded slightly. Ragul's plan was cunning. The aunt of one of our most dangerous adversaries was a cantankerous old lady, he had told us, and quite powerful. She lived in style in the capital city, but she was rather withdrawn from society. Forceful of character, old, and a bit deaf when she chose to be, she lived in apartments belonging to Hagnot, her nephew, who was not only the powerful First Councilor but also the driving force behind the anti-experiment faction. Her chambers had a different entrance, and Hagnot and she lived entirely separate lives. While he searched the planet for us, for the present at least, we would be safest in the chambers of his aunt.

The shuttle-car came to rest, and the humming ceased. Footsteps sounded outside the car, and Ragul opened the hatch and stepped down with the greeting, "Lieutenant Nanoch, isn't it?"

I heard the man snap to attention. "Yes, sir, awaiting further orders from the First Councilor, sir."

"Due back soon, is he?" Ragul inquired.

"Not in person, sir, not till this afternoon, but we have been informed that revised orders are imminent."

"Damn!" Ragul sounded irritated, but we knew the reverse. "I can't wait that long, where's your com room set up? I might be able to contact him."

Eager to help and bored of kicking his heels, Nanoch offered to show Ragul to the office, where a communications room had been set up for the alert.

This was the chance Ragul had planned for us! As their footsteps retreated and disappeared, Rill and I scrambled to our feet and peered out of the window. Satisfied, we hurried to the front and stepped out through the hatch.

"Left," I hissed urgently as Rill hesitated a moment, then we darted forward and around the tall cement corner into a narrowing corridor that ended in thick metal double doors.

I nervously smoothed my skirts down and slowed to a more normal pace. Rill seemed to have no qualms at all as the doors swung open and we entered a marble passageway and rounded a sharp bend.

Sure enough, there on the right was the door Ragul had described and the sign he had drawn for us: a stylized pregnant female in gold. Even on this world, there were separate washrooms, but the two groups were fertile females and everyone else! The second door bore a silver circle.

We went into a utilitarian and unpretentious set of rooms, but they were clean and adequate. The row of mirrors and countertops were similar to Earth's, but other things were not, and they seemed meaningless in their anonymity, like the small, empty niches in the blue and white tiled walls and the white unit the size of a wastepaper basket that lay on its side on the floor with a large hole facing into the room.

On the other side of the room and running along the wall were the toilets, a long, thick shelf with regular holes along it and no partitions. They continued around the corner, as did the red knobs in the wall that Ragul had told us never to touch, without explaining why.

I perched on a stool before a glass and smoothed my hair toward the knot at the back of my head. It was braided tightly, so few hairs had escaped during our ride.

"Once in the building," Ragul had said, "try not to be seen together until we reach our destination." So Rill had moved down the room.

The door swung open, and a plump, overdressed woman entered, followed by a very pretty girl with a pale complexion. The girl, I decided, had relented to wiser counseling than her companion and was dressed simply in a pink tunic over a pale yellow under-dress with a pretty embroidered sash. Her black hair was braided around her head and she wore no jewels, unlike the woman, who was festooned with dully glittering baubles.

"Now do stand straight, Lena! If you slouch along like that, only a holder will wish to keep you!" the woman admonished.

Lena raised a pair of embarrassed eyes in my direction, and mine met hers with sympathy. She smiled tentatively.

"Hurry, girl, we're lucky your father could come by and pick us up with all this fuss on, so best not keep him waiting!"

I reapplied some powder and stood up as if to examine my dress in the glass before leaving. The skirt of the creamy under-dress swung about my legs as I moved. A green tunic covered much of it, with the edges embroidered in greens and cream. The gold belt around my waist was echoed by the band around my head and the sandals on my feet. Rings sparkled on my left hand—two fine emeralds entwined on one finger and a small jade on another—but my right hand was bare, as was the custom for ladies not yet held. Yet again I wondered at the amount of female apparel at Ragul's holding. I had discovered that earrings were unknown here, a fashion I thought they sorely lacked!

When the girl and her mother left, I slumped back onto the seat, already emotionally exhausted by my fears. "How much longer do you think, Rill?"

"Soon." She spoke from across the room. "You go first." I nodded, but she continued. "You remember what to do?"

"Yes, I'll be off then." I left quickly, with my head held high and no anxious looks to the left or right. Grimly, I forced myself to slow down and walk in the languid way that became my pretended status.

Typically, town buildings on Selene had parking on the roof. Only this one, like expensive dwellings on our world, had security guards to keep out the sightseers. Lieutenant Nanoch had taken the man's place, it seemed, during the alert that had been called to find us, though it seemed that was not public knowledge. I was to walk down the corridor to the lifts and take one of them to the seventh floor where reception was, along with several very expensive little shops, a cafe or two, and sitting areas. While pretending to browse, I would await Ragul and follow him at a leisurely pace and distance.

As I reached the end of the corridor, the elevation-tube doors opened in front of me, disgorging three men. Two men in leggings and short tunics were listening intently to a third, older man who wore a long, black robe over his grey and silver formal vestments, which denoted high rank. They passed me by with barely a glance, and gratefully I entered.

When the doors opened onto the reception area, I wanted to shrink back into the lift! Before me lay a glittering array of sumptuous, moving colors that resolved themselves into finely robed people, fluttering streamers, gay stalls and booths, and flowers.

The noise level was low, muffled by thick carpets and the fabric partitions of the shops.

Two people hesitated as they were about to enter the lift. "Are you going down?" the man asked. The girl clinging to his arm ignored me.

"Ah, no, thank you." I stepped out past them, smiling brightly, and strolled off to the right, as if I knew where I was going.

The room was very large, and there was a quiet elegance in the quality of the furnishings and the beige and gold background. It was laid out like a fan, with a round reception desk and the elevating-tubes at the narrow end and the rest radiating out beyond them. Along the walls were permanent stores with head-high fabric walls shaped in half circles. Other spaces contained festive stalls. The seating looked divinely comfortable and elegant, with fountains and plants adding to the ambiance.

I was headed toward a large booth of cream and brown fabric that displayed jewelry. I bent over plastic domes that protected bracelets and displayed rings. It all seemed to be hand-worked, and no two items were the same.

A neat but plainly clad girl appeared at my shoulder. "Can I help you, lady?"

I saw the mark on her neck denoting a sterile person.

"I'm just looking, thank you." I moved off, wondering if all humanoid worlds were basically the same. Then I caught sight of him. Ragul paused at the reception desk, speaking to a plainly dressed man who spoke into a communication device and then nodded.

Ragul strode back to the tubes, and as Rill emerged, he entered. I watched her move to a booth that displayed paintings, casually looking them over before drifting on to the next.

I had paused before a booth selling small posies, enjoying their sweet scent.

"Lady," came a voice behind me. Despite knees that threatened to turn to water, I turned slowly. The man was not tall nor young, but he smiled sweetly, and taking a posy from the display, he offered it to me. "It's not as beautiful as you, but please accept it anyway."

Damn! What was the normal thing to do here? Did acceptance mean anything? Was rejection a terrible insult? I glanced from the man to the flowers and back, his slight flush giving me a hint.

"Perhaps we should ask my future husband?" I looked vaguely around as if to find him.

"Oh, no! Indeed no, lady. I apologize, I'd no idea." He backed away discomforted, while the stall woman held out her hand for his coin.

At that moment, I saw the man from reception approach Rill and murmur something. As she moved toward the tubes, I followed suit, anxious to leave this social minefield!

When we exited the elevation-tube we were faced with a hall curving away on both sides. As I hesitated a security man at a small desk rose to greet us.

"Who do you seek ladies?

"Lady Garola."

He looked at the screen on his desk. "She is not expecting anyone, did you call from the desk?" My heart leaped into my throat, I had no idea what to do!

As I hesitated he turned to answer a summons from the console.

"One moment." Turning to me he asked, "Are you the Lady Rowanna?"

At my nod he gestured down the long curving corridor to our left, "Ninth door."

When we reached the apartment, Rill touched the panel by the double doors. Moments later they opened and a girl in a simple, pale yellow tunic bowed us in. Ragul came and led us into a stately room of palest blue with coordinating furniture.

Sitting on a low dais was a very large and elderly lady. Her hair was white, as was her skin, but her black eyes sparkled with interest.

"Here they are, Lady Garola," Ragul said, "this is the Lady Rowanna." We moved forward to where she sat, and I bowed as Ragul had taught us and touched her fingers to my forehead.

"Rona, ha!" she snapped.

"No, Rowanna," Ragul corrected her loudly.

"So!" She ignored him and scrutinized me. "He's stolen you away from your mother, has he?" I looked anxiously at Ragul. This wasn't the story! He shrugged infinitesimally, but his eyes gleamed with success.

"No," I said. "Ragul is escorting my sister and I at her request!"

"Ha! I know his clan," she snorted. "So he'd hold both of you, would he? Well, his father was just such a one too, and he got away with worse, but I doubt the boy has his abilities."

I looked aghast. Would this mean a change of plan? What would we do now? But looking again at Ragul's calm expression, I realized with a start that this was exactly what he had intended her to think! Why else claim her protection rather than one of our mother's relations?

Ragul just laughed and introduced Rill. Lady Garola beckoned her imperiously. "Come here, girl! Stop standing there like a block."

Rill smiled slightly and moved forward to bow in the same way I had. I admired her ease and grace. No one would have guessed that she was a wolf disguised as a red setter.

"Well, Warlord and holder of Tenem and Harth," she said somewhat dryly, "it seems you have excellent taste. Never thought Meranna's daughters would turn out so sightly. Though neither looks meek enough, I'd say!" Rill and I exchanged glances.

"But you have always been such a model of temerity, madam, perhaps you judge too harshly?" Ragul smiled quizzically down at her, and then he added, "And would your lord have wished you any different?"

"No, boy, he would not. Nor would you have dared to sauce me in his presence!" she snapped with grudging approval.

Ragul stepped forward and raised her fingers to his lips. "You will do as I ask?"

"Yes, yes," she replied. "Though more to spite Meranna than to oblige you!"

She caught my wondering look and Rill's puzzled one. "Your mother contrived once, when we were just coming of age, to invite so many important guests to her party that I was placed below the fruit!" she proclaimed in awful tones. We looked properly horrified, and I wondered if it was like being below the salt in medieval times.

"Well, if she has not been sorry many times since, you certainly have the power to make her so now," I commented.

"So I think," she agreed with satisfaction.

"Are your staff to be trusted, Lady Garola?" Ragul inquired.

"Yes, yes. Stop fussing boy! Not the lords that hope to hold them, nor their relations, will have a notion of where they are."

At last she motioned us all to sit, and we assumed the cross-legged and straight-backed posture that Ragul had taught us was proper for the low dais still used by the older generations. Mine was covered in a fabric in which blue birds flitted around in a paler blue sky or sat on improbable dark blue flowers.

It was good fortune our temperaments did not hinder our sitting almost motionless while Ragul and the old lady carried on a desultory and occasionally muddled conversation. Rill had the discipline of a warrior, and I was naturally restful—or indolent!

At last the old women clapped her hands and another yellow-clad girl appeared pushing a trolley that was made of three clear plastic circles, one above the other, and each loaded with succulent things to eat.

My mouth watered with the appetizing smells. The girl served Lady Garola first, taking things from the trolley and putting them on a plate on the dais beside her. The drink she chose was placed there too. The settles stood only four to six inches above the thick carpet. Ragul had warned us that many old families preferred to keep this fashion of furniture, rather than the more modern pieces I had seen, and that the two kinds had existed side by side for nearly a hundred turns. I couldn't help wondering why such an old lady would choose to be so uncomfortable!

When the trolley stopped by my side I decided, regretfully, to avoid the cooked dishes of thick lumpy stew, lest I made some silly mistake when eating. However, the tiny savory baked goods with their pale green pressed curds smelled delicious, and the small fancy cakes looked delightful. I pointed out my wants and chose a long, cool fruit drink Ragul had introduced us to the night before.

Surreptitiously, I watched Ragul and Lady Garola, who picked at her food, to avoid making a fool of myself or betraying us. So I was unprepared for Lady Garola's exclamation of disbelief and her surprised regard of Rill. Looking up anxiously, I could see that the meal spread around Rill was designed for nourishment rather than elegance. Rill smiled back at her placidly from behind her spoonful of thick stew.

Understanding flashed across the old woman's face. "How long did it take you to escort them here?" she asked with interest.

"Long enough, Lady Garola," he replied. She looked at him with greater respect. Then she turned back to look me over. I became fiery pink and unnaturally intent on my plate.

Ragul laughed. "It is just possible," he admitted to the unspoken question. I hadn't thought it was possible to get redder, but I was wrong.

He had chosen only a light meal, and when he had finished it, he made his excuses to Lady Garola and rose to leave.

"Yes, I've heard of the alert, even in here, Lord Ragul, and I am sure you are anxious to be back at your duties."

"Yes. Even though this is a civil matter, I do have an obligation to assist. Indeed, I have a meeting with the First Councilor in a half segment." He glanced at the band on his wrist.

Coming back to us, he took me by surprise, taking my face in his hands and kissing me hard on the mouth. He gave my shoulder the merest squeeze before releasing me. Rill fared the same.

Somehow, when he left the room, he seemed to take my appetite with him, and fear took its place. I stared unappreciatively at the little pink cake in front of me.

"Stop pining, girl, he's hardly left the room!" the old woman declared crossly. With a glare at the plate before me, I lifted the small cake and bit it viciously in two.

Chapter Six

The room Lady Garola had allotted us was, unlike the rest of the stylized apartment, a thing of quiet beauty. Unobtrusive and expensive, as everything here seemed, this room had a touch of something extra. Instead of being just a frame, it had become part of the picture. Alone at last, we looked about us, seeking to understand this environment.

An illusion had been achieved that made the bedroom seem to be outside, in a secluded garden, beneath an afternoon sky. Yet the quantity of plants growing in the room were comparatively few, and the "grass" was a pale green carpet that gave way to the greenish grey tiles around the fountain. The flowers were minimal, only a few pink and cream blossoms floating in the pool. A low sleeping dais had a central position, with some leafy plants around half the room giving texture and beauty.

The fountain splashed quietly. The faint stir of leaves, the elusive scent of warm, damp earth after rain, and the smell of growing plants made the effect uncanny. It really did seem like a garden.

"The lighting," I commented, "that must be it. It isn't just the sky effect, there's the peripheral illusion of a large walled garden, even the faint movement."

"Yet when you look directly at it, it's not there, like the Natura," said Rill.

"What's a Natura?" I asked.

"Whatever fear that obsesses you," she said, shrugging.

I nodded, appreciating her remark. "How deep. How perceptive," I said. "Could you use that deep perceptive quality to spot the clothes she mentioned?"

Rill grinned. "How did she say it? 'You might condescend to use some of the gowns you find there.' And in such an autocratic voice. I rather like her." As she talked, she prowled along the edge of the room least furnished with greenery. "Do you think it will be a concealed entrance like at—"

"Yes," I said quickly, feeling that it would be better if we *never* spoke about the place, so that we would not slip up. "A plaque in the wall would detract least from the room."

Rill glanced at me with interest, but she said nothing as she continued her search. We each found a plaque at the same time.

The whole room was textured surfaces, and her matte cream plaque in the matte cream wall was as hard to see as the rippled green one I found between two tall ferns.

The plaque slid open when I palmed it, and I peeped into a room that contained a jungle of green plants, all intent, it seemed, on flinging themselves into the most beautiful sunken green marble bath I had ever seen. Crystal taps glittered, and floor-length mirrors endlessly reflected the bubbling, swirling waters therein. A Jacuzzi! I moaned ecstatically.

Rill's laughter came over my shoulder, and I turned to her, grinning foolishly. Quizzically, she said, "You get more excited by bathing than by a man, don't you?"

Turning back to the room, I responded, "Baths are a more enduring pleasure." I tried not to remember my heart slamming against my ribs when Ragul kissed me.

"Really?" She looked at the bath with a renewed interest. "We don't have them at home," she admitted. "So far, I have always chosen a shower, and you must admit, this is different from anything we've seen here."

With a last lingering, hungry look at the Jacuzzi, I palmed the door shut and followed Rill across the room to a series of open doors. Between them, artlessly arranged bushes spilled out onto the carpet. There were four doors opening into one long walk-in closet. Hanging on shaped and padded hangers were myriad gowns in a galaxy of colors for a host of occasions.

"Oh goodness! Every season must be represented here," I commented as I walked down the row of clothes, my trailing finger disturbing their beauty.

"Seasons?" queried Rill, holding up an overdress of a stiff gold fabric.

"It's just a way to describe different skin tones. Named after the seasons of the year," I explained.

Rill still looked puzzled. "What *are* seasons?"

"Oh." I looked blank for a moment. "I guess you don't have them. My planet tilts as it turns, so the weather changes four times a year, and so does the state of the vegetation. Each change is a season."

"By the lights of Darrox!" gasped Rill. "That's terrible. How do you survive?"

"Actually," I said, laughing, "we rather enjoy it!"

"You're mad," she said, but with grudging respect.

Deciding not to disillusion her, I started to hunt around for accessories and soon found them at the end of the cupboard in a series of glass-fronted drawers for easy viewing.

I spent a rather happy half hour selecting clothes and putting them together at the accessory end of the cupboard.

When I had finished, I was rather surprised to find that Rill had been observing my choices with interest from her comfortable position on the bed.

"At first there seemed no reason to your choices, but now I see a pattern." Rill rose from the bed. "When you have the time, will you show me what mine would be?"

I nodded, pleased to teach Rill anything!

The knock we had been expecting came, and without waiting for a reply, the old lady entered our room as we turned to greet her. We remembered to bow only, as no formal brow touching was necessary after a first meeting nor in this informal setting.

Her bright black eyes stared at us intently for a few moments.

"Well, at least you look presentable. I thought I would find puffy faces and red eyes ... your mother was a watering pot," she said with some satisfaction.

"In your care, we surely need not fear our relatives?" I said, smiling.

"Relatives?" snorted the old woman. "I was referring to your young man."

I opened my mouth, then closed it again.

She observed this with considerable enjoyment. "Well, come along then, and meet a young visitor of mine."

"Is that wise?" asked Rill.

"I wouldn't have suggested it if it wasn't, impudent wench!" she retorted.

She turned and stalked from the room, gesturing for us to follow, which we did after an exchanged glance.

The large reception room seemed empty when we returned to it, and our hostess looked plainly at a loss and increasingly annoyed. "Where is the boy?" she complained. "I left him standing here only a moment ago."

A noise of strangled nervousness made me turn to look behind us. I looked up a long expanse of olive uniform before I came to a flushed, boyish countenance. There was a look of acute embarrassment in his face, along with a forlorn appeal for understanding in his amber eyes.

He was about eighteen and had the awkward, gangling appearance of one who has grown too much, too soon. He seemed all bones and angles, and his cuffs and tunic length betrayed him by their shortness. The yellow braid on the green material looked bravely military, but the flushed wrists sticking out of them belonged to hands that twitched in an agony of mortification.

I guessed that the poor boy had a made a dash for the necessary as soon as the silly talkative old lady had left him, and he hadn't quite made it back in time.

"Well, will this young man do?" I asked.

"Heavens, what are you doing over there, boy?" she exclaimed, looking somewhat startled.

"He seemed to be picking up those blue pebbles when we entered," I said.

His eyes flared with unspoken thanks, and he seemed about to smile when his demeanor became unnaturally solemn.

"I apologize, Lady Garola, for having knocked them over, but," an eager smile peeped out, "I believe they are all picked up now."

"Gad boy, you did give me a start," she commented querulously. "But never mind that. Come and make your bow to the Ladies Rilla and Rowanna." She waved him forward. "My dears, this is Lord Matul, the clumsiest of my grandsons."

With this encouragement, Matul executed a bow that had the polished grace of a courtier and was at total variance with his age. I was surprised at this, and also at the eager, tentative smile that accompanied it.

As we made our responses, a servant appeared and announced Senator Hagnot's request to visit with Lady Garola, if it was convenient.

My startled look encountered Rill's, but Lady Garola showed no hesitation in admitting him. In a very few moments, the man most desirous of seeing us dead was smiling formally at us and giving us a bow in exact accordance with our assumed rank. I had expected a more aged, less vigorous person than the tall, broad-shouldered man standing before me.

Turning to Matul, he frowned slightly. "Ah, I see by your insignia, Matul, that you are in Jossand's wing. I gather that you have decided to let your agent continue to hold Omat while you serve in the wings for a few years. A sensible choice. However, I am surprised to see you here." He paused significantly.

Matul stiffened into the formal stance of a soldier. "It is at Jossand's command that I am here, sir," he said simply.

"Oh?" Hagnot waited, then comprehending Matul's silence, he turned to Lady Garola. "Young but not stupid. A promising lad, my dear."

She nodded, a half-fierce, half-proud look on her face. "Not all flash and foolish," she admitted grudgingly.

"My business won't take too long," Hagnot said after a pause in which Matul looked uncomfortable. "Have you been down to your estate recently?"

"No." She looked intently at him. "I rarely leave the city these days, why do you ask?"

"It would seem," he said carefully, "that certain conspirators have helped some dangerous criminal elements to escape, and it had occurred to me that they may have thought I'd never think of my own property, or that of my relatives, as being a hiding place." Strong brown fingers tapped momentarily on the large clasp of his sash.

Lady Garola looked astonished. "Do you intend searching here?" she asked with astonishment.

"No, no. These criminals need confining and maximum supervision." His teeth flashed in a savage smile. "At least there will be no mistaking them when we find them."

"Why?" I asked the question aloud unintentionally, a merest breath of sound that he caught and heard. He turned to look at me. I must have looked the picture of girlish horror, for he looked with momentary irritation at my pale face and parted lips. Then his annoyance vanished, and his eyes fell to the rise and fall of my breasts beneath the thin green fabric of my tunic. His lips curved, and his eyes held a gleam as he raised them again to my face.

"Lady, do not distress yourself. They could never approach you here." Glancing toward his aunt, he added, "Your guests have not been here long, I think."

Lady Garola watched him with a speculative smile. "Not long enough, perhaps, to realize how safe they are in my care." Hagnot nodded in understanding.

A servant approached Lady Garola and extended for her inspection a tray of polished wood bearing blue goblets and fluffy pink crackers. After a critical glance, she signaled with her bejeweled fingers, and the girl passed among us offering refreshment.

Before they reached me, another girl approached Lady Garola informing her, to that lady's obvious irritation, that Lady Uronia had arrived … accompanied.

Hardly had the girl made this quiet announcement than the plump lady of the washrooms and her pretty daughter came tripping into the room. She advanced girlishly toward her hostess with outstretched hands, declaring coyly that she wouldn't have come if she had known Lady Garola was entertaining such distinguished guests, that the silly old book could have waited to be returned. She cast a fawning glance at Hagnot and would no doubt have continued in the same vein had not a third person entering the room expressed his surprise.

"But dear Lady Uronia, I mentioned the fact to you myself in the foyer downstairs!" the newly arrived officer said and smiled maliciously.

Lady Uronia had the grace to flush, which did nothing to improve her countenance, and her daughter was cast from shy embarrassment into an agony of humiliation that her mother's next words did nothing to alleviate.

"Captain Essoth, whatever will you say next! I never heard you, if you did, I'm sure!" she retorted with brittle gaiety, and she added rather viciously, "Perhaps I assumed you were talking to Lady Lena, for I am sure I would never delay an officer on duty, and you do seem to keep popping up at her side no matter what your duties are!"

But Captain Essoth remained unabashed, and he discomposed Lady Uronia by assuring her that as his duties placed him at Hagnot's disposal—he nodded to the senator—his escorting them to Lady Garola's, where he had been told the senator was, in no way infringed upon his duties. Having thus dealt with her, he bowed over Lady Garola's hands.

I somehow felt this wasn't quite what Ragul had planned. Phrases like "lives retired," "never goes out," "a bit of a recluse," and "seldom sees her nephew" had figured largely in his description of her. Now, here we were, Rill and I, up to our ears in the very people we were hoping never to meet and who were rapidly dashing any hopes we might have had of remaining unsuspected and alive. The chances were increasing swiftly that either we would make an unexplainable gaff or be recognized for what we were, or that we would be denounced by someone who knew the real daughters of Lady Meranna!

Lady Garola, however, seemed to have considered the difficulty and, dispensing with a formal introduction with an excess of testiness, merely referred to us as her two young guests, the Ladies

Rilla and Rowanna. Then, without taking breath, she demanded what Lady Uronia could possibly have to see her about.

Lady Uronia rose to the occasion admirably and, after returning a book to Lady Garola that she seemed not even to remember owning, asked for her ladyship's invaluable advice on marrying off one's daughter to just the right sort of person. She engaged to include Hagnot in the conversation, dropping many hints about Lena's youth and beauty, her breeding stock, and her mother's earnest desire to see her held by an older, more experienced man, along with her firm conviction that Lady Garola would have some excellent advice on the matter.

When the servant approached us with the tray, Matul peered into his goblet and groaned. Grinning in sympathy, he offered me one. "Trust grandmother to serve Gorange! All the elderly ladies do, have you noticed? I wonder if it is a sign of age, like going grey, or perhaps it was all the rage when they were young." He grimaced at the taste and said, "Though that's hard to believe."

I sipped mine tentatively and found it very weak, an insipid, faintly fruity drink reminiscent of diluted lemonade. He smiled shyly at me.

"Have you been with my grandmother long?"

"No, in fact I don't really know this town, or any people here … we live in the country." I glanced toward Rill, who seemed to be developing an absorbing interest in her refreshment rather than in the nearby conversation between Lena and Captain Essoth.

"Ah. Then these persons of considerable interest," his said, his eyes twinkling mischievously, "are unknown to you?" He nodded imperceptibly toward the distinguished older man. "Senator Hagnot you'll have heard of, of course. It's a pity his sister was ever rescued from a Natog ship, for I think it affected his judgment of the experiment. However, it seems he was proved right." Matul shrugged dejectedly before indicating the other man. "Captain Essoth, I don't know him that well. He commands the Third Wing, but he's not … well, let's just say I would not want a sister of mine to be held by him."

I nodded. A good-looking man, very fit, with a narrow intelligent face, but the mouth was thin and haunted by a bitter curve. Somehow I felt he would not prove a good friend in bad times.

"He burns to hold Lena from what I've heard, but he stands little chance. The queue is long, and the mother has larger fish in mind." Matul grinned as we watched Lady Uronia deftly remove Lena from the captain's sphere and draw her to the side nearest Hagnot while continuing to chatter to Lady Garola.

"Unprincipled," he murmured wickedly.

"But in such a good cause!" I teased. "Has she many daughters?"

Matul looked startled. "Does anyone have many daughters?"

I cursed my thoughtless tongue. "Don't forget I'm from the country. We are told you city folk can do anything!" I rolled my eyes comically, and Matul laughed, causing Essoth's eyes to rest on us.

He moved languidly toward us. "Ah, Matul. Been busy since the eclipse conferences?"

Matul acknowledged the officer's presence and gave an easy reply. Essoth paused to consider me. "We haven't been introduced, I believe." He smiled and seemed about to embark on the long list of family that formal etiquette required when I interrupted hastily.

"No, we haven't, but don't you find all that formality wearisome?" I trilled lightly, and then I continued, "You know, with so many new faces I really am becoming rather confused, and there seems to be some sort of alarm on. Do either of you know what it's all about?"

Matul pressed his lips together, but Essoth smiled unpleasantly, and glancing toward Hagnot, he remarked, "Well, it's all rather hush-hush really, though how you can hope to conduct such a vast search without arousing comment I don't know." He seemed amused at Matul's increasingly angry glare. "Don't scowl at me, boy, it's an open secret, and if you ask me they would be found quicker if a public announcement was made!"

"Well, no one is asking you," Matul snapped. "And if fewer people went around blowing their mouths off, it would be more likely to remain a secret."

Essoth's eyes glinted. "How secure you must feel as the Councilor's second cousin," he taunted softly.

Matul flushed with anger and mortification, and he would have rushed into a dangerously fatal speech had I not managed a doltish giggle, which drew the angry and astonished glances of both men.

Essoth's look was penetrating, but I managed another giggle and exclaimed, "I never knew the city would be *so* exciting! I mean, at home this sort of thing could never happen in a ladies' salon."

The random shot hit home as both men looked uncomfortable, and I babbled on, "And when I think how quiet and formal mama said this stay would be, due to Lady Garola's age and health, but really it seems it's not at all like the country!" I finished breathlessly, viewing with satisfaction their embarrassed countenances.

At that moment, Lady Garola, ignoring the attentions of Lady Uronia, advanced toward me, casting a somewhat forbidding look at Captain Essoth. "Well now, girl, what's put these two in such a pucker?"

"My foolishness, Lady Garola, I asked about the alarm, and it seems no official statement has been made, which makes a reply rather difficult," I admitted.

"Ha! Officials wait to find out what the people know before they almost admit to half of it being possible! Insane criminals indeed. More likely they are after a band of men who have discovered a means of avoiding disturbance taxes! Or some poor simple who parked his craft in the Councilor's area!" she snapped contemptuously.

Lips twitched as some of her listeners seemed to recall the relevant incidents. Then Matul looked grave as he remembered the reason for his presence in his grandmother's apartments.

"Lady Garola, have you decided on a reply to Jossand's request? Every hour's delay might be vital."

She glared at him. "Is it indeed! Well, I consider the idea all foolishness. Fugitives hidden on my estates indeed! No one would dare. However, it seems my nephew is of the same mind, so you may as well have my men search, as well as yours, though why my own people are not able to do so alone escapes me!"

Her blatant disregard for secrecy clearly pained Matul, who bowed formally to his grandmother and begged her permission to retire and take her agreement to his commander. He continually surprised me with his mature and polished responses, which were so in variance with his appearance.

With his departure, Lady Garola whisked me away from Essoth with the rudeness only tolerated in the old, the rich, and the powerful. Trailing Rill in her wake, she told the room at large that we were tired from our journey and were retiring, and she promptly left the room with us, muttering audibly that she rather hoped they would all have gone by the time she returned.

She waved Rill and me toward our room as she swept on down the corridor. Rill palmed open the door while giving me an inquiring look. "I don't know," I confessed. "I was glad she got us out of there, of course, too great a risk. But why *she* felt anxious I really don't know, perhaps some of them know our relations." I realized how serious the situation was. While some of our minor social gaffes could be written off as the sort of mistakes country-bred girls could make, if we were discovered to be imposters, we would be in great danger—the public outcry could draw Hagnot's attention, and that would be fatal.

"Perhaps," agreed Rill, "but perhaps not."

"Why else?" I asked in surprise.

"Have you considered, Rowhan, that first Matul seems to find you attractive, then her nephew leers at you, and next two young men seem to be getting mad at each other in your presence. Of course," added Rill with a grin at my horrified countenance, "it's only a thought."

"Really, it wasn't like that, Rill," I said. "Her nephew is her own problem, but Matul was only grateful that I'd saved him from an embarrassing situation. The quarrel between Essoth and Matul had nothing to do with me, it was over a breach of security!"

"A good thing he didn't hear what Essoth said to Lena then," Rill commented as she twirled across the room, leaving her remark to tantalize me.

"Well, go on then, what did he say?" I asked.

"Only," said Rill, palming open the bathroom door and disappearing within, then continuing in a muffled voice, "that these aren't the first escapees, and that some people are beginning to wonder what's going on."

I rushed to the bathroom door, stopping my headlong flight by grabbing the open doorway. Rill's clothes were falling to the floor around her, her red skirt like a pool of blood out of which Rill rose like a goddess of war.

"What else did he say? Rill, think about what this means!" My voice lifted in an agony of suspense.

She smiled. "How do you use this bath?" She was enjoying my frustration.

I relaxed a little. After all, she was smiling, so it couldn't be bad news. "If you don't tell me the rest, Rill," I said, looking at her long length and lazy smile as she lifted an eyebrow. "I'll ... I'll weep and simper and anything else nauseatingly 'female' that I can think of!" I threatened. "And I'll be pathetically brave too!"

"Oh, the Gods forbid," groaned Rill in mock horror. "I'll tell all, but only after you tell me how to use this thing."

"Easy," I said as I shook some pink crystals into the water from a scoop lying in a beautiful cut glass bowl that was one of many within reach of the bath. "Just step down into it, and lie with the water up to your neck, relaxing. Now, if you please. What's this all about?" I plopped myself down on a wide marble ledge as Rill cautiously lowered herself into the steaming, fragrant water.

For a moment, she lay there stiffly, the water bubbling around her. Then she relaxed with a moan of ecstasy, and I grinned. Another groan, a ragged sigh, and she slowly opened her eyes. "By the forks of Dejan, you're right!"

I laughed and allowed her to enjoy it a little longer before returning to the attack.

"Alright, you calm and excessively smug warrior of Dejan, perhaps now you could deign to tell me your news?"

Rill opened one eye, looked at me, and then closed it again. "So be it. Captain Essoth, a man I would not trust, was saying that Hagnot has demanded that the military aid him in finding some missing persons. He was complaining that it was his unenviable task to ferry Hagnot around."

"Why did he tell her this?" I questioned.

"A combination of explaining his presence and a desire to appear superior to those taking the situation seriously, I think," Rill answered. "And then he went on to say that there are so many conflicting accounts of who's missing, and why they are wanted, that many of the lower echelons are posing some pretty cynical questions."

"Go on," I pressed.

"Well, how could there be insane criminals? No one can remember any being hunted, let alone caught and imprisoned. And," Rill said, sitting up to emphasize a point, "if they are as insane as Hagnot says, *how* could they escape, and *why* would anyone help them?"

"Damn. What conclusions are they coming to?" I insisted.

"It seems that since this alarm, some people are remembering a rumor, a couple of months ago, about some experiments going missing. It was quickly hushed up. Now some people are wondering if all the experiments were the failures they were reported to be, and if not, what happened to them?"

"Experiments? What experiments?" I asked irritably, visualizing atomic bombs or death rays.

"Us, idiot, us," Rill said, sighing.

"Us!" I squeaked, coming to my feet. "Do they have any idea of who we are? You know, pictures being circulated and that sort of thing? Do they know how sane we are?"

"Sit down," Rill snapped. "No, of course not. These are only rumors, sitting room whispers, most of which never get to the ears of officialdom. Take Hagnot, he is absolutely convinced that the experiment was a total, and I mean total, failure. He is sure we were all insane and not fit to breed with. No one could ever convince him, I gather, of anything else, and he is the main power behind the hunt. But to get the help he needs in hunting us down, he has said he is trying to recapture insane 'criminals.'"

"Why does he have this conviction?" I queried more calmly as I sat down again.

"No idea," replied Rill, rising from the tub, "so now let's hear what you gleaned."

"Only that Hagnot has decided that his estates and those of his relatives must be searched by the military. He had a hunch that someone might think them a jolly safe spot to hide criminals. And that," I added, "was a little too close for comfort."

"A lance that just misses brings home no dinner," quoted Rill as she toweled herself down.

"No," I agreed. "But I find his obsession with our insanity a little more reassuring. Although I suppose we wouldn't be in this mess if we were accepted as sane ... or would we? I'm a bit confused. Is being sane synonymous with being dead, in our case?"

Miserably, I watched Rill go into the bedroom. The tub water had completed changing itself. It sparkled and fizzed. What I really needed, I decided, was a lovely hot bath.

Later, I lay where I had flopped onto the bed. I always stayed too long in baths and invariably felt totally enervated when I got out.

I moved a finger experimentally. The effort didn't exhaust me, so I tried a foot. Just a wiggle, but I was pleased that I didn't drop off to sleep again after the exertion. Perhaps, I thought, I should risk opening my eyes, or even stretching ... or was this being too daring?

Before I could come to a decision, hard fingers were thrust into my sides, and I leapt from the bed with a shriek. I whirled on a grinning Rill. "Never," I said slowly and furiously, "never, do that again. Many things I take calmly, go ahead, break something, I don't mind. But never do that again." And I meant it. Anger pounded through my veins, and I was half crouched as if to attack. I took slow deep breaths and made myself straighten. Rill looked interested.

"It's not that I hate being tickled," I tried to explain. "My feet, my back, I adore it! It's just my waist, it always has been." I could feel the tremors of reaction dying away. "I mean, everyone hates having someone grab them by the neck and pretend to squeeze. Well, this is the other thing I hate," I finished lamely, now feeling rather foolish at my response.

Rill continued to look interested. "You actually moved quite fast," she said. "And the stance, most unfeminine, almost aggressive." Her eyes laughed at me.

"Well," I said, "I had a bit of military training when I was at university. It's surprising what sticks. It wasn't as if I was one of their more enthusiastic pupils."

Rill's head fell back in laughter. "I'll bet," she gasped.

I bristled slightly. For heaven's sake, I wasn't Loona!

While I had slept, Rill had selected her clothes for the evening meal. During our intensive cramming, we had been shown many pictures of costumes, codes of behavior, and customs, so we had a reasonably good idea of what to wear for most occasions. There was the usual simple tunic over a long, full skirt. She had chosen an orange skirt and a tunic of rich browns that warmed her skin to a pale gold and brought red-gold highlights to the loose curls of her short auburn hair. She had taken a long string of beads, like topaz, and knotted it to form a loop around her brow, and from the knot at the back, it fell down each side to join in front as long beads. It was clever and in keeping with the local theme. I nodded my approval. "And is this how you dressed to go hunting?" I asked with a show of innocence.

She grinned. "On occasions."

I felt compelled to at least match her initiative, and at last I twirled before the mirrors reasonably satisfied with my efforts.

A creamy satin skirt swished around my legs and a deceptively simple tunic of swirls of beiges, gold, and peach complemented it. A thin gold belt encircled my waist a couple of times, and I had a golden band around my brow, with beads hanging from the sides and back to hold my long, wavy hair in place.

"Nice," said Rill. "If we live through the next few weeks, we may well find our talents useful."

Dwelling on her words as I followed her down the hall, I felt considerably less pleasurable anticipation of the meal ahead.

We had believed we would be dining alone with Lady Garola. She had mentioned the fact, and she had given her advanced age as an excuse for quiet living. So it was with fear and dismay that I saw Hagnot rise and bow his head to Rill, taking her hands to touch his chest, as was correct for a lady as yet unheld. Ragul had told us of this, and that it was rarely done, except by the most exacting and old-fashioned.

Then he turned to me. I am not a vain creature, I don't think all men desire me, but Hagnot definitely had the look of a hunter as he advanced toward me. His lips curved into a smile of triumph as my fingers trembled in his. Irritation welled up in me. The conceited, arrogant idiot couldn't tell a timorous virgin from a frightened rabbit!

I glanced at Rill, her steady look held mine. I couldn't read it. It conveyed caution, yes, but not the condemnation I dreaded nor the anxiety I felt.

Hagnot was leading me to the long, low dais he had risen from. I cast an anxious look at Lady Garola. We were supposed to be taken! But she and her nephew seemed to have come to some sort of agreement, for she sat straight-backed, a small smile on her lips.

She beckoned Rill to a place near her, so our platforms formed three sides of a square facing inward. We assumed the cross-legged posture, and at a gesture from Lady Garola, the servant came forward with low tables, finger-bowls, and napkins.

The meal presented a thousand new agonies. Each small course presented new dishes with their specialized cutlery, and it needed the inventiveness of the damned to delay eating until Lady Garola or Hagnot had started. Then came the course that Rill and I were served first, and the others waved away. It looked like a soda float topped with cotton candy. The piece of cutlery resembled a long silver toothpick with a tiny fork at each end.

I let my hair fall forward to hide my face. Perhaps in pushing it back I could contrive to upset the small table and its wretched dessert.

Strong fingers soothed back my hair, and I glanced up anxiously into Hagnot's face.

"A favorite dish of mine," he said, smiling.

"Then why don't you have any?" I asked, playing for time.

"I intend to." His smile was definitely disquieting. Then he leaned forward to lift up the slender fork and deftly wound a small portion of the candy floss around the tines, then dipped it into the creamy mixture and lifted it to my lips. I had no choice—it was going to drip on me if I didn't open my mouth.

It's very odd how being fed by Mogan made me feel like a loved child, whereas being fed by Hagnot was altogether too intimate for comfort.

Turning the fork deftly, he prepared the other end, and then slowly, watching me, his lips closed over it.

"Actually," I gasped, "I think I am a bit full. In fact," I added firmly, "I know I am."

Lady Garola chuckled across from me, and Rill dug happily into the confection, seeming to ignore my plight.

There was only a slight pause before the still smiling Hagnot straightened.

"There's no need to look so militant. I told him you were both taken. However, as we all know, until the files are recorded … whoever can hold can have!" A crusty smile moved her features.

"Whoever would have thought the arrival of you girls would give me so much entertainment?"

"You did," grinned Rill. "Otherwise you wouldn't have done it."

"Oh, hoity-toity, and how do you explain that?" Lady Garola demanded.

"Well," Rill responded calmly, "even if we were dead bores, you still have the pleasure of seeing our mother having a fit, possibly several."

At this a genuine smile of glee touched the old lady's face. "That's true," she said. "Very true!"

Hagnot was no sweaty-handed youth. He made no further attempt during the short evening to single me out. He talked to his aunt while we listened, very much more eagerly then our dutiful faces implied.

The look in his eyes was calm and certain. He could afford to wait; the end was inevitable. If anything, he found my resistance amusing and interesting and to be savored while it lasted. I found him male, arrogant, powerful … and deadly.

On returning to our room, Rill blessed the gods of Dejan for making old ladies tire easily. The ordeal after dinner had been short, and once Hagnot had left, Lady Garola had waved us off to bed.

In a loose red robe, tissue thin, Rill counted off on her slim fingers the information we had gathered to date about the search. I lay on my stomach on the bed watching her and nodding as she went over the points.

"It was Hagnot that called the alert, and he is getting the military to search likely places, including the lands held by his relations." She paused her pacing for a moment. "People have been told the experiments were dying one by one, and that it was a failure. However, no one believes the insane criminals tale at all, and they are starting to wonder if there is a connection to the aliens. Especially as there are now rumors that some of the experiments have gone missing." After a pause, she added, "Of course Hagnot has to kill us. Not only does he believe we are mentally damaged by the virus, if the people found out he has lied about our deaths, he will be ruined. From something Torren told me, I think he also thinks breeding with aliens would be disgusting, even if they were viable. Can you remember anything else?"

I just shook my head. I was still feeling vulnerable and frightened from the events of the evening, and I cuddled into my long cozy robe like a child. Rill sighed and continued pacing. It was like this that Ragul found us when the servant bowed him in.

Our reactions were different. I rolled off the bed, clutching my robe tightly around me, and Rill paused in her pacing to look him up and down.

Ragul strode up to Rill as calmly as you please and, slipping his arms around her waist, pulled her into him and kissed her long and slowly, evidently enjoying every minute of it.

There was a giggle from the doorway, and the door softly closed behind him. Slowly, he raised his head and grinned at us.

"Why didn't you say you were coming?" I said to hide my confusion.

"A holder's rights," he said, grinning wickedly. Then more seriously, he said, "And a holder is what I must be seen as and must actually be … as soon as possible."

"Be patient with Rowhan," Rill advised him, turning within his arm to look at me. "She's suffering from a surfeit of Hagnot."

"Hagnot?" said Ragul, looking startled. "What was *he* doing here?"

"I gather it was meant to be a brief and formal visit, until he saw Rowhan." While Rill explained, I clutched my robe around me and watched him with big eyes. "And now his intentions are decidedly obvious, and his aunt has no objection," she finished.

"Damn," said Ragul, wheeling away from us. "Of all the wretched pieces of work!" He swung round on me. "Of all the men on this planet, you had to attract him! By the eggs of Nerta, what possessed you? Do you dislike living so much?"

"It wasn't like that!" I snarled. "Whose stupid idea was it to bring us here? 'She lives retired,'" I mimicked, "'Never sees anyone.' The place has been like bloody Piccadilly Circus!"

"Like what?" Ragul and Rill asked together.

"Everyone in and out all the time, they practically crawl out of the woodwork," I said furiously. "And if you think for one minute that I encouraged that arrogant, conceited, Selenese son of a bitch, you can—"

His two swift strides forward made me pause. Lowering his head, he searched my face.

"I'm sorry," he said after a pause. "It was rather a shock. I just don't think you are aware of the danger you are in. Hagnot is the main, some say the only, man against the experiment. He is very powerful, and on this subject, not his usual impartial self. Believe me, no matter how beautiful your big blue eyes are to him now, if he discovers your identity, he will kill you."

I kept trying to swallow the sobs that wanted to come. Ragul drew me to him.

"Why is he so against us?" asked Rill.

Ragul cradled me in his arms. "His sister was rescued from an alien ship after transformation." His face was grim. "That's why even the sterile holds are decontaminated now, before we open them, so none are left alive."

"So? We have been transformed," I murmured against his chest.

"Yes, but you aren't Selenese, and even you weren't your best for a while," he replied.

I raised my head to look at him. "Does being Selenese make that much of a difference?"

"Yes," he answered grimly, "a horrible difference. The Selenese brain synapses fail, and the body can only survive hours even with life support. The screaming is terrible, though we are told they can feel nothing."

Ragul's depression seemed contagious.

Chapter Seven

The light stirred across my eyelids as I lay curled in the large, soft bed. My eyes remained firmly shut. It had been a long night—infinitely more wearing than the night of passion that our hostess no doubt had imagined we'd had.

It was a subconscious niggling that made me sit up and look around. I was the only one in the room, but that wasn't it. It wasn't the faint breeze nor the barely audible stir of foliage—I'd gotten used to that yesterday and liked it.

I frowned at the beiges of the bedspread and found my solution there. The random patterns of light and shadow stirred and moved across the bed. Looking up, I could see no branches to cause them, but the ceiling was glowing as if with the light of early morning. Rippling glints of light reflected up from the pool. Enchanted, I realized how subtle the arrangement of light, water, and bed was to achieve and extend the illusion of sleeping and waking in a garden. Looking again at the crossing and recrossing light and shadow on the bed, I saw their origins in the ripples caused by the fountain.

Fully awake, I stretched and bounced out of bed, feeling much happier and more refreshed than I had a few minutes before.

Rill was obviously at breakfast—a voracious appetite, that girl—and Ragul had left in the early hours. I didn't really want breakfast nor to be quizzed by Lady Garola, and I was eager to see what I could remember.

The evening before, Ragul had firmly sat us down and introduced us to the Selenese alphabet. Basically a phonetic language, many of the sounds of the thirty symbols were exchangeable with ours. The C, H, Q, and Y letters were not there, but some of our letters, the vowels for example, had two or more symbols, one for each sound. The SH and CH sounds had their own symbols too. In many ways, it was simpler than our alphabet, and spelling was much easier.

Ragul made us softly chant the learning songs as we awkwardly inscribed the symbols over and over again. We had barely mastered them when he hurried us on to our names, which included, when written, our numbers and file codes.

Rill had rebelled at this point. Her written language was very different, and the Selenese alphabet had taken an incredible effort on her part. The name she could memorize, but the added number symbols, which were meaningless to us, were a horrendous task in the middle of the night.

Ragul remained adamant. Our lives might depend upon it. Naturally, the numbers with our names were made up, but it would take time to check them out, time which could prove vital.

"Well, even if they do turn up blanks, we can always say we'd made a mistake and give them another," I pointed out.

His glance was stern. "No one ever forgets their number. It's almost the first thing you learn as a child, especially a fertile female."

"How can a child be fertile?" I asked.

"By a gene test, normally taken at any time after eighteen days into the pregnancy," he retorted with exasperation. "Now, first your title, then your names, then the number, and lastly the code, got that? Try it again."

Bullying, praising, and explaining, he compelled us to write most of the night away till tears of weariness blotched the paper and distorted the letters. At last he seemed satisfied and set about gathering up all the used pieces of paper, including his examples and our copies.

"Not all of them," cautioned Rill as she stretched and flexed her fingers.

"Yes, all of them," was Ragul's firm reply.

"But I'll never remember them all," she countered sharply.

"You'll have to. It's too dangerous to leave them lying about. Rowhan, dispose of these, will you?" he said, handing me a sheaf of papers while he stooped to gather those that had drifted to the floor.

"Where?" I asked, stupid with sleep and clutching them in a rather dazed way.

"Over there, the niche in the wall." He pointed to a textured green wall as he checked beneath nearby furniture and plants.

Following his gesture, I noticed a small niche, barely a foot square, halfway up the wall. It was empty. In a rather dazed way, and with a mental shrug, I stuffed the papers in and removed my hands. As my hands left the niche, it hummed faintly and the papers vanished, leaving only a wisp of smoke to be drawn away in moments by some concealed means.

I don't know how long I stood there, staring at the niche. It was Ragul, coming up with the last bunch of papers, who glanced at me, and asked what was wrong.

"Why didn't it hurt my hands?" I asked through a tightening throat.

"Domestic ones have a sense screen around the opening and won't turn on if there is anything living in them. Prevents nasty accidents," he said as he reduced the papers to nothing.

"Do you feel anything?" I asked as if from a great way off. "As your feet disappear, and then your legs, and then …"

I don't know what he replied. For the second time in my life, I fainted.

I shuddered away from the memory of the room at the institution and looked about for the small pile of paper left for guest's use by Lady Garola. Sitting cross-legged at the low desk, I carefully wrote out the Selenese alphabet, whispering the names as I wrote. Then I inscribed my signature and was rather pleased with the result. I debated keeping it to chuckle over with Rill on her return, but Ragul's fears were contagious, so steeling myself I disposed of it in the niche.

I was just beginning to wonder what had happened to Rill when the door sighed open and she came in, her swift strides hampered by the long olive green shirts of her underdress. She was halfway across the room before the door had closed.

I raised an eyebrow and cocked my head inquiringly.

"Your unwanted suitor is proving a problem," she stated. "I'm glad you didn't come to breakfast. He was there. Asking a lot of questions." She must have seen me grow pale as she continued swiftly. "No, he has no idea … yet. His aunt had told him who we are supposed to be, but he was recalling members of the family, talking of places we've supposed to have been. I had to keep my mouth full so I could answer with nods, smiles, and shrugs!" Her voice betrayed her tension, and she began to pace the room with urgent strides.

"Ragul said he would be over as soon as he could this morning," I reminded her, my anxiety growing to match hers. "He'll have some ideas."

"Will he?" Rill asked bitterly. "I rather thought this was the best he could come up with."

"It would have been alright if Hagnot hadn't seen me. Indeed, Lady Garola had promised to keep us hidden. We weren't meant to see anyone!" I protested.

She conceded the point with a shrug and flung herself into a large chair.

There was a heavy silence while we both considered the problem. "I think," I began tentatively, "that Ragul will take us away as soon as possible when he becomes aware of Hagnot's persistence. Indeed, he may already have made plans to do so. So," I said more firmly, "I think we should get dressed for going out."

Rill looked thoughtful. "Yes, in the things we came in. I wouldn't like to be hounded for stealing a dress on top of everything else!"

"Just so," I agreed. But we were not entirely ready when Ragul entered the room unannounced. He took in our preparations with a glance and nodded approvingly. "Good. Be swift. I haven't told Lady Garola yet, and I won't until we leave, as she might be tempted to inform that nephew of hers." He looked strained and fell to pacing as we finished our preparations.

"Where will you be taking us?" I asked, a little irritated by his continued silence.

He looked up, gazing blankly at me for a long moment, then as he recalled his thoughts, we were interrupted by the knock and entrance of one of the serving girls.

She bowed to him and gave him a message. "The First Councilor, Senator Hagnot, requests your urgent attendance at the war chambers with all possible haste, sir, and in anticipation of your assent he has arranged for your conveyance to be on the roof by the time you receive this message." She bowed again and left the room.

A shocked silence filled the room, and then Ragul threw back his head and laughed. "By the many children of our forefathers, if it were not for you two, I'd admire his tactics. But I'm not that easily stopped. A friend will take you; he'll not know of that till it's too late." Without more than a wave in our direction, he left the room with long strides and the look of one who is rather enjoying a duel to the death.

Rill and I just stared at each other. What on earth, or in this case Selene, were we expected to do? Just sit there until someone came?

I dropped forlornly into a chair, expecting that at any moment Lady Garola would enter and inquire why we chose to sit in our room in the walking dresses we had arrived in instead of keeping her company, formally dressed, in the salon.

Barely twenty minutes later, a girl came to tell us that someone awaited us, and as we entered the salon it seemed that Lady Garola had no idea we were about to leave. She must have assumed our absence was due to a fit of the sulks, and she happily left us to it, believing that hunger would bring us out in due time. So it was that when we entered the salon Lady Garola was looking more surprised than we were at Torren's breathless explanation that Ragul had asked him to take us to visit his mother.

"I was led to believe," her voice rose in anger, "that they were to lead retired lives at present! Now I am to gather that they may come and go as they please!"

"Not at all, Lady Garola, rather Councilor Ragul was concerned that their presence was too much for you, living as quietly as you do, and that you might be increasingly plagued by all sorts of people attempting to pursue their acquaintance. Lady Uronia, I gather, is one such," he added with a straight face.

Lady Garola eyed him suspiciously. But her ill humor was subsiding, and she grudgingly admitted, with a somewhat cynical smile, that the boy undoubtedly knew what he was doing.

Turning to us, she continued, "Well, you've been nothing but trouble, however, if you need a refuge, I shall not mind having you again." She gave a chuckle and said, "I can't wait to see my nephew's face when he finds you gone. As I said, if you are not happy there, come back. Your visit has taken passes off my age."

So it was that soon afterward we were stepping out of the elevating-tube into the large foyer we had been in the day before. Nothing had changed, but it seemed less intimidating. Rill and I gazed casually around as Torren made a call from a public visi-booth. I could have watched the changing patterns of people and colors for hours, but Torren hurried us down to the streets below where an air-cab waited.

"The Garage of the Seven Doves," Torren told the woman as we climbed in. She nodded, and we rose swiftly from the ground as another cab swooped in to take our place.

I swallowed a dozen questions as there was no privacy in the scruffy air-cab. The pilot continually decried other air users, the awful traffic caused by the unusual activity of the Wings, and the inevitability of the Senate raising the cost of air-cab licenses to help pay for their lavish standard of living.

I gazed out of the window, fascinated by the rose-colored stone buildings. Some older ones, judging by the weathering, were shaped like the steps of a pyramid, while newer ones rose to nearly fifteen stories. Every window had heavy metal shutters, more serviceable than elegant, and the tops of the buildings had one or more levels of parking. One fine building stood in a small park and had colonades and long windows that looked down the sloping city to the glittering sea. To the right, a large river cut through the edge of the town edged in many places by public gardens, judging by the numbers of people in them.

In minutes, we had reached the Garage of the Seven Doves, which proved to be a public parking area busy to the point of congestion. Having paid off the air-cab, Torren assured us that even if we could be traced to here, no one could tell when we left, or in what, or where to. He guided us to a small red and white air-car and helped us to climb into the rear of it.

The windows were tinted, allowing us to sit up and gaze about had we wished, but our attention was on Torren, who was attempting to talk to us and maneuver in a three-dimensional queue at the same time.

"I got a call from Ragul from a public visi-booth at the top of the old lady's apartment block." He swerved, accelerated, and edged into a higher stream. "He said, 'I'm unable to make it for lunch, war meeting, could you run my errands for me?' Of course," he engaged more thrusters, a steeper rise, and made a curve to the right, "I guessed what he meant. So I raced over."

A large, plain, red stone building loomed ahead. The traffic streamed around it to the left, all going in the same direction, but we edged to the right. As we did so, I realized I had seen no advertising, not on the buildings nor the air-cabs. When we got past the building, we turned off into a maze of little streets, but we were about eight stories up.

"He said this morning there was no time to be lost in getting you away from Hagnot." We slowed as we approached an unassuming building block. "It was bad luck, his taking a fancy to you. You sure you didn't encourage him, not knowing who he was and so on?" He set the air-car down in a small parking space and said, "He's active with females, of course, but he hasn't looked at a lady since his own died some time back." Torren killed the engine and turned to look back at me.

"Well, he's looking now," I said between gritted teeth, "and I did *not* encourage him!"

Torren looked unconvinced, but he shrugged. "Oh well, you can't put a bird back in its shell. Let's get you inside." He opened the hatch and, helping us alight, urged us into the building. Several floors down, we passed through bare and silent corridors lined with anonymous doors. At one, he put his hand on a plaque that read his palm.

The door hissed open.

As it closed behind us, we found ourselves looking around a room that would compare well only to a rabbit hutch. It was almost clean; the furniture, while sagging, was still in one piece; and the lack of pictures or decorations ensured that no one would be offended by the owner's taste.

"Will we be safe here?" I asked, cautiously selecting a chair.

"Oh yes. Belack is a good fellow, a friend of mine, but you won't be seeing him. Played a joke on a senior wing officer, so he's got a month's extra duty on decontamination. But he said I could always bunk down here anytime."

"Besides Belack, are we safe from anyone else?" asked Rill drily.

"Oh, I see what you mean." Torren gave a nervous little laugh. "There's nothing to connect Ragul or any of us to this place. Not really his kind of district. Though I must say he never pulls rank, he's not stuffy, if you know what I mean. It's just that being a Warlord, a councilor, a lord holder and a commander, and of excellent family, well, no one would blame him if he was," he explained irrelevantly.

Rill and I looked at each other, thinking the same thing.

"How long will we be here?" I asked, "and will we be keeping you away from your duties?" If we were locked in here with him, we might well commit murder. I couldn't remember him being anxious and babbling when we were all with Ragul on the island.

Torren looked uncomfortable—perhaps he felt the same way about us. "We hope to have made better arrangements in a day or two," he admitted, "but I mustn't stay here. I'm only off duty till after lunch, so I can get food in and so on, but after that I must stay away. It's safer."

Rill watched him. "Do you fear us, Torren?" she asked quietly.

He answered her seriously. "No, not in that way. The idea of your having been without minds does make me a little uncomfortable, now that it's sunk in," he said, "but it's not that. Most of our ladies are," he hesitated, searching for the right word, "more helpless.

"You are both so beautiful and you, Lady Rowhan, are so small and delicate. But I can't forget the weapon Lady Rill made, nor the chemicals you were carrying when we found you. You are both capable of killing." He paused, trying to explain. "It's like—"

"Discovering your old family tabby cat is really a tiger?" I asked, proceeding to explain what each was.

"Yes, exactly," exclaimed Torren with relief.

Oddly enough, I liked him better for his admission.

He departed soon after that, promising to be back as soon as he could. That left us to explore a room not more than eleven feet by ten, not counting cupboards.

Along the length of one wall were cupboards and closets; the end door of the latter opened into a tall, narrow compartment with a shower fixture in the ceiling and a handle in the wall that pulled out a drawer that had a top surface with a large hole—a toilet! Pushing it back emptied it in some way. On the wall in front of that was hand soap and spray and a body blow-dryer. The floor was a maze of tiny holes, and we later discovered that it had the dual ability to suck away water or circulate air. It wasn't the kitchen.

In fact, nothing proved to be the kitchen. There were shelves of clothes, junk, and souvenirs of heavens knows what. There was a half shelf of books we couldn't attempt to read whose pages were of thin plastic that had a tendency to stick together. There was an assortment of old pills and potions whose labels had long since been rendered illegible or lost. There were even a few items of female clothing ... but no kitchen.

Rill had also come to this conclusion by the time Torren returned. "Where," we asked in unison, "is the kitchen?"

"Kitchen?" returned Torren in surprise. "You don't expect a single to have a kitchen, do you?" Then, seeing that we did, he explained, "It's never any point in cooking for one, you just buy a load of singpak meals, whatever you fancy for each meal. Here, I'll show you." He dumped the armload of bags he was carrying onto a chair and, rummaging in them, emerged with some rectangular boxes, each about two and a half inches deep.

"Anyone want vegetable stew with necca buds or venta pods with rich tenin sauce?"

I nodded cautiously and watched while he showed us how to lift and remove a tab near the base on one side, rather like a pop can lid. It was a vacuum. When the air rushed in, whatever was in the base heated, and after two minutes he peeled back the lid to reveal a hot meal, ready to be eaten. A tentative mouthful led to the delightful discovery that it was delicious. Torren grinned at my surprise.

Then I asked the question that had occasionally popped into my mind, but that I'd never asked. "Torren, I haven't recognized any of the dishes we have eaten. Tell me, do Selenese eat meat?"

"Meat?" He looked puzzled.

"Yes, you know," I continued foolishly, "flesh."

He didn't go green. First he went pale, then he flushed, and under our interested gaze he dashed for the cleansing closet. He didn't have time to close the door properly, so we were left in no doubt of his feelings.

Rill shook her head reproachfully at me. "That was unkind. Hadn't you noticed that we have *never* been served meat?"

I was defensive. "There have been so many things in my food that I haven't recognized. The food is delicious, the textures vary greatly, and the herbs, spices, and flavors are largely unrecognizable! I may well have been eating meat and not recognized it!"

"Meat," stated Rill unarguably, "is meat. And there is nothing," she added dreamily, "nothing at all like a portion of barely cooked zanderbeast with the bloody juices running down your fingers."

Torren had shown signs of emerging, but at this he reeled back and shut the door firmly.

It was my turn to look reproachful, but as I ate my venta pods with rich tenin sauce, I was thinking of a thick, juicy, rare steak, a lobster's tail, and a dish of melted butter.

We had the rest of the day to ourselves, Torren having left abruptly soon after emerging from the cleansing room. We discovered in the bags some children's reading books that he had thoughtfully bought, which made me feel sorry that we had made him so sick, along with writing tools and paper. I struggled through the Selenese version of *Peter and Jane* while Rill wrestled with the alphabet. My store of Dejan curses was increasing by the hour.

In the evening, Rill emptied the bags and discovered several other goodies. There were self-heating drinks and multipacks for breakfast. There were also plastic juice containers, and a hunt in the cupboards revealed cups, and a game that, after much poring over the rule card, seemed like a simple version of chess. I was rather good at chess, and having come to the smug conclusion that

Rill's world was a bit primitive, our first game was short and my humiliation complete.

Rill, whose opinion of my namby-pamby world had been no more complimentary than mine of hers, condescended to explain that on her world they had a similar game, but it was in three dimensions. She smirked.

My dander was up. I resolved to do better, and I did. It took her all of five minutes to beat me in the second game. The third game lasted eleven minutes—I think she dozed off—and I was nearly in tears of self-disgust. Rill came round and gave me a hug, and looked deep into my eyes. "Don't fret, little one. Even on my world, I am considered a master," she explained.

I felt better. I sniffed and sat up straighter, and at last I grinned.

"You beast, I bet you enjoyed that," I said.

Rill's grin grew. She wrinkled her nose and gave several small nods.

"Oh, you can be irritating." I laughed, and throwing a cushion at her, I made a dive for the bathroom before she could catch me. It was my night for losing. After being firmly removed, I had to wait while she made her leisurely ablutions before I could follow suit.

We needed our sleep, and we didn't wake as early the next morning as usual. In spite of that, the next day seemed long and proceeded uneventfully. I progressed through several of the children's primers that Torren had brought, and I helped Rill through the first one. It was during this that I discovered that Rill's spoken language bore no relation to the written one. Indeed, she had two written languages and three spoken ones, and none had ANY relation to the others. The commonest written language, I gathered, was a bit like hieroglyphics. No wonder she found the transition to Selenese difficult. But as I pointed out, anyone that good at chess would soon master it.

I decided to try my newly acquired abilities on the books we had found in the room. I chose one with the biggest print and the brightest cover, deciding it was probably written for young children.

I painstakingly and with increasing bewilderment worked my way, word by word, through the first page. By the second page, Rill was casting odd glances at my pink face. By the third page, my gasp of disbelief, combined with my casting the book down, caused her to ask what I was reading.

"Rill," I said, stunned, "I didn't even know that it could be done that way! Or by so many!"

"What?" asked Rill, rising and coming over.

I glared at her, tongue-tied.

"Well?" she asked.

I bounced up and handed her the book. "Understand this, Rill, with the right man, I might be able to do some of it, but I'd curl up and die before I could sit down and explain it. You read it!"

The light dawned on her face, and she turned the book over with interest. "We don't have any books like that on Dejan." She seemed thoughtful. "Those who become very experienced teach others. I thought it was like that for all people. How can you learn tenderness or timing or control from a book?"

"Rill," I said, feeling a little better, "that book isn't intended to teach, it's written to titillate."

She looked puzzled for a long moment. "If he has a woman, he doesn't need a book. If he has no woman, doesn't this make him feel worse?"

I shrugged.

So the day passed in eating, reading, writing, and getting up to stretch before settling down again. That evening, I cut up pieces of paper and taught her a version of Scrabble, and with the aid of the reading books, we did quite well. Except that Rill felt the words should be allowed to go upward and in reverse too. Such was her persistence that I agreed, and after that the game was more evenly matched.

We were woken in the morning by the chiming at the door. I saw no way of knowing who was outside. Torren could get in without help. I looked at Rill. She shook her head.

"Belack's friends probably know he's not here," I whispered, "but Ragul chose this place because he's *not* one of Belack's pals."

While we stood there, the chimes stopped. We found ourselves waiting for them to resume. The stillness was tense. Gradually, we relaxed.

"You were right," I conceded, "probably just a passing friend."

We had barely washed and dressed when the small vidi-screen buzzed. Fear flashed through me. If they were that persistent it was probably his parents or something. If they descended on us, they'd want to know who we were and what we were doing in their son's room!

Rill just stared at it till the sound ceased. Silence filled the room.

"Hang on!" I said with inspiration. "It couldn't be his parents, they'd have palm print access!"

"Would they?" Rill seemed surprised. "Would a single male want his parents to have walk-in access?"

"Hmmm," I said, admitting the validity of her argument.

Suddenly the console below the vidi-screen began to click rapidly, and a strip of paper emerged. At the beginning was a long line that included the word "Belack" and some numbers. Then, in big letters, "OPEN THE DOOR - RAGUL."

I could read it quite easily, but I only felt overwhelming shame at my fears.

I need not have. When the door chimed next and we let Ragul in, he commended us on our good sense and his stupidity in not having considered the problem and arranging a code.

"I just thank the gods you were able to read the message!" he finished. "I doubted that you could, and our plans would have had to be put off till tomorrow."

We explained Torren's purchases and our efforts over the last two days. He remembered he had mentioned the books to Torren the night he had left us, but had had no hope that we'd make such progress.

"Now," he said, looking around in a businesslike way, "we must remove all evidence of your presence and then we'll be on our way."

"Where to?" Trying to ignore the knot forming in my stomach, I rinsed the cups in the hand soap and water spray of the bathroom.

He grinned as he threw food boxes into a niche in the wall we hadn't noticed. "You, Lady Rowanna, will be in a house of correction for young ladies. You refuse to be held by the man your father has chosen for you." He swept up the scattered bits of paper as Rill made the bed and pushed it back into the wall.

"You will be left alone to think over your behavior, with a few improving books, and no overly rich foods that might incite further willful behavior." His lips twitched.

I felt indignant at the prospect and stuffed the cups into the cupboard without drying them.

"And Rill? I suppose she is going to be imprisoned for disobeying her holder," I teased.

Ragul looked around, impressed. "I hadn't thought of prison! They'd never think of looking there."

"Thanks," Rill murmured, giving me a look.

Ragul laughed. "Don't worry, a lady can't be sent to prison unless she refuses to bear children, but it was an excellent idea."

When the room was restored to its original state, Ragul checked the time. "Torren's late. I know he'll come as soon as he can, but I can't afford the delay." He looked at me irritably. "I had intended to take you … but if Rill doesn't leave soon, she won't arrive in time." He paused to think, and we didn't interrupt him to ask what it was she could be late for.

As he rubbed his chin thoughtfully, he came to a decision. Putting his big hands on my shoulders, he looked down into my face.

"My dear lady, it's important that Rill leave at once. I'll have to take her, and once Torren arrives, he will take you. Don't worry, you won't be left here. Even if Torren has an accident and fails to arrive, I will check back and find you here." He searched my face to be sure I wasn't worried.

As Ragul turned and went to the door, Rill gave me a searching look and a twisted smile. I don't think she liked leaving me alone. "Beware of your soft heart, little one," she warned, and she left.

The room seemed very empty when they'd gone.

Barely twenty minutes passed before Torren burst into the room, apologizing for being late. He seemed surprised at my being alone, but he accepted my explanation and seemed eager to leave. He didn't think to check the room, he just rattled on about how the alert was mucking up everyone's schedule.

We walked along the depressingly plain corridor and ascended to the roof by the small anti-gravity lift we had come down by. The day was grey and the wind fresh. It tugged my clothes around me and whipped my hair across my face. I hadn't realized how depressing the windowless room had been until I was out of it.

"That must be a problem with incredibly long hair like that," Torren said as he leaned slightly into the wind and took my arm to aid me. "The wind is always worse on the top of buildings," he added unnecessarily.

I was astonished. The last time I'd seen him, our eating habits had revolted him. He had fled, pale and shaken. The wind ceased abruptly as I entered the cabin of the air-car, then Torren climbed in and shut the hatch. He turned and grinned at me.

"Okay, Torren, why the change in attitude?" I asked.

He looked momentarily uncomfortable at the memory of our last meeting, then his smile returned.

"Loona is pregnant!" His open palm slammed onto the sturdy console with his expression of joy. "In less than sixteen more days, we will know if the child is fertile. Normally we wait longer to do the test, but in this case the results are vital, so they'll do them as soon as possible."

"They?" I asked.

"A top-class gynecologist, of course, we don't want her to have any problems." Then seeing my expression, he said, "No one looks at the face or number of a pregnant lady too closely till the child is born, Lady Rowanna, that gives her time to ensure she is legally held by the time she gives birth. There are many men of excellent family who insist the lady give proof of her conceptive ability before they will officially have and hold her."

"And if she fails the test?" I asked, guessing the answer.

"Her next suitor will be a less exalted one," he replied. I watched his hands move over the console, setting the machine in motion.

"Well, I'm glad Loona's pregnant, but I'm still a bit surprised it made you feel so differently."

Torren looked at me a moment before returning his attention to the controls. "For the joy of a child," he said quietly, "I would eat meat myself."

Chapter Eight

Torren's sincere response left me feeling curiously humble. It brought home to me, as none of the facts had, that many people on this planet were forever denied the joy of holding their children in their arms or watching them grow.

I had borne five children. They were the joy of my life. They were also occasionally my sorrow, a nuisance, and a drain on our finances, but what would my life have been without them? I flinched away from the thought.

Our air-car was joining a stream of traffic and rising to a higher level when, with a short burst of static, a crisp military voice came from the small speaker. "Wing Second Torren, isn't it?" Before Torren could do more than look wildly around at the nearest vehicles sweeping past, it continued, "Divert, I repeat, divert to RADA Complex immediately. General recall."

Torren found his voice. "I have a passenger, sir."

"Good, we need all the help we can get." The connection went dead.

Torren paled and looked at me grimly. "I can't disobey a direct order, especially in an emergency like this." It was a statement, not a defense.

"An emergency like what?" I asked.

"There is only a general recall when there has been a penetration of our space, and that means an impending invasion." Although his voice was steady, the skin of his face seemed to have withdrawn tightly to the bones.

"So what are people grabbed off the street supposed to be able to do?" I asked.

"They can release military personnel from routine jobs so they can man the ground teams and defense craft," he answered, his mind obviously racing, trying to think how best to deal with the problem of me.

"Even breedable females?" I asked in surprise. Usually they made such a fuss about protecting them.

"Well, you'd be in the lower chambers, of course, unlike the more expendable folk." He looked surprised I'd needed to ask.

The RADA Complex was within the city, unlike Earth's military installations, and there were few precious moments for Torren to brief me. He was not even able to come to the accepting building with me, as all passengers had to be dropped off and the air-car flown to its allotted space.

I was curiously fatalistic as the orderly crowd swept me through the huge doorway. There were many military people among them, obviously called back abruptly from leave judging by their various and somewhat hurriedly donned attire. The heavier fabric of their olive tunics with their insignias clashed with mismatched hose, bulged over brighter garments, or hung open as the wearer changed. There were civilians in fair numbers as varied as their clothing. Many had the heavier coarser hose and tunics of manual workers, the reds, browns, and earth tones contrasting with the brighter and lighter fabrics of the others. Some of the older men wore robes and hose, but others wore an open robe over a long tunic and hose. The women wore a gay variety of tunics over loose hose or, more commonly, over underskirts or dresses. Dotted here and there were ladies dressed as I was. There were no patterned fabrics, and about a third of the shifting crowd wore some kind of head covering. It seemed unrelated to rank.

I was in one of the many lines forming before a long counter, where on the opposite side, a number of people in uniform either sat asking questions and writing the answers or hurrying about on various errands in an atmosphere of orderly chaos.

The tall man in front of me left, and I found myself looking down on the balding pate of a small man with rolled-up tunic sleeves, who, without looking up from his forms, said, "Name, number, experience," in the voice of one who has ceased to expect a straight answer.

But he wrote down what I said, still without looking up, made no comment about my lack of experience, tore off a portion of the sheet, and handed it to me as he turned over the next sheet and said, "Third on the left. Name, number, experience."

I moved out of the queue and looked uncertainly around. The three stone, windowless halls formed a T, with the counter being parallel with the top, at the junction with the short entrance hall.

I wandered off to the left, wondering exactly what "the third" was. It proved to be a busy descending flight of stairs with massive steel doors that stood open. At the bottom were two uniformed men. As I reached the bottom, one grabbed my arm. He pointed across the steady flow of people and said, "Down those stairs over there, ma'am." He resumed his scrutiny of the descending populous.

These stairs, again with massive doors, were less crowded, and the man at the bottom sat at a makeshift desk on which were piles of forms. Civilians were stopping at his desk.

"Paper."

At my turn, I handed him the one I had been given. He glanced at it, jotted down my name on one of the forms, and scribbled something on mine and then handed it back to me. "Stores, to the right at the end."

Most of the people down this corridor were in uniform, even the women, and as I walked past the open doorways, I felt my gay clothes to be inappropriate.

At the end, I found another long counter, but this time those being served carried away various items. I stepped up to the counter and handed over my small form. The girl looked at it impatiently. "Not here, you go through that door, at the end." She turned away to the next person.

Dutifully going through the door indicated, I found myself entering another part of the store room that was being used as an office. A frail elderly man with the sleeve of a missing arm tucked neatly into the front of his grey tunic took my note and read it. "Well, my dear," he said slowly, "do you think you could help Genna put the lighter supplies onto the shelves in the storeroom?"

Before I could reply, the girl from the counter bounced in and stated, "Sir, if you don't mind, could she do the written work? She'll be more trouble than she's worth out there!" Grabbing up a box of straps, she flounced out again.

"Well, well, of course," said the old gentleman, smiling. "I should be happy to have your help."

I looked at the piles of paper with horror as he sat me down, but fortunately he didn't seem to expect me to fill them in. "They're a bit complicated, my dear," he explained kindly. My job, it seemed, was to count the bits of paper exchanged for, let's say, flight boots and subtract it from what the file card said was in stock at present, and then tell him how many were left. At least that's what I thought he said. Actually, he was only explaining what we were doing. I was only to count the bits of paper and tell him. After wondering to myself why they didn't have scanners and computers doing this, we set to work. I could now read Selenese numbers, but I found them horrendous to work in, so I surreptitiously counted them in our numerals, jotted it down, converted the file numbers to numerals, did the sum, and then converted it back.

"There are 2,006 personal air filters left," I announced as I passed on to the pile of boot liners. I had finished counting them and was subtracting them from the translated file number when the old man asked me to repeat what I had said.

I glanced down at my scribbles. "Two thousand six, sir," I replied, adding, "And there seem to be only forty-six pairs of boot liners left." I reached over and began to count the requisitions for pairs of foam ear cushions for head sets. I felt better. I was coping, and if I was a bit slow, well, so was the old man. Anyway, I was a lady, and nobody seemed to think they could do anything.

Happily, I called out the next numbers. "One thousand eighteen foam ear cushions left. Pairs, that is." I scooped up the next pile, webbing service belts.

"One moment, young lady, how many boot liners?" he asked.

I felt a moment of fear—were my translations wrong? But then I guessed that he must be a little deaf. I looked at my scribbles.

"Forty-six pairs left, sir." I wanted him to feel better, so I added, "I do speak softly, I know, I'm sorry."

He got up and came over to me. "I can hear you perfectly, lady, so now perhaps you can explain how you arrived at the answer so quickly."

I looked at him blankly. Of all the criticism I had expected to receive, thrown into this crazy situation as I was, overcompetence was the last! He looked at me and then down at the scribbles on the paper. He waited a moment more.

"What do these mean?" he asked patiently.

"Well," I said, swallowing hard. "I was never very good at my sums, much slower than everyone else, so one day I thought of this way of doing them, and when they're done I put them back into proper numbers. I hope I haven't done wrong."

His smile was very sweet. "Wrong, dear lady? I wish you had been one of my pupils in the long ago. I'm too old now, sadly, but I'll not let you waste your time here. I have three old pupils in the level below this," he said, chuckling as if at some private joke, "who will not have forgotten me and who will hear you out for my sake. And probably several more times for their own."

I gazed at him in dumb misery, and then I begged, "Oh, please can't I stay here? I could explain it to you."

"I hope you will one day, if you would be so good, but these are times when every Selenese must do their duty, and the time saved by your idea may someday be vital. Now compose yourself while I compose a note to Benot." He smiled at his little sally.

"If any wish to detain you," he continued as he wrote, "tell them you are on the business of Canar Lessand." I barely noticed that he gave two names, and it was only later that I discovered that "Lessand" was the highest honor the Selenese could bestow on anyone, and more than a year would pass before I found out what he had done to earn it.

Chapter Nine

I traversed the length of the hall again, passing the incurious girls at the counter and the indifferent man at the makeshift desk, and walked down to the other end where, I was assured, the flight of stairs led down to the last level of the RADA Complex.

The most noticeable feature of these steps was that they were much narrower, and they had two huge doors at the top and two more halfway down. The stairs did a sharp U turn, and the first metal door was just halfway around the narrow bend, so that it was like the continuation of the wall, and the second was just around the bend. Besides rendering a traditional battering ram useless due to the lack of space, the second door could only be opened outward. If someone blew up the first door, it would block the second door. Cute, I thought, but I was reminded that the Natog were a force to be reckoned with.

Just within the second door, the passage was cut from the bare rock and narrowed abruptly again, barely allowing room for two people to pass. At their base, the stairs widened out and there a pair a guards halted my progress.

"I'm sorry, but you must have an official release to enter this area." The guard really did sound apologetic.

"Well, I don't mind," I assured him, "but I have been sent by Canar Lessand with this note for Benot." I smiled at him. "Perhaps you could deliver it?"

They looked doubtfully at each other. "We're not allowed to leave our posts," admitted the apologetic one, "but if you are on their business, then I suppose a release form isn't necessary." He looked for confirmation to the other guard, who nodded solemnly. In all the time I was there, I never did hear him speak.

I poised to move off. "Well?" I encouraged, "where do I find him?"

"Oh, he could be anywhere, you can't miss him … he's just like his holos." He turned back to the stairs to delay another victim.

I moved off without any real idea of where I was going, but just wanting to get away from the two guards. There were the sounds of general activity ahead, beyond the bend in the passage. Rounding the turn, I emerged into a large cafeteria-type room that doubled as a common room. Surprising numbers of people were sitting and eating, moving around, or talking in groups amid the rather cheerful clatter of dishes and voices. It reminded me of university.

Someone made a noise of apology behind me, and I quickly moved aside to let them pass.

This confusion might be to my advantage. I walked up to a girl who couldn't possibly be Benot and smiled winningly. "Excuse me, I'm a bit lost. I've been asked to deliver something to Benot, but I couldn't find my own mother in all this. I don't suppose you know where he would be?"

The girl grinned back. "Grim, isn't it? I was really confused the first few days. As it happens, I can help, I saw him come in not long ago." She peered around the room. "Ah, there he is, see? That table over near the far corner."

I looked, and then I pretended to look faintly puzzled. "Are you sure? He doesn't look quite like the holos!"

She laughed. "Who does? I think they cut his hair and tidied him up especially for them, but he's still short and dark, and you must admit, you can't miss the nose."

I grinned my relief. "That's true! Thank you so much."

"Anytime. I'll tell you what, if you are in for dinner, come over to my table and I'll introduce you to some nice people. They'll help to keep you sane anyway!" she offered.

I thanked her again and moved across the room toward the table she had indicated. I scrutinized the occupants as I approached. "Short, dark, scruffy, and with an odd nose," I repeated to myself.

There was only one person at the table who seemed short, dark, or scruffy, but his back was to me, and he was talking animatedly. I paused a pace or two from the table, gathering my courage. However, he became aware of my presence, or one of his listeners had indicated it, for he swung around and appraised me for a moment.

"Well? What can I do for you?" he asked abruptly.

I felt betrayed by my assumptions. His was a plain face, all angles and tough-grained skin, under a thatch of coarse black hair, but the nose … oh, that nose would have had Michelangelo groping for his tools. It was a nose of perfection.

"Do you, if fact, have anything to say?" he asked with growing annoyance.

"Steady, Benot, the child is obviously terrified out of her wits," cautioned an older man from across the table.

I threw him a grateful look and held out the note to Benot. "Canar Lessand asked me to give you this." I spoke quietly, in deliberate contrast to his manner.

Benot took it and read it quickly. He glanced at me, and then he read it again more slowly.

"Well, I'll be … but Canar Lessard is not a man to make mistakes." He studied me with considerable interest, then, as abruptly as his previous behavior had been rude, he smiled. Hooking a vacant chair from the next table, he swung it into an empty space beside him and invited me to be seated.

Eyebrows were raised in surprise around the table, and the older man again spoke. "Perhaps, Benot, you would be so good as to enlighten us."

"Our illustrious and retiring mentor has sent us this young lady because she has devised a method of calculation that is vastly swifter than any used at present, he says." He waved his hand theatrically at me. "Not precisely in your fields, Sendal, Foust, but very much in mine."

Then, before Sendal could speak again, he turned back to me and asked, "Could you do one now, or do you need special equipment?"

"Well, if it's a big sum," I answered hesitantly, "I'll need paper and writing tools."

"Paper and writing tools!" He smiled benignly at me. Feeling in his tunic, he brought forth my requirements and laid them on the table before me. Somehow, in spite of his change in behavior, I felt that he was still hostile toward me.

I took up the stylus and poised, waiting. I looked at him inquiringly.

"Try this," he paused, then continued, "If an air-car uses two demic of fuel to fly sixty meteg, how much fuel will it need to fly seven hundred and twenty meteg?"

"Are all other variables constant?" I asked, not believing the sum was that easy.

"Of course," he responded.

"Twenty-four demic," I responded without recourse to the paper.

His teeth bared in a smile. "It's not often a lady has those figures off by heart. Evidence of a misspent youth!"

I rose to my feet and carefully pushed back the chair, I had no desire to stumble as I made a grand exit.

"No. The only evidence here is of a closed mind," I said quietly. There was total silence at the table as I turned and left.

I was halfway to the door when I heard him call. I ignored him and succeeded in gaining the passage before I heard the sounds of his approach.

"Wait, damn you!" he snarled as he grabbed my arm, pulling me around under the shocked eyes of several people about to enter the common room.

"I'll wait for you on a Natog ship, you arrogant son of an egg waster." Not for nothing had I listened to the scraps of conversation in the long queues of the upper hall. "And if you don't let go of my arm this *instant*, you will never be able to breed with anything!" I hissed furiously.

Surprisingly, he did, eyeing me with considerably more respect. Oblivious to the small crowd gathering, he spoke again more mildly.

"Well, standing here won't save any eggs. Come and sit down and we'll discuss it."

"Discuss? With you? I never wanted to leave Canar Lessand, and I'm damn well going back to him. He's a gentleman ... in *every* sense of the word." Whirling away, I continued toward the stairs.

I heard him curse under his breath as he followed, but he made no attempt to touch me. As I turned to go up the steps, he spoke to the guards, "Hold this lady." Without hesitation, the silent one moved between the steps and myself. Only for a moment did I think of trying to slip past, then I turned and glared at Benot.

He watched me intently for a moment and then tried again.

"Lady, I was unpardonably rude." He hesitated in the face of my stony silence. "I apologize. Even if you had not been sent by Canar Lessand, I should never have said, nor implied, the things I did."

He folded his arms across his chest and regarded my glacial expression with his head slightly to one side. The silence lengthened, and even the whisperings of the newly arrived were hushed.

"What can I say? He sent you to me because *if* you have found a quicker way of figuring, what you have discovered *is* vital. That has not changed. You are not giving your discovery to me, you are being given the chance to help Selene. Few have the opportunity to offer what it appears you can."

I had not been idle during his soliloquy. After some quick thinking, I had arrived at a conclusion. When I was caught, as there was little doubt I would be, it would be preferable to have friends to stand by me rather than enemies to condemn me. Also, this wouldn't be the first place that Hagnot would look for me. Indeed, it might never occur to him to look here at all. I might just be able to bluff it out until Loona was proved sane and fertile.

I allowed my face to soften, a look of indecision crossing my features. Eagerly, Benot noted the seeming effect of his words, and careful to hide his triumph, he made a grand gesture. He stepped aside and held out his hand to me.

I made myself hesitate a moment longer, and then I stepped forward and, without looking at him, let my fingers touch his. His fingers closed around mine surprisingly firmly, and turning, he led me down the corridor in a direction I had not previously taken.

The small crowd dissolved quickly before us, and I was able to note that we passed several doors, some of which stood open to show small rooms, labs, a meeting room, and a momentarily open door gave a glimpse of banks of electronics and other equipment with glowing screens and flashing lights. The hum of electricity ceased as the door shut.

At last, he paused at a door and opened it. Bowing, he gestured for me to enter. Within, I looked around with a sense of deja vu. A brilliant friend at university with me had also lived in such a state of disorder and downright mess. However, my friend had assured me he knew where everything was, and he did. More evidence of total recall than of a superior filing system, I had thought, and I expected this would also be the case with Benot.

With great care, he lifted several overlapping piles of papers and a shabby robe from a seat and placed them beneath it. When I had seated myself, he took an empty chair by the overflowing desk and turned to face me. He eyed me warily for a few moments.

"I'm not sure Canar Lessard mentioned your name in his note, and as I've left it at the table anyway, perhaps we should start afresh." His strong, blunt fingers tapped momentarily on the wooden arm of his chair.

"I am the Lady Rowanna." I made no attempt at the long formal introduction that admits a person to your social circle. This was to be a solely working relationship, and my brevity indicated it.

Benot nodded. He couldn't have expected anything else after our inauspicious start.

"Well, Lady Rowanna, perhaps you could show me how you did that sum, and then we can go on to more subtle and difficult areas." He turned and pressed one of several buttons on his desk console.

The blank wall above his desk seemed to flicker and then glowed into life. He lifted his chair over some papers and set it down near mine. Handing me a black oblong, rather like a TV remote, he sat back waiting. At last, he seemed to realize my confusion.

"Sorry. You haven't used one before, is that it?" He didn't seem surprised when I nodded. "Well, it's quite simple, you press this button to write and this one to erase. The others need not bother you yet." He demonstrated with a few squiggles on the screen and erased them, then handed it back to me.

"It isn't going to be that easy, " I said at last. "You are making the assumption that I have adapted what we have. I haven't. I scrapped the lot."

He sat up with a jerk. "Are you saying that you can perform some tricks with little sums but that you can't use or extrapolate your method on anything beyond that?" He waited for my answer with growing anger.

"No, I'm not. And you are making more assumptions on little or no evidence, *again*!" I answered with rising irritation. "Just stop a minute. We can't achieve anything if we don't make some attempt to be mutually tolerant. If my method was obvious and simple, someone would have thought of it eons ago. So please show a little patience! Anyone with your ability with our present method will be able to compute any equation with this method and go far beyond anything I could ever dream of doing with it. Isn't that worth a little patience?" I finished on an almost pleading note.

Benot slowly smiled, the first genuine smile I'd seen on him. "Yes, Lady Rowanna, and may I say you are a most unusual lady?"

I smiled back ruefully. "Well, you won't be the first, my mother thinks I'm unnatural!" Lifting the remote, I wrote numbers that appeared on the screen. "I use these basic symbols. Although I guess you could use any number of them, I use ten of them because as I child I got used to working in that base due to the number of my fingers."

I glanced at Benot, who nodded in understanding.

"Each symbol represents a quantity. This one represents nothing, this one one, and this—"

"Wait a moment, if it means nothing, why have it at all?" he asked.

"Well, sometimes the absence of something is as important as there being something, and its presence effects all the other symbols, depending on where it's put." I went on to give a quantity to each symbol. "Now, here are some more symbols that show what you intend to do with the numbers. There are a few of them, but we will just start with these. This one means you will add together the numbers, this one shows that you will take them away from each other, and this shows that the following numbers are the answer, not part of the sum. Clear so far?" I looked anxiously at Benot, but he just nodded slowly, staring at the screen.

"So let's try a concrete situation. If you have two tokens in your pocket and three in your hand, how many would you have altogether?" I said, writing it on the screen in our numbers.

"Five," said Benot easily.

"No. You are right, of course, but you are doing it from memory, from your memory of the present way. Look, I'll put dots under the symbols to represent their quantity, and down here I'll write the sum again as before, but in dots."

Benot leaned forward, watching intently.

"You do the dots in the same patterns. Two dots, three dots, and the five are four with one in the middle. Do you stick to those patterns?"

I nodded. "Anyone can internalize patterns up to ten, and these are very helpful at first." I waited while he stared at them.

"Supposing you had five tokens and five tokens. How would you manage that?"

"Alright. In dots that would be two five patterns, and that's as high as you will ever need to go. With the symbols, you have completed your base of ten, so you go back to the beginning in a way. Look," I said, writing for a moment or two. "You have one block of ten and no extras left over. See how the nothing, the zero, comes in handy?"

I looked at his intense expression. "Five and six would be one block of ten and one left over, six and six would be a block of ten and two left over, and so on." I handed him the control. "Now you do some, just little ones to get the hang of it."

Benot had successfully completed two or three sums, increasingly quickly, when the door beeped, and Benot yelled admittance while continuing to concentrate on the screen.

Two of the men who had been at the table in the common room entered, the younger somewhat cautiously, and stood gazing at the screen after shutting the door.

Benot turned to me. "What happens when the number is greater than one block of ten and nine left over?"

"Guess," I said, quickly seeing his face darken. "You'll progress quicker if you work it out for yourself, it is a logical step, truly."

He turned back to the screen, staring at it. The two men continued to wait—they seemed content to do so, and used to it.

Suddenly, Benot struck the arm of his chair and whirled around to me. "*Two* blocks of ten! Right?" he shouted triumphantly.

I grinned. "That's right, and so on, up to any number you could dream of."

He swung back to the screen, but before he could explore the idea further, the older man interrupted him.

"Benot, my good fellow, while I hesitate to interrupt," he said, his cynical smile betraying his words, "I feel impelled to remind you of our discussion prior to your meeting this young lady." He slightly stressed the personal pronoun, and he bowed in my direction.

Surprisingly, once he was made aware of their presence, Benot tuned from the screen with the barest show of reluctance and attended to them.

"Sendal, Foust, this concept," he said, waving at the screen, "is fascinating and very well thought out. I have a gut feeling this is *it*. This is what we've been feeling for intuitively all this time." He turned and smiled at me. "Young lady, while you will have seen holos of these two, I would like you to meet Sendal." The older, taller man stepped forward and bowed slightly, raising my hands to chest level. His long gray robe was of the unfastened kind, revealing a dark tunic, light leggings, and a sash of silver cloth. His left hand bore an unusual ring shaped like a shield.

Benot continued, "And Foust." The younger man was slender and of medium height. His green tunic had embroidered edging, and he wore a soft leather sash. He raised my hands to his bowed head, from which I gathered that Sendal was equal to Hagenot in station and that Foust was not, as yet. I had spent such a short time in public on Selene that I was a little shaky as to the more casual greetings, and so I responded with the forms Ragul had taught me.

"All seems peace and harmony," Sendal commented after the introductions, smiling thinly. "Had you not been a lady, one would have expected to walk in to see your grisly corpse on the floor and Benot laughing wildly."

Benot grinned and gave a slight laugh. Foust looked shocked and stepped forward to reassure me. "Not at all, lady. Sendal himself said it would do Benot good to be paid back in his own coin for once, and he delayed his coming to give you both time to restore communications between you." Benot raised his eyebrows at this and looked over Foust's head to Sendal.

"My own coin? My old friend, do I detect a hint of criticism?"

Sendal merely smiled and turned the conversation. "Do not hope to distract me again, Benot. I am very short of good men, and you do not give Annot enough work to justify having him. I could request him officially and get him, but I would rather come to an agreement with you."

Benot waved his hand at the screen. "If this proves to be a breakthrough, I can give him more work than he could do in a lifetime. I need the math to make our own ships and take them into space to confound our enemies, Sendal, and you know it!"

"And you know we have an enemy within. Sterility. Without people, your space ships can't be built or manned," Sendal returned grimly. "I need Annot to work on viral reproduction, and I need him now."

"Oh. That's clever!" I said, hoping to cool the brewing row.

Both men turned to look at me. "What's clever?" snapped Sendal while Benot glared at me.

I looked from one to the other. "Well, what he said. I wondered if it was possible, but as no one had ever said anything about it, I didn't like to ask."

"What's she blathering about?" Sendal turned to Benot for explanation.

"I don't know," said Benot slowly, staring at me, "but whatever she says, you can't have her. You can have Annot. Not her."

"Why in the name of all the eggs on Selene should I want her?" demanded Sendal.

"I have no idea, but she's an original thinker, and very logical, and you can't have her," Benot said.

Sendal turned to me in exasperation. "Would you please explain your cryptic comment? Though," he said, a smile twisting his lips, "your timely interference seems to have been to my advantage. I have been after Annot for some weeks now."

I had no desire to make a fool of myself, but I felt I must explain my evident misunderstanding. "I thought you meant you were growing implants," I said humbly.

Sendal looked incredulous. "How?" he asked, too astonished to be sarcastic.

"The translation virus, of course. I thought you were taking cells from an infertile female, checking the DNA, choosing those with fertile genes, and then making a translation virus using them. Then some isolated living organs would be infected with the virus, and when they were perfect and free from the virus, they could be safely implanted into the original cell donor and ..." I faltered to a halt. The three men were staring at me. "I'm sorry. I don't really know anything about the subject, I'd just wondered about it in the past, and when you said viral reproduction, I sort of made the assumption ... Sorry."

There was silence. At last Benot said in a whisper, rising from his chair, "Sendal? Would it work?"

Sendal turned slowly toward him barely shaking his head. "I don't know. I don't know! No one has ever thought in that direction. To get the virus to work for us and not against us! It's unbelievable." He paused and unconsciously pushed back a lock of gray hair. "It couldn't work quite as she suggests, but I believe there might be a way ... you couldn't just infect some organs and expect them to be made over, of course ... but if you ... it just could ..." He turned toward the door, and then swung back to the other two, his robe swirling around him. They were still standing open-mouthed. "By the eggs, Benot, do you know what this could *mean*?"

Benot gave a grudging laugh. "I know what it could mean, it means we could conquer the enemy within and without. It also means we must prevent anyone trying to educate her at all costs." The mathematician was running his hand over the thick black mane as he spoke.

Sendal seemed shocked. "With her natural abilities, she could go far, in spite of being a lady. It's not like you to inhibit someone with ability, Benot."

"Don't be an idiot, Sendal, I'm not trying to inhibit her. But her value lies in her original thought. Left in ladylike ignorance, she has thought new thoughts, in new ways. Educate her, and she will lose all that and will just become a poor edition of ourselves!" explained Benot in exasperation.

"Excuse me," I interrupted some what bitterly. "This ignorant lady is exhausted by the experience of listening to such exalted beings as yourselves, and intends to have something to eat. Alone!"

Under their astonished gaze, I left the room, and I heard Benot say, as I closed the door, "Was it something I said?"

I half expected one of them to follow me, to prevent me from being contaminated by someone intelligent, but the door remained closed. I rounded the far corner and came again to the common room. There were far less people in it, but there were several queuing for food. As I approached the counter, I became obsessed with another worry. Ragul had not seen fit to give me any tokens. He could not have visualized this situation. I was hesitating before joining the queue, hoping someone would say "charge it," I suppose, when I heard familiar strides behind me. I swung around and found myself in the arms of Ragul, who caught me and held me steady. All I wanted to do was throw myself onto his chest and weep with relief!

"How in a Natog ship do you get yourself into these situations? We're getting out of here before anyone pays you much attention," he said without waiting for a reply.

"Ragul," I began tentatively, "I think they've already noticed me, one or two of them, just a little."

He groaned as he moved me toward the door. "Who's fallen in love with you now, half the Supreme Council?"

"Well, I don't know if any of them are on any councils," I said, rather stung by his tone, "and I don't think love could be further from their minds, but I don't think they'll like my going."

"I don't give a damn if they like it, you are not staying here." Ragul could be very forceful, and it wasn't as if I wanted to stay. We turned the corner into the passage and all but bumped into Benot, Sendal, and Foust. Ragul gave them a nod of recognition and moved on to pass them, still holding my arm firmly.

Sendal looked puzzled, and Benot moved to intercept us.

"Well, Ragul, it seems surprising to see you here when you weren't at the last council meeting," Benot commented.

"The world turns without me, and my presence was needed elsewhere," Ragul returned easily, showing no inclination to stay.

"I see you know the Lady Rowanna," Sendal added, looking at his hand on my arm.

"Yes." Ragul lifted his brows. "But I was not aware you knew her, Sendal."

"Oh, but I do, Ragul, and so does Benot and Foust. We are just joining her for dinner. You do intend joining us, I hope?"

I quailed under the glance Ragul gave me. "I am afraid that is not possible. The Lady Rowan and I are engaged elsewhere. Perhaps soon?" Again Ragul moved to pass, but Benot's next words stopped him.

"Ragul, I don't know what she is to you, but she is vital to Selene. She must be kept safely down here."

Ragul turned me from their view and his eyes asked an unspoken question. I shook my head minimally. He turned back to Benot. "She is my lady. I hold her, and the files are being processed." His voice was calm and reasonable as he dropped what appeared to be a bombshell. The effect on the three men was astonishing.

Benot seemed annoyed; Sendal looked surprised and scrutinized me more closely; and Foust stared at me, an incredulous look dawning on his face, only to be wiped off a moment later, leaving it quite empty of expression. Oddly, it was Foust who left me feeling the most uneasy.

"Well," said Sendal at last, "I can understand your desire to have her to yourself then, but Benot did not exaggerate her importance. Her method of mathematics is unique and, Benot tells me, far-reaching. She has also put me on a track unprecedented in my field. We really do feel that to remove her from here would not be in the best interests of Selene."

Foust saw the conflict on Ragul's face and said quickly, "Well, it need not be decided at this moment, let's all have dinner and discuss the matter. It's possible Ragul's claim can be protected, while keeping the Lady Rowanna safe here." Somehow we found ourselves being ushered back into the common room, and despite Ragul's obvious reluctance, we were seated at a remote table and our orders taken.

When the server had gone, Benot tried to explain to Ragul the concept of my math, such as he had mastered it to date, but Ragul seemed too concerned to concentrate. Sendal began to explain to him the idea I'd had about using the transfer virus, and Ragul just gave me a look bursting with things unsaid.

"My, you have been busy," he said at last, forcing a smile to his lips. I could barely meet his eyes. It wasn't my fault, or was it? He turned back to Sendal, and then looked at the other two.

"I'll be blunt. Hagnot wants her." They looked thoughtful.

Sendal nodded. "I appreciate your problem, Ragul. He hasn't looked at a lady in years; if he wants her, he'll intend having her. And he will have the parent's support. His vote beat yours in the last Supreme Council vote. At the moment, he is the more powerful."

"On the other hand," interrupted Foust, "is he likely to search for her here? Is her intelligence known? Would he not be more likely to seek her in the sealed halls?" His eyes flicked a moment to mine and away again. "I think, if we chose to do so, we could keep anyone from knowing she was here."

"Even after that disagreement in the hall?" Sendal asked dryly.

"All the better!" Foust exclaimed. "No one else knows her name, and if we give out a false name, the only girl they will talk about will appear to be the wrong one."

"Her beauty is unusual," Benot objected mildly, ignoring the frown that Ragul gave him.

Ragul said somewhat dryly, "Might my coming and going not arouse some comment? He knows I hold her." They ignored my blushes.

Benot frowned in concentration. "Not … not if you are seen to be coming to me. We are known to be collaborating on altering the hyperdrive in the larger ships. You can keep bringing me more information, and I can keep asking for more."

"And I suppose," I said tartly, "that people of his rank always run around as messenger boys!"

"True," commented Sendal. "I think we're approaching this in the wrong way. We can't stop it from being known that he holds her, but we can ensure that people are misled about who he is holding. I think Foust may be right in thinking that your quarrel, Benot," he said, ignoring Ragul's look of querulous inquiry, "might be of help.

You have two nieces do you not, who are ladies and are not known here?"

Benot began to smile. "Indeed I do, and who but a relative would dare to be so impudent?" he said, quickly catching on. "Though neither would be expected to catch such an illustrious eye, a bit plain, both of them."

"Excuse me for asking, but would anyone care? There has just been a general recall because our space has been invaded. Isn't everyone going to be a bit too busy to even notice?" I interjected.

They all looked at me with surprise. Ragul explained, "You know it's always six or seven days before interception, and much of the work is routine to the personnel."

"But haven't we rather fewer ships than before?" I asked, hoping to cover my slip.

"So?" said Benot. "We'll fight them within our atmosphere and on the ground, it won't be the first time. Though the first time this decade, with so little space support, I'll admit. We have one or two little tricks they haven't seen before."

The men were still smiling rather grimly when the food was brought to the table, and the conversation became more general while we ate.

Chapter Ten

That night I slept in the small, hastily vacated room of two lab assistants, who presumably had been squeezed in elsewhere. I'd had a long evening with Benot, who had quickly grasped addition and subtraction in the "new" concept and was barely restrained from keeping me up all night by the combined efforts of Ragul and Foust. Ragul's motives I could understand, but Foust puzzled me. Besides Ragul, he alone asked me no questions.

I was stifling my yawns as Ragul escorted me to my room. I was unsurprised when he entered it too. No doubt he was going to be cross with me for getting into another mess.

He closed the door and looked into my tired face. Then he took me by the shoulders and gently shook me. "What's your name?"

"The Lady Ninerta, Nina to my friends." I swayed sleepily.

"Stay awake, please," he remonstrated.

"Can't." My eyes closed and seemed glued shut. "In fact, I think I'm already asleep."

I felt my head being tipped back by firm but gentle fingers. "Well, perhaps it's best this way." I could hear the laughter in his voice, but it seemed too difficult to puzzle out. Then I felt the warmth of his lips gently caress mine. A gentle stroking back and forth. I opened my mouth to protest, but somehow those firm lips parted mine further, and unresistingly I let his seeking tongue invade me. His strong arms slid around me, holding me against him, which was just as well since my knees seemed about to betray me.

I don't remember how I got onto the bed, but I do remember thinking with irritation that a damn sight too much experience went into giving a man that much practiced ease. And that was the last time I was irritated by it that night, for I had not realized that I was once again a maiden. Instead of the pain, frustration, and humiliation of my wedding night with my long-dead husband, I had the most wonderful and fulfilling night of my life. My only embarrassment was the nasty feeling that the person making all those soft and ecstatic moans had been me.

I awakened in the soft glow of a light that had not been turned off. I lay against him, tucked into his arm, my head on his shoulder. I breathed the very masculine smell of him and trembled—his presence disturbed me. His dark curls gleamed in the soft light, his lean, tanned profile stood in stark relief against the white pillow and the curved firm lips did nothing to belie the strength and intelligence of his features. I stared at his sleeping face, wanting to imprint it on my memory forever.

The lips stretched into a smile, and the eyes opened to look straight into mine, an amber devil dancing in them. "Well, my dear lady, am I forgiven?" His quick arm tightened around me, and I was unable to hide my furious blushing. "I can see I am, and I am glad."

He drew my head down and kissed me. Suddenly rolling us over, he now grinned down at me with a decidedly amorous twinkle in his eyes. I couldn't prevent my arms from sliding up around his neck any more than I could stop the little gasp as his nuzzling face found my neck.

His breathing was rough, and he pulled me tightly against him. When he raised his head to look down at me, his face had changed completely. "If you were taken from me now, Rowhan ..." He didn't complete his sentence. There was an urgency in the next few minutes that I never dreamed I could enjoy so much.

Curled in the bed, I watched him shower. I watched the muscles of his broad back as he dried, my eyes slipped shyly past the tapering hips to the long, muscled legs. He even had nice feet. He scooped his clothes from the floor and in a few fluid movements had them in place, his curls firmly subdued.

He came over to the bed and one strong finger flicked my pink cheek. He stooped and kissed my forehead.

"Did Torren tell you about Loona?" he asked, sitting on the bed beside me. I nodded. "In nine days, the fetus can be tested, and then you will be safe."

"Only if it's fertile, I expect," I said gloomily.

"That's why it's important that both you and Rill conceive, my lady. Even one of you carrying a fertile child would be sufficient."

"Well, I'm sure you are doing your best!" I snapped, remembering that I was sharing his favors with Rill.

He laughed and, tipping up my chin, smiled down into my hostile eyes. "I am indeed, and I had no idea it would give me so much pleasure." And very gently, he kissed me.

After Ragul had gone, the room seemed small and confining, so I rose and showered. I had no other clothes with me so I had to put on the slightly crumpled clothes of yesterday. No doubt they would expect me to send out for my clothes, only I had nowhere to send to. Another problem for Ragul to deal with. I would let them think my clothes were with him, and they would have to send him a message. Suppose they offered to send directly to his house? I thought I could see a way around that.

The crowd in the dining common room was thinning by the time I arrived, and as Ragul had given me several tokens the evening before and explained their value, I was able to purchase breakfast with few qualms. My trio was not to be seen, and I was just about to take a place by myself when the girl I'd met yesterday touched my arm.

"Excuse me." She seemed more constrained. "But if you don't want to sit by yourself, you can share my table." She almost seemed to expect a rebuff.

"Why, thank you. I like having a friendly face across the breakfast table."

"Hmm. Yes, we did hear about your tiff with your uncle. I must admit, I hadn't realized you even knew him."

I forced myself to laugh. "And now you think we are the best of good friends and live in each other's pockets?"

A reluctant grin reached her eyes. "Well, no one's ever heard anything like it. Him in a temper, yes, but not the other way around."

"That's the trouble with family squabbles, they tend to be so spectacular. But really, we tend to get along usually," I said between mouthfuls.

"Well, you're very lucky to be working for him, and he seems to value your contribution." She waited hopefully. Her short hair fell rather prettily around her face, her fingers winding a strand between them.

I was saved from replying by the arrival of Foust, who seemed to be relieved to have found me. He whisked me away from my unfinished breakfast by explaining that my uncle wanted me, now.

We traversed the long hall toward Benot's office, but I was surprised to be led firmly past it and into another room, further down on the right.

I looked around the room, empty but for ourselves. "Perhaps, sir, you would explain your action in bringing me here," I said rather frostily.

"It is very possible that you do not know that I am one of the leading psychologists of this world." He paused a moment—my silence must have said a lot. "When the aliens were brought to this planet, I was not put in charge because, it was said, of my revolutionary ideas and my extreme youth. Igan and his assistant Snard were put in charge. Although refused all access to the aliens, I have been permitted to follow their 'progress.'" He paused bitterly. "By means of reports. There were even a few holos."

He stared at my pale face. "Fortunately, there is little resemblance, but why take chances?" He could see my bewilderment. "Igan and Snard arrived this morning. With all the experiments being dead or missing, they chose to return here when the alarm was given."

I turned blindly toward the door. I had some half-formed idea of leaving the building and running somewhere … anywhere.

"No, Lady Rowanna, you are safer here!" His words stopped me. "Have you conceived yet?"

I whirled angrily back to face him. "How in the hell should I know! You tell, you seem to know all the answers!"

A slight flush touched his cheeks. "Ragul hasn't given you some PreVal tablets?"

"Ragul hasn't even given me a change of clothes!" I snarled.

"I can remind him about the clothes, and I can get the tablets quite easily. They are totally harmless. Take one each day, the urine becomes pinker as your fertile period is reached, and if conception takes place, it turns the urine blue." He paused again and looked a little anxious. "You *are* Ragul's lady? He does hold you, doesn't he?"

I didn't have the opportunity of answering. The door opened behind me, and a voice brought back the image of a short, fleshy figure with soft, full lips.

"Ah, Foust, I thought I saw you come in here. Igan requires your presence. If the lady can spare you, of course." He added the innuendo effortlessly.

I turned slowly and looked into the face of the man who had tried to kill me.

Chapter Eleven

During the next few days, I wondered whether aliens on Earth would have remained unsuspected in such a small society as I had here in the secure level of the RADA Complex. I decided that the elite did not notice my oddness because they were odd themselves, and the lesser folk assumed that if someone was accepted by the elite, they must be alright. I also concluded this would be the same on Earth.

Avoiding Igan and Snard proved impossible, but they showed no interest in me at all. I had feared that when they heard of my unusual ideas from Benot and Sendal, they would consider the situation strange, to say the least. However, it seemed that they were totally absorbed in their coming meeting with the Supreme Council.

Ragul, coming and going as his duties permitted, proved less sanguine. Had it not been for Foust's constant reassurances, I believe he would have found some way of removing me from the complex. Perhaps it was only the fact that my presence aroused less attention than my disappearance would have that stayed his hand. He had accepted Foust's penetration of my identity very much better than I feared—it seemed he had a great respect for the young psychologist. However, I was excessively glad Ragul was not present when Hagnot arrived.

***

I stretched as unobtrusively as possible in the uncomfortable pretense of a chair and regarded Benot expectantly. He was staring fixedly at the screen, occasionally drumming a finger on the wooden arm of his more hospitable seat. Abruptly, he turned to me.

"The dot between the numbers represents a fundamental difference between the two sets of numbers, although they may have many aspects in common. In this particular case, the numbers to the right of the dot are less than one whole unit. Is that correct so far?" He frowned in concentration.

"Yes," I said, smiling ruefully. "I wish I'd been able to condense the last hour or so that neatly."

He ignored the irrelevant. "I can see we have 524 pies, but what are .362 pies? You say they are less than a pie, but how?"

For the next hour or so, I explained the concept of dividing things equally by ten or one hundred. Having arrived at the end of my explanation of the third decimal place, I drew in a deep breath and asked anxiously, "Did you get that?"

"It would take one thousand small slices to make one whole pie?" he asked thoughtfully.

"Yes, *yes, yes!*" I exclaimed joyfully, my relief knew no bounds. I was abysmal at math and dreaded the fast-approaching moment when he began to ask all the questions I wouldn't be able to answer.

"How very handy. What on Selene did you need it for?" he asked with interest.

"Um, well, mostly for dividing up pies on a picnic," I admitted.

Benot threw back his head and laughed. "Well, I shall find a better use for it, Ninerta. Is there more to be learned about this aspect?"

"Not just yet perhaps, but I think you should do some adding and subtraction and so on in decimals before we go on to algebra," I said tentatively. I hadn't finished swotting up on my algebra yet.

"Algebra?" Benot asked quickly.

"No," I said firmly, "adding and subtracting decimals first! Besides," I added hastily, seeing him put on his persuasive look, "I'm stiff and tired and hungry. Very hungry!" I added for good measure.

It was at this fortuitous moment that the door buzzed, and at Benot's call, it opened to reveal Foust with a somewhat sheepish half-smile.

Benot and I looked at each other inquiringly, then back at Foust.

"I thought," he said tentatively to me, "you might like to have lunch in your room, so I put your lunch in there. Then I thought Benot might want a working lunch, so I put his there too. But I knew Ragul wouldn't like that much, so I put mine in there as well." He smiled at us.

"While you were doing all this thinking," Benot asked drily, "did you ask yourself why we should not eat in the cafeteria as usual?"

Foust nodded his appreciation of this point, while the small smile twitched at his lips. "Well, I *thought* that if Ragul knew that Hagnot was in the cafeteria having lunch with Igan and intended on seeing you after that, he might possibly insist on taking Lady Ninerta away."

We were on our feet before he had finished speaking, and Benot was pivoting him toward the door.

"My dear Foust. You think of everything! Do not believe those who say you are somewhat slow in getting to the point. Get out there and tell us if the coast is clear!" Foust laughed as we ejected him into the hall.

"It's alright, they've only just started lunch, and I assured him you would not be available for at least another hour."

Benot merely grunted, and none of us dawdled on the way to my room. None of us had any doubt that Ragul would remove me at once, and with good reason. It would take just one small thing to jog the perceptions of Igan, Snard, or Hagnot, and they would recognize me for what I was! I tried not to think of how fine a line I was walking.

**

Lunch proved to be quite a light-hearted meal, with Foust giving us a very good imitation of Igan's blustering denial of incompetence to Hagnot.

"Did he admit that any of the rumors were true?" I asked, carefully casual because of Benot.

"Which ones?" said Foust with a shrug of his shoulders. "There are so many rumors. He can't very well deny that recently three of the experiments were removed by persons unknown, not after that attendant, Maton ... Mardon ... well, some female, let out a screech that got to the ears of the Council."

I was momentarily shocked. Mogan? Why would Mogan have us hunted? Unless she believed someone had taken us and might be ill treating us. But surely she believed us to be dead?

"What about the others?" Benot asked around a mouthful of apple.

"The others?" I looked at him with interest. "I've heard a hint of a rumor about others, but no details. A couple of quarters ago, wasn't it?" I pretended interest in a rather tasty vegetable pastry.

"Just over, I believe. Mostly from Garlan, but a few from Tenit," he answered easily.

Foust's head jerked up. "Really? Where did you hear that?"

"One of the young officers who brings the flight information for the stress charts has a cousin who worked there. Fellow called Gant. Sent there to rehabilitate and instruct the aliens, I believe." Benot chucked the core toward the inevitable niche in the wall.

The pastry seemed harder to get down as I remembered the resentful, cross man at the institute who had given up on us so soon.

"Humm." Foust looked thoughtful. I had noticed he had a habit of rubbing a soft fold of the leather sash between thumb and forefinger when he was thinking, as he was doing now. "I don't think Hagnot knows anything about that, not for sure. Igan certainly won't tell him."

"What about Snard?" I suggested. "He and Hagnot seem to have very similar ideas when it comes to aliens. He hates the very thought of them."

"But not the thought of staying alive. If someone else has been stealing them and making a success of them where he failed … he'd be left out, bound for the Natog."

"Oh." I guessed they didn't need capital punishment on Selene. "But why Garlan and Tenit? Any special reason?"

Benot looked at me impatiently. "Don't you ever read hard copy? Or watch visi-cast? They were thought to be the most hopeful. Most of the others died hours or days after the transformation. Or had such homicidal tendencies they had to be restrained."

I didn't reply. If Garlan was Rill's planet Dejan, then Tenit must be Earth. Where were they now, those others who had gone missing? Were they tucked away somewhere safe and pregnant? When would they come out of hiding? I chewed my lip thoughtfully.

"You are not going to sulk, are you?" I looked up at Benot, who was glaring at me suspiciously.

"No," I replied. "I was just wondering what anyone would want them for."

"Well, I could think of a few reasons," began Benot, but Foust got up from the edge of the bed and consulted his wrist.

"Well, I'd love to hear them, but I believe Hagnot will be breathing down your neck any minute, and I have a meeting to attend." He turned to me. "I feel you would be safer to remain in this room till Hagnot leaves the complex, good lady."

"And how will I know when that is?" I asked somewhat tartly—I had the feeling Foust's interruption had been deliberate.

He bowed formally. "I shall inform you personally." With that, they left, Benot striding down the hall, already thinking a thousand other things, and Foust carefully closing the door, leaving me alone with my thoughts.

***

The lights in the secure level of the complex could never be turned out. They could be dimmed as mine were now, but never completely off. I eased onto my side and studied Ragul's broad back. His breathing was light and even, and the soft light outlined the muscles of his arm and those of his back. His skin had the glow of health; it wasn't just the tan they all had. It actually felt smooth beneath my lips, and the smell of him was good enough to eat.

I lent over and peered down at his face. I delighted in his aristocratically straight nose. The eyelashes were black and thick, but the rest of his face seemed in this light to be all planes and angles carved from oak. I realized suddenly that Selenese men had no facial hair! Indeed, there was almost no body hair at all. I looked again at his features, strong, almost harsh in repose. Around those curved, firm lips there were traces of humor ... and in the lines around the eyes. My gaze wandered on to the nice, wide brow, the vibrant, dark hair, and then back to the rock hard chin. I tried to imagine him with stubble, but was glad he didn't have any. I had always got a rash from stubble.

***

I lay back against the pillow. What would he do when I told him I was pregnant? The PreVal tablets seemed to have responded positively. They had reacted just as Foust had said they would. So here I was, pregnant … and frightened. Four days ago, there had been just me … now there was us. I moved restlessly against the pillows, and then I turned back to stare at Ragul's shoulder. So strong, so solid. So asleep!

Turning away again, I stretched out an arm and drew the paper and pencil from the small table. If I couldn't sleep, I might as well get on with Benot's damn algebra.

Chapter Twelve

The alarm buzzer woke me, gently intruding into my dreamless sleep. At first I was dismayed by the sight of the empty space beside me, then I saw Ragul through the fluted plastic shower door. He emerged wet and grinning.

"Missed me, my lady?"

"Only your attentions." I grinned as he swooped to kiss me.

"Indeed, and is that why you delay in telling me your news?" His eyes laughed down at me.

"How on Earth?" I asked in wonder.

"You went in the night, my very dearest lady—"

"And I couldn't flush for fear of waking you!" I groaned. "Blast those PreVal tablets!" But it was very hard to sound annoyed when someone amazingly sexy was nibbling my neck.

"How long has it been?"

"Two days," I admitted breathlessly as he got to an especially ticklish bit.

"Why, you sweet, mad Earthling, did you wish to hide it from me?" One big hand cupped my breast, and the other moved down my thigh.

"I thought you'd be up and off to Rill," I admitted, blushing slightly.

He raised his head to look down at me, a puzzled look on his face. "Why?" A smile spread slowly from his eyes, curving his lips tenderly. "You look very different from the girl who tumbled down a slope to my feet, but my very dearest lady, it was that brave, generous, good, and excessively wise lady I fell in love with. And courage! You didn't even whimper when your arm broke. I just wanted to take you into my arms right then."

"A jolly good thing you didn't, with that fracture!" I said, trying not to grin.

"And did you encourage me, dear my lady?" Ragul asked with mock grimness, holding me still more tightly. "Or did you run from me as from a Natog hunting ship? I think you deserve to be eaten, but by me." He lowered his head and kissed me with rough, possessive thoroughness, his hands and body demanding a response of my melting limbs.

The door buzzer sounded. I clung to him as he kissed me.

"Ragul," Benot demanded through the door.

Ragul's breathing was deep and harsh. "What the nard is it?" he roared.

"Ninerta!" bellowed Benot. "Sendal's called a meeting. It's important, and it's *now*."

We looked at each other as Benot's steps retreated down the hall.

"What's all that about?" I asked.

Ragul cursed softly as he sat up and, reaching a long arm out, scooped up his uniform. "It must be the tactics meeting he mentioned. Though why he should schedule it for this hour of the morning only that egg waster would know."

I rose quickly, and after a one-minute shower, I donned the rose underskirt and sandals. Slipping the ivory tunic over my head, I smoothed it down and wound the rose and gold sash around my waist.

Ragul succeeded in forcing his still damp legs into a Selenese version of trousers only used in uniforms, and then he glanced at my progress.

"Don't bother to dress your hair, we haven't time. Just leave it loose."

I paused in my brushing, and then shrugged. Normally, he didn't like people to see my hair unbound.

However, as we hurried down the corridor, he kept glancing at it with irritation. "Your hair is too damned erotic!" he burst out at last. "Why don't you just keep it plaited or something?"

"I was going to! You stopped me. If you want I'll go back and do it now!" I halted crossly.

Grabbing my arm, he propelled me forward. "Not now, we're almost there." And a moment later, we were entering the conference room. Benot and Sendal were already seated at the large oval table. Two young men in uniform sat talking together several seats away, and Foust looked up from his task of apportioning paper and writing tools. He looked surprised.

"Ninerta, what are you doing here?" He was beginning to look anxious.

Benot interrupted, "I told her to come, she has lots of good ideas." He grinned at me, and even Sendal bent a smile in my direction. The two young men looked on with interest. Foust swung round to the youngest. "Amar, didn't you say your father was coming to this meeting?"

Without waiting for an answer, Ragul gripped my arm and turned me toward the door. But it had already opened, and two men stood there. The first, a man of about fifty, began to smile slowly.

"Indeed I am, Foust, surely there are no objections?" said Hagnot as he smiled down into my eyes. "And to think I had been told Ragul had formed a new attachment, to a budding genius in fact." He gave a low chuckle.

Sendal looked annoyed, Benot infuriated, but Ragul's face seemed carved from ice. Without a word, Ragul turned and led me to the table. The young men rose, and the tall, stocky blond bowed to his father. His hair was short, like all the military men I'd met, as was Hagnot's.

"Greetings, Father."

Hagnot nodded as he took a seat across the table from me.

"Greetings to you, Amar. Despite your comments, I believe this ideas meeting will prove very interesting."

Amar flushed hotly, betraying his youth.

"I only meant, sir, that we tend to end up doing much the same thing as the time before."

"That's only because the methods are tried and true, and despite each new innovation, they seem to give the best results."

Foust seemed to remember the common civilities. "Lady Rowanna," he said, giving up the pretense of calling me Ninerta, "this is Wing Commander Jossand of the Second Wing, and this is his youngest officer, Amar, Hagnot's son."

"Gentlemen, this is the Lady Rowanna." They rose and bowed. "And now if Sendal wishes to start …?" He looked inquiringly at Sendal.

Foust sat down as Sendal rose at the end of the table. I glanced at Ragul's rigid profile.

Sendal looked around the table. "I believe Gossot is coming, but I don't think we need wait after all," he said. "It's just the same old things. However, Benot has been working on a new kind of shell that may well pierce the hulls of the hunting ships. And I, gentlemen, have been working on a nerve gas that, if released in the Natog ships, would make their capture very much easier. Used together, we believe they will make a contribution to the coming conflict."

Leaning forward, Ragul tapped the table. Sendal nodded.

"Sendal, how soon will we have the shells, and how many of our ships have been modified to take them?"

"We have six trial models and twenty flight models to be finished in the time available. But that's the limit, we have no more of the necessary metals readily available. Only the ship with the flight model you had fitted is ready, but we hope to have two more ships fitted within schedule."

Jossand tapped the table. At Sendal's nod, he said, "The ships we capture will be refitted for our use, but what about trying to salvage some metals from Moran?"

There was a murmur of disapproval around the table. Jossand flushed. "Well, the dead city isn't *sacred*, is it?" The silence lengthened.

At Sendal's nod, Ragul smiled at Jossand a bit wryly. "No, Jossand, it isn't sacred, just not dead enough. Those who have attempted it die of the sickness, nothing seems to cure it."

I opened my mouth to suggest lead-lined suits, but I closed it again. They didn't even seem to realize what radiation sickness was!

Benot observed my movement. "Ah, dear Lady Rowanna, I felt sure you would come up with something." Everyone turned and looked at me with varying degrees of expectation. Hagnot was merely smiling derisively.

I looked a Benot blankly. Then I smiled at him. "Benot, I understand that you want to get nerve gas on to the Natog ships, but why by shell and why nerve gas?"

There was indulgent laughter from the end of the table. Amar leaned forward to kindly explain, but Benot waved him silent.

"Go on." He wasn't smiling. He looked intensely interested, and so did Sendal, though more cautious. Foust looked faintly anxious, and Ragul squeezed my knee tightly.

"Well, I can see you want more ships ... but wouldn't it be fun to really do them some harm? What we really need is a very deadly virus." I stopped thoughtfully.

"I think you will find I have several of those," Sendal commented.

I brightened. "Do you? Oh good, in that case it should be easy!"

"Enough." Hagnot turned to Sendal. "I thought this was to be a serious meeting. As much as I admire the Lady Rowanna," he had the gall to smile, "I do not feel that she is contributing anything to this meeting."

"Do you not?" Sendal asked rhetorically. "Well, I beg to differ, and this *is* my meeting," he said somewhat childishly. He nodded to me to continue.

"Do you have any materials that can exist within an animal without harm for two or three months and then decompose?" I'd been thinking hard, and the Trojan horse appealed to me.

"Yes," Benot spoke up. "At least three sorts of plastic will do that, one sort is used for internal stitching I believe."

"Good." I talked slowly, looking for errors as I went along. "Suppose several pregnant milk beasts due to give birth in about four months were each given a pellet ... no, they'd regurgitate it and chew it ... they would have to be implanted. Yes, each having an implant of a hollow pellet containing a virus. When captured by the Natog ... they would be injected with the transfer virus and made sterile. However, the virus within the pellet would remain unaffected. When the Natog return to their planet, they will naturally keep the animals for the last week or two before they give birth so they would have twice as many animals … and then it would be too late." I looked up from contemplating the table. I hadn't expected any bouquets, but the silence was unnerving.

"Of course," I added a bit lamely, "you'd have to calculate the incubation period and the time of maximum infection, and then adjust the disintegration time accordingly, and perhaps you could avoid pushing the milk beasts at them, sort of give them up with a struggle …" My voice died away. They all just stared at me.

Benot slammed his palm down on the table forcefully. "By the Eggs of Nerta, I told you she'd do it, Sendal!"

The older man's face slowly creased into a wry smile. "It's so simple. So incredibly *simple*! Why didn't we think of it?"

"I told you," Benot said, beaming, "she's an original thinker!" He turned to Hagnot. "And that's not all she's done, she's been a real help here, she—"

Foust interrupted loudly. "Ragul, can it be done, giving them the milk beasts without it looking suspicious?"

Ragul took up the change of conversation eagerly. "Without difficulty, Foust. We know their ways. We might have to put up a stiff fight to prevent arousing suspicion, and we'll have to try to take a ship or two in the usual way, or with the nerve gas, but we must be very careful to let the right ones escape!"

Amar put in eagerly, "We could use Tellick's positive identifier!" He turned to Jossand. "He's the chap I told you about. He's made this machine that can tell the difference between two identical craft just by the sound they make."

"Wouldn't each ship need one?" Hagnot asked, and Amar flushed to his sandy eyebrows.

Benot looked up from something he was scribbling. "How many hunter class ships are we expecting this time?"

"That depends on the number of mother ships. We are poor pickings and have seldom rated more than two for many years now. So that's twenty-eight hunters." Ragul glanced over at Jossand and said, "It has been confirmed there are only two, hasn't it?"

Jossand withdrew a flat plastic rectangle from his pouch belt and pushed it across the table to Ragul. "Yes, this is Marinner's report. They seem to be swinging in around the outer planets as usual. It's a much longer way. I don't have a guess as to why they take that route."

Benot smiled. "I do."

Everyone turned to him with interest.

"Think of the force that keeps us on this planet," he continued. "We believe that all planets must have this same force, but while our experience is limited, we have discovered that the forces vary considerably. We have found it much safer in our travels, " he said, bowing toward Ragul, "to avoid all large bodies in space. But suppose we were able to calculate accurately, and quickly, the force around each of the planets that are roughly on our route. Could we not save fuel, and so go much farther, if we were able to use the planet's force to swing us from one to the next?"

"Crushed to death on the planet's surface more like!" Amar started hotly.

Ragul waved him quiet.

"Are you suggesting the calculations could be so accurate that we could arrive at the right distance from the planet, remain at that distance for the *exact* amount of time, and then leave, going the correct direction for the *next* planet?" Ragul sounded doubtful.

"We couldn't, of course, but with the new math Lady Rowanna has invented, I believe so. In fact, I have concluded that these calculations may have been the purpose of several of the puzzling bits of equipment removed from captured ships. You'll find this hard to believe, but I don't think they use mechanical computers."

He ignored the sounds of disbelief and surprise. "Remember, we have *never* found a mechanical computer on their ships, and they must have some method for computing the math." He looked around the table. "After the emergency, I intend on concentrating my efforts in this area, and I intend going over all the alien equipment that was removed from the ships again." He looked around defiantly.

Hagnot lent back in his chair. "You seem much impressed with the math you say the Lady Rowanna thought up. I would inquire further into this. But as to the equipment, none of it worked. In the laboratories, they failed to do anything when power was restored to them. You did many of the experiments yourself."

"Well, you couldn't expect them to work, surely!" I blurted out indignantly.

Ragul's fingers squeezed my knee painfully. I relapsed into silence.

Hagnot sat forward and pressed his fingertips together as he contemplated me for a moment. "Dear Lady Rowanna," he said softly. "You are full of surprises. Tell me, why do you think they would not work? I assure you they were removed very carefully, nothing was lost."

Beneath the table, my hand grasped Ragul's wrist. I was tempted to dig my nails into him, but he took the hint and removed his painful clasp.

"Hagnot, they probably lost the only thing necessary for them to work: power."

"We restored the power," Benot assured me.

"Yes, but it was too late. Think of a brain, it may be like that in some ways. If a brain doesn't get what it needs from the blood, the person falls unconscious. If the brain was without it only a tiny amount of time, the person may be alright. If it was longer, the brain would be damaged. You could try to teach the person things again, but your success would depend on the extent of the damage. A mechanical computer wouldn't have the same problem, but a solid state one would. "

Benot looked delighted. "A solid state computer? I like that. And what you say may well be possible. It's certainly one of the areas I'll investigate! I have one or two ideas of my own I'm rather eager to try. I remember in my student days doing some experiments and discovering in passing that some crystals had a curiously regular response to an electrical charge. However, that has nothing to do with this meeting. Sendal, what conclusions are we come to?"

Sendal carefully rose to his feet and unconsciously smoothed back his shoulder-length gray locks. "A most fruitful meeting. It seems there are no objections to Lady Rowanna's idea of sending a virus back to Natal," he said, "and there seem to be no insurmountable technical problems involved. I suggest therefore that the proposal be put before the Supreme Council for ratification, while Benot and I supervise the making of the necessary capsules. I have no doubt the military men present will arrange the necessary diversion to facilitate our endeavor?" He received their nods and continued somewhat bitterly. "No doubt it will be the requisitioning of the necessary milk beasts that will cause the greatest problems."

Ragul caught his eye with a quick tap on the shiny wood. "It might be best if several different kinds of beasts were implanted. There's more possibility of several getting through."

"And a way of identifying those that were *not* taken, or you will end up with the virus!" I added hastily.

There were nods of agreement around the table. Sendal began to round off the meeting, but just then the door burst open and a tall fleshy man stormed into the room. His olive uniform was badly creased, and he looked tired and angry.

"Who do you damn well think you are, Sendal, calling a meeting at this hour of the morning? Either exhausted men aren't up yet after a short sleep or they haven't got in from night patrols and inspection tours. If you think I'm going to ratify some minutes I haven't damn well been present for, you'll find you're mistaken!"

"I appreciate your position, Gossot, but you will be relieved that with two members of the Supreme Council present, the ratification of another Councilor will not be necessary."

Gossot's jaw dropped open as he swung round and observed Hagnot and Ragul at the table. His face darkened in anger. "I take it that as Ragul is also the other War Councilor, I should be grateful to have been asked to come at all!"

Hagnot took pity on the weary and irascible man and made an effort to calm him. "Come now, Gossot, you've had a long and wearing night on inspection ... you do alternate days with Ragul till all is in place, don't you?"

"Yes, and I would have been long back if it hadn't been for you," Gossot snarled.

"Me?" Hagnot looked genuinely astonished.

"You're still trying to find those experiments, aren't you?" Gossot baited.

***

I was lying alone in the crumpled bed. After an exhausting day, I had retired early, hoping to make up for last night's lack of sleep. Instead, I found myself tossing and turning restlessly. The meeting had ended in an explosion of activity. Gossot had heard rumors that strange people had been seen in the Denton Swamps.

He had gone to investigate, and the people he'd questioned seemed unimaginative sorts who reported hearing screams from the swamp, and twice a man had been seen in the distance pulling a woman back into a stand of rushes. However, no one had wanted to venture far into the swamp to track them as the going was treacherous.

Hagnot stated his intention to go there at once. Ragul, encouraging this decision without being too obvious, was disconcerted by Hagnot's request for his help. It went without question that the emergency came first, but the attack was not due for three days, and Hagnot's request for an airship and trackers didn't seem unreasonable.

In minutes, Hagnot was gone, preparing for two days in the swamp. Ragul smiled at me. "I thought I was going to have to whisk you off after the meeting. As it is, I can get some work done and collect you tonight."

"Tonight! He'll be gone for two days," I argued, loath to be dragged off into the unknown again.

"Or he may get done a little early," Ragul countered, and he stooped to kiss me. I slipped my arms around his neck and clung unashamedly to him. He nearly squeezed the breath out of me before releasing me and taking a step back. "Saying good-bye to you can be damn frustrating." With this parting shot, he turned and left.

I wasn't allowed the luxury of gloomy reflections or the chance to go into a romantic decline. Benot whisked me off to his room to teach him algebra.

"Think of a number of symbols that everyone knows and that have no numeric value," I began.

"The letters of the alphabet?" he suggested. "Or the symbols of the craft halls, the signs of each of the councilors, or—"

"Enough! Let's use the letters of the alphabet." I had no idea what the other symbols he mentioned were. "Suppose we had $2a+3a+4a$. If you add up the numbers you have nine, and what do you have nine of?"

"Nine lots of a?" Benot responded, unthinkingly ruffling his black mane of hair as he considered the problem. It stood almost on end, but as his tunic looked as if he had grabbed it from a clothesline, it wasn't really noticeable. Benot was clean but very scruffy. You just didn't notice it because of his vibrant personality.

"Yes. Now let's try this. If you have one pimm fruit, two apple fruit, and another one pimm fruit, what do you have?"

"Either two apple fruit and two pimm fruit or one cool summer drink," Benot replied.

I laughed a trifle desperately. And so began a long morning of explaining that each letter represented something. It might be a very tangible or a very illusive something, but each different thing was represented for the duration of the equation by that letter. Finally, I said, "So you can see that you can only add, subtract, etc., numbers with the same letters. Any questions so far?"

"Yes, why do your concrete examples nearly always revolve around food?" Benot asked with real interest.

"I'm on a diet," I said and grinned.

***

The day passed very well, with many diversions into other areas of math to tie in what we had already done. I was rescued for lunch, but by evening Benot could be given a sum with exponentials, brackets, multiplication, division, addition, and subtraction, and he could do it. I felt very proud of both of us. I hadn't lied when I said I was lousy at math.

So now here I lay in the low light of my room, pleasantly full of dinner but disastrously alert. I banged my pillow into a new shape and pondered. There was no point in preparing tomorrow's lesson—I wouldn't be here to give it. But perhaps I could leave some notes for Benot. It would give me something to do.

The door buzzed. It couldn't be Ragul, he could palm it open. I rose and slipped on a shapeless tent the Selenese consider a bathrobe and went to open the door.

Hagnot didn't wait to be invited in—he pushed past me and closed the door as I gasped a protest. He leaned against it and looked down at me. "Well, well, Lady Rowanna, you are a bundle of surprises."

"So are you," I said. "I thought you were to be at the swamps for the next two days."

"Yes, Ragul still does. But in fact, my men searched it thoroughly only a few days ago and discovered its inhabitants. Alas, not those I seek, but they have proved useful." He smiled down into my stiff face. "My dear Lady Rowanna, you prove to be more and more fascinating with each meeting. From what I have heard, you really *have* been some use here. Extraordinary for a lady, and such a beautiful one. Though except for your glorious hair, I'm having to rely on memory." He reached out his fingers and twitched at my robe.

"You will have to continue to do so, and I am not your lady. Ragul has me and holds me!" I said.

"Like nard he does, not till the papers are on file, and it's surprising how things get delayed during an emergency." His eyes wandered down from my face. "And as for the having …" As he stepped forward, I began retreating, glancing around for something to hit him with. I lunged for the stool by the desk. I could hear him laugh as he grabbed a handful of robe and jerked me back against him, his arms pinning me to his chest.

My kicks were ineffectual with my legs swathed by the heavy robe, and at last I ceased as he just stood, gazing quietly down into my face.

The moments were passing. He held me without effort, and I saw in his face more than passion or even male amusement at my helplessness. I was looking at grudging respect.

Lowering his head, his firm lips softly teased mine. He began kissing my eyes, my hair, his lips making a trail down my neck, and then, shifting me in his arms, he kissed me full and hard on the lips.

I whimpered and began to struggle again. Then he was lifting me and lay me down gently on the bed, covering my body with his. He was a big man, and I felt myself sinking into the mattress beneath him. I could feel his strong fingers gently slipping aside the robe and sliding up my thigh. I tried to wriggle away, but my movements only seemed to excite him. His breathing was harsh and hot against my ear, my throat. I tried to push him off and shouted in his ear for good measure, and he jerked back in surprise. I wriggled free, but before I could escape from the bed, he grabbed my hair in one strong hand and pulled me back.

"Hagnot," I gasped. "Let me go. I'm pregnant. You'll hurt us."

"So quickly? So conveniently? I'm old enough to have heard that one before, my dear." I felt his tunic rough against my breasts as he pulled the robe open. "Before the Gods of the Old Ones, Rowanna, I'm going to make you the lady of the most powerful man on Selene!"

I was saved from that future by a power outage. The glowing light only flickered, but the buzzer started, and the door opened. With a curse, Hagnot rose from the bed to close it. I swung up behind him. As he approached the door, I gave him a tremendous shove, and he staggered through as I palmed it shut.

He pounded on the door while I sank to the floor and wept.

Chapter Thirteen

I awoke at my usual time the next morning. I stretched and was surprised at my feeling of well-being. After my storm of tears last night, I had expected to feel jaded, not to mention depressed. Instead, I felt joyous anticipation … Ragul was coming this morning to take me away! I would dress with special care, I thought with a happy squirm of anticipation.

I was still feeling cheerful as I dried after my shower and arranged my hair in the demure coil of plaits he so approved of. I hummed a happy little hum.

In the cupboard, a long Wedgwood blue underskirt caught my eye. It had wild flowers and grasses embroidered up from the hem, as if they were growing. There were lemon yellow flowers, and scarlet, French lilac, and pale pink. The grasses all had a hint of yellow.

I found the matching blue overdress, a short one with narrow half-length sleeves. The sash was of the same color with flowers, soft and long. I twirled before the mirror, pleased with the result.

I sat carefully in the chair and glanced at the bar clock. I had often thought their clocks looked like horizontal thermometers, with the pressure constantly rising as the day progressed. There were twenty main segments, totaling one revolution of the planet. The red line was about a third of the way along, so nearly seven segments had passed. Normally, I would have had breakfast and would be starting work with Benot. I bit my lower lip thoughtfully. There would be no harm in having breakfast; Hagnot wouldn't attack me in the cafeteria! I could jot down some of the notes for Benot I'd intended to last night. I shuddered away from last night.

Benot would be working on the virus shells with Sendal so … breakfast was rather a good idea. I grabbed up some paper and pencils and left my room only slightly less jauntily than when I got up.

By the time I had broken my fast, I had covered several sheets of paper with notes, examples, explanations, and some suggestions of the more advanced uses of the different areas of math we had covered. Benot was a brilliant man, and in a couple more days, he would easily outstrip my meager knowledge.

Suddenly, I slammed the plastic beaker down. Packing! I hadn't packed a thing! I jerked my chair back, and sweeping up the papers, I headed for the disposal with my tray balanced uncertainly in one hand. I dumped the remains of the food and the tray and headed for the door.

"Lady Ninerta! Or is it Lady Rowanna?" My friend from the queue greeted me. She smiled merrily and leaned forward conspiratorially.

"Which one do you intend having?"

"Name?" I asked hopefully.

She squealed with laughter. "No, silly, which man, which Councilor, which *hunk*!"

I could see what she meant —they both seemed to have a lot to recommend them. What I didn't see was how she knew Hagnot was in the running.

"Of course, when there were general inquiries about a Lady Rowanna, none of us guessed it was you." She partially enlightened me. "But after that meeting … and then when he was so short with Amar, and of course … last night," she added.

"Forget about last night, nothing happened, but what happened to Amar?"

"I heard Hagnot left a bit abruptly." She grinned. "Amar asked his father what his intentions were concerning a Lady Lena. It seems Amar wants her, but the mother is hoping for Hagnot. Well, Hagnot just snapped that Amar could have a clutch of Lena's. He'd chosen his next lady, and it wasn't her!"

"I bet Amar was relieved." I grinned.

She smiled. "Well, actually, he seemed a bit anxious, and he asked a little tentatively if you weren't already taken. Hagnot just snarled something about there being a difference between having and holding, and then he stamped off."

I snorted. She laughed. "Spoilt for choice, that's what you are."

I grinned and left her with a friendly wave.

I hadn't much packing to do. The eight outfits, one for each day of the week, fitted easily into the heavy cloth bag. The accessories fitted on top, and the sandals all had their own little bags and nicely filled the larger bag. I closed it and, after consideration, stuffed the whole thing into the cupboard in case anyone came. I hadn't told anyone I was going. The bar clock showed nearly half the segments of daylight gone. I paced uneasily. A light buzzing interrupted my thoughts; I eagerly pressed the button by the small grid. "Yes?"

To my intense disappointment, it was Foust's light voice that came over the communicator. "Lady Rowanna, do you have any idea why Igan and Snard have been called away so urgently?"

"Igan and Snard?" I repeated blankly, opening the door. "I didn't even know they had gone!"

"Hmm." He paused in thought for a moment. "I'm going to be having a late lunch, care to join me?"

"Well," I said carefully, "that might not be possible … I'll do what I can."

"If you're expecting Ragul imminently, don't!" Foust leaned against the doorway. "He's run into a lot of bother over the defense plans. Gossot thinks the virus plan hasn't a chance of succeeding and wants to put explosives in the animals to destroy the ships here instead."

"Can't they do both?" I asked reasonably. "As long as they aren't the same ships."

"No, when ships begin to crash, the others would jettison their cargo and leave to think up a new plan."

"True," I murmured. "Who will win?"

Foust sounded guarded. "Normally Ragul would, easily, but the Supreme Council is not very happy with Ragul at present."

"Why, for heaven's sake?" I exclaimed.

"Hagnot has more influence in the Supreme Council than Ragul," Foust said. "And you stand between them. Lady Rowanna, if it was not for your origin, which would you choose? If it is Hagnot, might this not be a good time to tell him? Not the truth of course, but in a few more days you should be safe even from Hagnot's paranoia."

Ragul had been talking to Foust, I thought grimly. "But suppose I'm not pregnant with a fertile embryo, wouldn't that be my death sentence? Or are you suggesting that if it's not fertile, that doesn't matter!"

Foust sounded pained. "I wouldn't have suggested it if I thought that to be the case. Which man do you prefer?"

"Ragul, a thousand times ... Ragul."

He suppressed a faint sigh. "Very well. May I hope to see you at lunch?" he asked before turning away.

"Yes." I palmed the door shut, and the room was silent once more.

***

Lunch proved a surprisingly interesting meal. Had I assumed Foust and I would be dining tete a tete, I would have been mistaken. Whatever his intentions, the group at our table increased in size. Before I had sipped halfway down a frothy lemon drink, an annoyed-looking Amar seated himself at our table and glowered at our meals.

"Something wrong?" Foust asked.

"Wrong? What could be wrong? The lady I love has a mother who thinks to marry her to my father. And when I get my father's intentions sorted out, I have that upstart Essoth warning me not to have aspirations in her direction! Who in a hunter does he think he is!"

"An upstart who is afraid you'll get her?" I suggested. "After all, he wouldn't have bothered if he thought you had no chance at all."

Amar seemed to consider the point. Then he just grunted.

"I understand," I said, picking tentatively at a salad before me. "Being a tragic figure is *so* much more romantic."

Foust choked on a mouthful of vegetable roll. Amar looked astounded, and then he burst out laughing. "Oh, Lady

Rowanna, I wish my father did hold you. He'd never know a day's peace!"

"What a thing to wish upon your father!" I said in mock horror. "By the way, what are you doing here?"

"Oh, an emergency strategy meeting. Ragul has sent Jossand some preliminary plans to go over with the commander of the Fourth Wing, and some involved junior officers of the ground forces. I'll be leaving with Jossand to start getting it all set up as soon as he has finished. His wing may be called on for support."

I looked at Foust with raised eyebrows; he gave an infinitesimal shrug. Amar was staring across the room with pleased surprise, and he waved a hand. Turning in that direction, I was delighted to see Matul making his way across the room to our table, a shy smile on his thin face.

"Lady Rowanna, how delightful." His eyes were warm. "One does meet you in such surprising places!"

I laughed. He raised my hands to his head in a formal gesture seldom used in this subterranean world and I noted he wore a new uniform that fit perfectly—for now! "What brings you here, Matul? Still seeking insane criminals?"

He shook his head tiredly. "I think that falsity has been dropped, especially since two have been found. I brought Hagen, my half-sister, along with some viruses she has been working on for her father." He saw my blank look. "You know, Sendal. Her father."

I was glad Matul had mistaken my frozen look. Shock left me numb. Foust glanced at my face. "Matul, perhaps you could tell me about those two. You know of my interest."

"Of course. There has been a systematic search of all the properties around the institute by Essoth's Wings, but Hagnot suddenly decided they were to be searched again. The bodies of two experiments were found on Gossot's property last night, in a kind of lab, preserved. Igan and Snard have positively identified them as being among the ones taken two quarters ago."

"Gossot!" Foust exclaimed.

"Two quarters ago?" I blurted out.

Matul didn't seem surprised at our reactions. "Yes, you'd think they would have started the search ages ago. But Gossot swears he knows nothing of the matter."

Foust looked grim. "What did they die of?"

Matul looked faintly sick. "It seems there was some attempt to transfer their reproductive organs to Selenese women. Their bodies were found too."

I took an unsteady breath. Two quarters ago ... well, whoever the unfortunates were, at least it was not Rill or Loona.

Foust asked the question in my mind. "Matul, does this mean the hunt has been called off?"

"Alas, no. But it has been postponed until after the emergency. We all have military duties, and even Hagnot can't deny that." He remembered Amar's presence and looked a little embarrassed.

Amar smiled slightly. "No need to hesitate on my behalf. I am as weary of my father's obsession as everyone else."

"Amar," I said, leaning forward earnestly. "If the experiments had worked out perfectly ... would your father have been able to accept them?"

Amar considered the question seriously for some moments. "I don't know, Lady Rowanna. I wish I did. I like to think that for Selene, he would have put his personal objections aside ... but I am afraid he would have considered it to be for Selene's sake that he would have continued to be obstructive."

"Was it only because they were transformed? Or did he also object to their being aliens?" I asked.

"Both really. After all, aliens are just that ... alien! How could they be like us? It would be like copulating with animals. Our race wouldn't really have survived. It would have been altered, debased. Our civilization would have decayed before long, and we'd be easy picking for the Natog," he added gloomily.

I gasped at his assumption of superiority. Didn't they know anything about the planets we had been taken from?

"They were all taken from very primitive societies?" I asked.

"Well, I'm told that the ships that took them encountered no resistance at all, so they must have been," Amar responded.

It amazed me that the greatest mistakes could be so elementary.

"It might also have been incredible good luck." I rose from the table. My unfinished meal seemed suddenly distasteful.

The sound of a rapidly ringing bell filled the hall. It continued for some moments. When it stopped, there was a silence in the room. Everyone remained where they were: some standing, some sitting, even some with food halfway to their lips. They were all looking toward the small grid halfway up the wall.

"Citizens of Selene," came the official voice from the speaker. "This is the second stage of the emergency. The estimated time of arrival of the Natog hunting ships is twenty-two segments from now. That is the thirteenth segment of tomorrow. This leaves up to twenty segments for nonessential personnel to seek shelter. As usual, only grades of personnel three, four, and five may leave their posts. In sixteen segments from now, all grade two personnel can leave, and in nine segments, all grade one priority personnel are to be made secure. Thank you for your attention."

With the cessation of the voice, there was a momentary lull before the babble broke out. I raised my eyebrows slightly at Foust. He rose to the occasion.

"I'm not sure Ragul will relish you being secured here, Lady Rowanna. However, he has until the middle of tonight to remove you to another secure area."

I nodded, gritting my teeth against the thousand questions I couldn't ask. I forced a casual response. "Oh well. I've got notes to finish in my room. Nice seeing you again, Matul." I nodded to Amar and left.

The long corridor was busy with people. A thousand worlds rarely colliding. By the stairs, some final stores were being brought in, and a tearful young woman was clinging to a nice young man whose head bent protectively over hers. Being infertile, she would not be in the strongest hold.

I hurried past them to my room. In a brief opening in the crowd before me I saw Hagnot coming toward me, talking earnestly to Sendal. A glance about showed me a conveniently open doorway, through which I dove. "Damn, now they're sure to come in here," I growled to myself. But as it wasn't a French farce, they walked past without a glance in my direction.

I was considerably hotter and more prickly by the time I got to my room and palmed the door shut behind me. No one but Ragul could enter unless I opened it. Yearning desperately for another shower, I gulped water instead and sat down at the desk to finish up my notes for Benot.

Before long, the door buzzed. "Not Ragul then," I thought. Rising, I went over to it and touched a button at the side. I'd never needed to use it before Hagnot had found me. "Who's there?" But I hadn't really needed to ask.

"Let me in, Lady Rowanna. I want to talk to you." Hagnot's voice sounded firm and in control.

"Talk my foot," I sneered.

"Talk to your foot?" Hagnot seemed genuinely startled.

I giggled feebly. "You're not going to talk to me or my foot. So go away."

"Have you been at the emergency rations?" He sounded suspicious.

"Never a ration," I assured him. But I don't think he was convinced, for after a pause, I heard him give a grunt of annoyance.

"I'll talk to you again when you are sober. Try and sleep it off ... a good shower helps," he added.

As he walked away, I thought that he had seldom appeared kinder. Almost tolerant. I wondered if Ragul would be tolerant of a tipsy wife. I returned to my notes, but there wasn't very much I could add. I tried to rack my brain to recall something constructive about calculus. I could only remember the smell of the chalk dust and the gurgle of aging radiators.

The door opened as I sat there, chin in hand, recalling Mr. Denis's narrow back.

"No hello kiss?"

I whirled about to see the door closing behind Ragul, a grin on his face. He held out his arms, and I ran into them. There was a shower of kisses to return. At last I pulled back. I was still in his arms, but I could look up into his face. "I was afraid you might not be coming."

"I know. I was afraid that I might be too late." He squeezed me gently.

I carefully withdrew from his arms. "And there's something else. Hagnot got in here last night."

"Do I have to kill him? Or were you your delightfully resourceful self?" Ragul asked rather matter-of-factly.

"If you mean did he succeed," I said rather crossly, "no. But that was more by good luck than good judgment."

Ragul watched me curiously, his head tipped to one side. I glared at him. "Did you want him to succeed?" he asked. There was a hint of laughter in his voice I couldn't understand.

"Want him! That overblown, arrogant, pompous ignoramus? Are you mad?" I snapped. I never understood why he collapsed into the chair laughing.

"My very dearest lady," he said at last, holding out his arms again. I went over to him slowly, and he drew me against him. "I realize the sexual mores of your society must differ somewhat from ours, but I assure you, I would only have to kill Hagnot if he became eligible to hold you."

I probably looked puzzled, and he continued. "If you accepted his claim," he explained. "I am not prepared to lose you." My head was snuggled under his chin, so he kissed my hair. "And as to my question, dearest of ladies, do I not know you to be a woman of passion, fire, and honesty? You have never given me less than all of you, nor I given you less, but have we not both given others considerably less?"

I looked up in surprise. "Ragul, I've only been married once, and it was only ever him!"

He looked astonished. "Then I'm considerably ahead of you. I accept your rejection of him as a tremendous compliment!" There was a pause, and then he added, "And no trying to catch up."

"Is that a no-no for Selenese wives?" I teased.

"No, but it is for you." His kiss was so fierce it hurt.

"Aren't we meant to be leaving?" I asked breathlessly, long moments later.

"We have time." And his long fingers pushed aside the soft fabric of the top I'd donned so carefully that morning.

Chapter Fourteen

It seemed as if the whole world was pouring into the city. The lights of thousands of small craft made bright ribbons of color in the starless night. I gazed, fascinated, out of the darkened cabin of Ragul's air-shuttle.

"It's all so orderly, no one is panicking!" I was amazed. In a major city on my world, there would have been looting, senseless violence, and panic.

"Why should there be?" He maneuvered the craft deftly through the traffic.

I refrained from telling him about Earth. Instead, I asked a question. "What is this labyrinth you are taking me to?"

"Quite early on in the Natog wars, it was discovered that they couldn't leave their ships because of the fear of infection," he began.

"Why don't they just wear space suits and spray them with a decontaminate when they return to the ship?"

"Much of their fear is psychological, but also they would be very much easier targets on the ground. So we took to the mine shafts and the local caves, whatever we could find. But as the trips down them became more frequent, it was decided that proper facilities were needed. This became more necessary as the Natog attempted to use machines to go down the shafts. In this city, they broke through the inadequate barriers in two places, but they caused more havoc and injuries than captures, fortunately.

But it was the deciding factor, and action was taken to locate the subterranean caves and tunnels believed to be beneath the town."

"What sort of rock is it?" I asked.

"Some fifteen sneg below the surface of Jena," he said, indicating the city over which we flew, "is a layer of hard rock. It's very beautiful. It's believed to have come in the long ago from a volcanic disturbance in the low hills to the east of here. It had flowed slowly, and gases that had dissolved in the lava failed to escape through the quickly cooling skin of rock. These remained as cavities in the solid rock, which slowly filled with crystals. Some of them are clear, others an exquisite white or pale green, even a sort of pink or lavender. They come in many shapes. Some grow in blades, others in radiating needles, and one lovely common one that, cut radially, looks like a delicate snowflake," Ragul enthused.

"And you hide in these?" I asked, somewhat puzzled. On Earth, these cavities tended to be very small.

Ragul laughed and began to negotiate down toward and area of light. "No. They are much too small, I just find rocks fascinating. Below the hard layer of rock is a layer of soft rock. Oddly enough, between the layer of soft rock and the layer of hard rock is often a layer of beautiful rock that looks wonderful when it's polished. I wish we knew more about these things."

He stopped chatting briefly to respond to official directions coming over the communication system and then continued. "Anyway, there are three layers of hard rock. In some forgotten age, something caused an area to subside." He broke off again to respond to further directions. "Along that fault line, there is only half a meteg of hard rock that was drilled through to reach the softer strata below. The business was further aided by the fact that at some time a river had carved its way through some of the soft rock, leaving caves and passages."

"Does the water ever return?" I asked a little anxiously; I had a fear of drowning.

"No. It's thought that the fault that we find so advantageous cut off the river, and it is the same river that bubbles to the surface at the small town of Sina."

I clutched the edge of my seat as the floodlit ground rushed up to meet us. "Do all the cities have the same facilities?"

"No. Your hometown of Balla, for instance, has very much more primitive subterranean facilities." On the ground, a man with two lights was indicating where Ragul should land. "But your grandfather was an eccentric and spent much of his fortune on huge sealing doors that would have done justice to a town three times the size of Balla," Ragul said as the craft touched down.

I unclipped my restraining belt and reached for the door, feeling less than confident. He reached across and held my wrist for a moment. "Remember what I told you. Let everyone know you are pregnant. Pregnant ladies are often a little odd."

The man with the lights seemed impatient with our delay, and he jerked one up high. Ragul leaned over and kissed me hard on the lips.

As I stood watching his craft lift into the air, I smiled bravely and waved. In a moment, another craft was landing where he had been. All around me, craft were touching down to disgorge passengers and then rising swiftly into the night. Disconsolately I turned, my cloth bag bumping against my leg, and followed the streams of people making their way toward the large, floodlit building.

Many double doors stood open, and I passed into a vast room reminiscent of the old Victoria Station in London. The group I was following came to the head of a stairway that abruptly descended into the ground. They showed no hesitation in going down. The walls were tiled, and the stairs could take four abreast. A large door at the bottom stood open. Soon, there was a bottleneck as the corridor ahead abruptly narrowed to allow only single-file passage. Almost popping out the other end of it, I passed over a wooden drawbridge.

Peering around, I saw large slots in the rock above and below the bridge. Each was the height and width of a man and disappeared into the wall. I was impressed, for the door that used these to block the entrance when the bridge was raised stood massively to one side.

Ahead, a corridor formed a T with the bridge, and I turned left, following two young girls whose long skirts swirled as they walked, giving glimpses of brown ankles.

We emerged abruptly into an vast, softly lit room, containing innumerable seats and wide benches with groups of people either circulating, merging and parting with friends and acquaintances, or sitting and chatting.

I chose a seat opposite an elderly couple. They had evidently come prepared for a long wait, and as I had seen little of the ordinary people of Selene, I enjoyed the opportunity to covertly observe them. They reminded me of an old farming couple I knew in Brittany. She had a basket of food that was covered with a crisp white cloth. She spread green paste over the inside of a long roll that had been cut open. Lifting a clean red root from the basket, she proceeded to deftly cut spicy smelling slices from it and place them on the green paste, along with brightly colored and unfamiliar vegetables. The old man patiently watched her, and when all was ready and she had folded the oblong shut, she handed it to him. Carefully, he broke it into two and courteously presented her with half.

"Lady!" An officious voice spoke near me. I looked up to see the harassed face of a slender young man. "You should not be here. You must go down to a more secure level. This is only for third-degree citizens." I glanced at the elderly couple, who were watching me with mild curiosity, hoping they weren't taking offense.

"I'm new to Jena, perhaps you could tell me where to go. Oh yes, my husband also asked me to mention that I am pregnant," I responded gently.

The young man almost jerked to attention. "Lady, please allow me to escort you. This is the first level. You must go down to the third, but I assure you it is not too far." Eagerly and with great care, he took my arm.

Gently, I removed his hand and assured him with a laugh that if he could just tell me the way I would be able to make it on my own. But he insisted on remaining with me until we reached the third level and he had left me it the care of a rather matronly dame.

This lady proved far less impressed, I was glad to note, and having shown me to a bed and pointed out where food and the necessary were to be found, she returned to the group she had left.

The bed was unusually high, coming to my mid-thigh. I prodded the mattress, and it seemed comfortable enough. Looking around the room, I noticed that it was all given over to beds except for a long counter separating this room from the narrow room where food was prepared. On the other side of the room, archways led to the showers. The rough carpeting was woven browns complementing the walls, which were a pretty pinky beige—but the high ceiling glittered with masses of crystals!

I wondered where the polished rock was that Ragul had mentioned, then guessed that if it was marble, it had been removed to embellish buildings. There was a distinct chill in the air, and I noticed that the less prepared of my contemporaries had wrapped blankets around their shoulders. I reached for mine.

A low, familiar laugh jerked me around. "Rill!" I beamed foolishly at her.

"I gather Ragul overcame your qualms, or was it Hagnot?" She grinned wickedly at me.

I blushed hotly. "Ragul, of course. You don't mind, do you?"

Rill perched comfortably on the edge of my bed. "Mind what? Sharing Ragul?"

I nodded.

"Of course not. Why should I? When all this is over, no man shall hold me. I shall take what men I want and when," she stated calmly and softly.

I grinned at her and answered just as quietly, "That sounds like women's lib."

"What's women's lib?" she asked, looking at me curiously.

"It's a women's movement for equal, or more than equal, rights … er, where I come from." I glanced around nervously.

She raised an eyebrow. "That's the first intelligent thing I've heard about your planet. I don't suppose you were a member?" she added softly with a grin.

I longed to tell her I was a founding member or even that I'd gleefully burnt dozens of bras, but truth prevailed. "Well, no. Actually, I … er … wanted to stay at home with my children, so I did." I felt defensive, just like most other women on my planet who had made that choice.

Rill laughed. "Well, you've certainly come to the right place!"

It felt good to be with her again.

"Come on." Rill grabbed my hand and brought me to my feet. "Let's beat the rush and have our showers now." I followed her at a more leisurely pace across the room. Abruptly, I stopped. Rill must be pregnant too! My momentary shock dissolved; Ragul had done what he had to protect us and help Selene. If he had enjoyed his work ... and I had little doubt he had ... a grin twitched my lips ... well, so had I. I continued toward the showers.

It was not the turning up of the lights that woke me the next morning, not the low murmur of the wakeful. It was my crossly rumbling stomach.

I lay contemplating the virtues of a quick shower before breakfast or after it. Nerving myself for a before-breakfast shower, as the showers had proved cool the evening before, I bounced from my bed and padded across the carpeted room. It was surprisingly full; nearly every bed was taken. But with the ceiling being so high, it gave the illusion that the room was practically empty.

I erupted from my brief shower shivering, only to find Rill dressed and subduing her damp curls before a misty mirror. I dried myself vigorously with a towel from the piles of tan colored municipal towels and donned my clothes quickly. I'd kept my hair dry, so I only needed to pat it smooth.

"Breakfast at your bed or mine?" I paraphrased into the mirror.

"Yours, it's nearer," Rill responded as she gave her reflection a final scrutiny.

We collected our loaded trays from the long counter and made our way to my bed. I noticed that several people were eating, and that they sat on stools taken from beneath their beds. They had put the trays on them, which I now realized were about table height. I was delighted with the economy of the idea.

The trays were indeed full. As I sat contemplating mine, I was hard put to know where to start. There was red tumbler of rich, raw milk and another of purple juice from some fruit. There were inevitable warm breakfast vegetable pasties, two warm brown globes that smelled rather like mushrooms, large pats of green paste, a small dish of something like jam, several fruits, and on a still-warm plate lay six golden things like crepes in a golden pool of fruity syrup. The crepes won.

Each mouthful was a joy. "I don't know how they expect us to eat all this," I commented several crepes later, waving to the rest of the tray.

Rill had split open one of the globes and was slathering it with the green paste. "The engagement is expected to start in the thirteenth segment, so this is the last proper meal till it's over. That's usually late evening. Standard rations are available, of course. No one leaves till morning."

"Oh!" I wondered where she had gotten the information, and I suddenly realized that I had no idea where she'd been the last few days. "Where did you find that out?" I took a sip of my juice, it was cool and delicious.

"Ragul told me." She bit deeply into the vegetable roll.

"Really? See him often, do you?" I strived to sound casual.

"Not often, but as I was at his mother's house, one could expect to meet him once in awhile," she replied thickly, around a full mouth.

"His mother's! Isn't that the first place they'd look?" I sipped during her silence. After swallowing, she continued.

"Quite. So it was known to be clear of … problems. She's a nice old thing. Very bright. When he brought me into her room, she just looked at me for a moment and said, 'I wondered how long it would be before you brought one of them here.' He apologized and explained that he was running out of places to put us."

"Why would they help us? What about Ragul's father? Wouldn't he betray us?"

"Not at all. Her next husband, not Ragul's father, who died some time ago, was the leading light in the plan to acquire us," she said quietly as she glanced around.

I pondered. "Will he be able to help us if things go wrong?"

"Unlikely," Rill commented. "He committed suicide, or so she was told, when the plan failed. Even she, his widow, is rather ostracized."

"Does she know about Loona and me?" I queried.

"I think she could probably describe you in her sleep," was Rill's grinning reply.

Everything tasted even more delicious as I drained the tumbler. I was about to ask Rill another question when a light voice called my name.

Glancing around, I saw Lena sketch a shy salutation to me from several beds away. Her short, plump companion smiled slightly, and they rose and brought their trays over to us.

"Lena, hello! I hope your mother is well," I added politely as I gave an involuntary glance around for her nemesis.

"Amar holds me!" Her blushing smile betrayed her delight.

My mind boggled. Yesterday, he certainly hadn't seemed to hold her. She must have seen something of my confusion, as becoming even pinker, she leaned forward to explain.

"I expect it does seem sudden, Lady Rowanna, but our situation was not easy. My mother had intended that Hagnot would hold me, but fortunately your arrival prevented him from even noticing me!" I nodded my understanding, and she continued with lowered eyes. "Unfortunately, there were others who *had* noticed me." She glanced up shyly for my understanding.

"Captain Essoth?" I asked with a smile.

She nodded. "So we pretended I was going to a young ladies amusement each afternoon with a friend, and then we presented Mother with the news of my condition as soon as we were certain, last night. Mother decided to accept that a Lord Holder and son of a Supreme Councilor was good enough match after all! So here I am!" she ended happily.

"Have you moved in with Amar?" I asked with interest as I took another bite of the roll.

She looked shocked. "Oh no, Lady Rowanna. The claim can't be filed until after the emergency." I swallowed the last of the vegetable pasty with some difficulty.

Looking again at her companion, I thought she seemed familiar. "I'm sorry, I believe we've met, but I rather think I've forgotten you name ... so many new faces you see."

"I didn't expect you to recognize me, Lady Rowanna, for we've not been introduced. I have seen you in the secure levels of RADA, and my father has spoken of you ... endlessly," she said drily.

I looked at her for a long moment. "Good G ... um, I had no idea Benot held anyone! And you don't really look anything like him," I added kindly. Benot was not a pretty man, except for his nose.

"He doesn't. Sendal holds my mother now."

Lena waved a small hand at her friend. "Lady Rowanna, I present Lady Haoe, daughter of Benot, Primary Mathematician and the second son of Lord Holder Cobben. Lady Haoe is held by Canto, Councilman Dobo's son."

I responded as was proper and went on. "But I thought Sendal's daughter was Lady Hagen, the half-sister of Matul!" I noticed she used the more informal introduction.

The girls laughed. "That's just Hagen, Sendal's daughter by Matul's mother." I was suddenly aware of the huge gulf between the fertile and infertile. His daughter was just Hagen and had to work for her living. What would she have done if she had not been bright? Perhaps the families cared for them.

I replied. "I introduce Lady Rilla to you ... but you met her at Lady Garola's, didn't you?" Lena agreed, and the three exchanged nods.

Rill reached over and took my warty orange starfruit. I looked at her tray in amazement and discovered she had all but finished the enormous meal. She grinned at me and began to peal the fruit, the strong citrus-like smell making my mouth water.

Haoe waved to catch my attention again.

"We wondered if you could tell us what the plans are." She glanced at Lena and back to me. "We don't know where our men are going to be."

I looked as surprised as I felt. "I have no idea what the plans are. No one ever told me. I don't even know why they should have!" I began to suck a yellow fruit out of its hairy skin, just as Ragul had taught me.

Haoe looked disbelieving. "Benot said you made a major contribution to the plan, and when Hagen brought Sendal two high-security viral containers yesterday, he said using them had been your idea." Her look was accusing.

I didn't hurry my mouthful and then put the skin down slowly. "Lady Haoe, there is a difference between having a few abstract ideas for men like your father to use and developing and planning a detailed campaign. You two probably know more than I do. It wouldn't be hard. Didn't Amar tell you anything?"

Lena shook her pretty head. "Not really. He had to hurry off because of some last-minute changes in the wings."

Haoe turned to Lena. "It seems Essoth was thrown out of his command. He still wants to fight, so Matul's wing commander agreed to have him, but he'll have to be just one of the pilots."

Lena flushed slightly and smoothed the rose velvet of her tunic as she replied. "Yes, Amar said Jossand might have to take him."

I had been thinking back to something I heard yesterday. "Do either of you know if it has anything to do with the accusations made against Gossot yesterday?"

"What accusations?" asked Rill with interest.

"It seems two dead experiments were found on his property. Apparently, they went missing a couple of quarters ago."

Lena's flush drained into paleness. She leaned forward earnestly. "It's not true. He had nothing to do with it. He's told everyone that Essoth and Snard rented the buildings from him ... how should he know what goes on there?"

I raised my eyebrows and looked at Haoe.

She waved Lena's distress aside. "Gossot is a cousin of Lena's mother," she explained a little stiffly.

I didn't know what to say, and I was saved from replying by the arrival of the matronly women of yesterday who I could now see was about halfway through her own pregnancy.

"Are you Lady Rowanna?" I nodded. "The Councilor, Warlord, and Lord Holder Ragul sent this in for you," she said as she handed me a gray tube.

I thanked her and saw that it was a scroll sealed in a plastic film. Having looked me over curiously for a moment, she left. Haoe and Lena followed suit, as they showed a marked disinclination to discuss Gossot's problems.

I looked at the scroll. There was a white disk with a thumbprint along the sealed seam. As I punctured the plastic, it crumbled. The letter was not long, and the bold firm script was familiar. I read it in silence.

My very dearest Lady, know that whatever comes, I love you. Never doubt that you are the woman above all others that I would spend my life with.

The Lady Rill will be joining you. She is also pregnant, and I am confident that you understand. When the emergency is over, Torren will come and get you both. He knows where to take you. I would come myself, but my duties do not end with the departing of the Natog.

Should anything happen to Torren or myself, I have made provision for you and the other two. Try to be less conspicuous than usual. Alone with nothing to do, the ladies around you will be more inquisitive than ever.

Your Lord,
Ragul

"Well, what does he say?" Rill sounded slightly exasperated. I swallowed and blinked away the tears that threatened to come.

"Torren will be coming to get us after the emergency. If anything happens to either of them, he has made provision for us." I tried to make my voice light. "Oh yes, we must keep a low profile, the ladies here have the time to notice things." But not the inclination, I thought, when they must all have male relatives and spouses on the planet surface in danger of being harvested by the Natog!

"Hmm." Rill put her tray on top of mine and seemed about to take them both away.

"Rill, do you really not mind, about Ragul and I?"

She looked at me a moment and sat down again. "Men are essential for companionship, Rowhan, but when they belong to another woman, they are no fun."

I looked my surprise. "*You* think men are necessary?"

"Of course. Not part of the structure or hierarchy of an ordered society, you understand, they are too aggressive, violent, and emotional and so must be kept in occupations where they can do little harm. But as companions, yes." She spoke matter-of-factly.

"I'd have thought you would prefer women friends," I ventured.

"Don't be silly. Women can see into the hearts of other women. They see the hidden doubts and fears, they manipulate their weaknesses, and they are totally ruthless. Men are blind. They see little they cannot touch. So with a man, you can open your heart and mind. They can be a true friend and an unsurpassed lover."

I hesitated a moment, fascinated by this glimpse of the gender roles and relationships on Dejan. "But what about the men? Don't you feel that you are using them?"

Rill stood up and laughed. "The Gods of Dejan made them blind, so we do not abuse our powers ... any more than necessary," she said softly.

Chapter Fifteen

In writing of these events, I have my husband's pledge that he will help me with the technical aspects of the Natog attack and how the various plans have been carried out, and what their long-term and short-term effects are, both on the Natog and the inhabitants of Selene.

Knowing my Lord, I'm sure he intends to honor that pledge, but if I delay this work until he is able, our children will be grown with children of their own, and the story old or forgotten.

I sit here, looking out over the gardens of a land that seems so similar and yet different from my own, and I think about the things that absorb my husband now.

The information now being retrieved from the Natog "computers" as I shall call them, for they serve that purpose, reveals several Homo Sapien inhabited worlds in various stages of development. Some are shared with other dominant species, some not. Some are holding on by a thread, while others thrived before the Natog and are fighting back.

One of the things my husband is passionate about is contacting and sharing knowledge with these worlds, thus paving the way for an alliance. But the other project is as urgent, and that is where he is now.

He and a stalwart group have gone to Earth to make contact, share information, and find wives—or at least eggs for Selene's future. He thought this would be an easy matter, but I pointed out that the Natog had taken Earth by surprise, and now that Earthlings were aware of the threat, it would be much harder to approach the planet, especially as his ship is a converted Natog ship! Earthlings would need a lot of convincing, and he would have to stand off and negotiate for some time. I tried to explain that Earth has no real unifying authority or leader, or it didn't when I was taken, and all the peoples would be fearful and want something different. I also pointed out that religious groups were very resistant to the idea of intelligent life on other planets (I can still hear his snort of derision) and, lastly, that Earth would never hand over oodles of women just because he wanted them! Especially young, fertile ones.

He listened closely, this husband of mine, and while he remains positive, I fear it will take longer to reconcile the politicians and the corporations and interest groups than he thinks, but at least the journey has started, however long it takes.

The sun slants its long afternoon light across the wide lawns and under the huge shimmering woomina trees that remind me of stories of elfin forests of old on my world. I can hear my daughter's eager questions and my son laughing with his nanny, and I know it will soon be time for me to nurse him. But I linger here, remembering the thick atmosphere of apprehension that grew in that huge room as the fateful day advanced. It was not for ourselves, but for those above that we worried.

I can't withhold a sigh for the memory, for little did I know then that, for me at least, the worst was yet to come, and there were deadly forces at work that would result in deaths close to me and my being held by the most powerful man on Selene ... and it began the next day. A day that had started so well.

Chapter Sixteen

I woke to the cheerful laughter and bright chatter of women released from the burden of unselfish fear, compounded as it had been by the enforced inactivity of the previous day. There was not even the subduing effects of survivor's guilt, as no one here had suffered a loss in the raid.

The Roll Calls still blinked reassuringly on the screens that encircled the high walls of the room.

Stretching beneath the light coverings, I glanced at the bar clock on the far wall. The sixth segment was barely past, but there were already empty trays being carried back to the disposal area, and nearly half of those around me were well into their breakfast. Rill gave a smile and a wave as she headed toward the serving area.

I had never suffered from morning sickness with pregnancy, but I tended to lose my appetite, often for the entire duration of the pregnancy, and live quite happily on milk (gallons of it), fruit juice, raw vegetables, and some fruits. Listening with resignation to the messages from my stomach, I realized I had embarked on that phase of my pregnancy. A long shower, vegetable nutrients, and water was what I lusted after. "I sound like a plant!" I grinned to myself as I headed toward the showers clutching a change of clothing.

I was munching on a vegetable stick when I joined Rill some time later, a glass of cold, tangy water in my hand. She was finishing something that looked like a cross between a waffle and a crumpet that was covered with a creamy sauce and a slightly viscous golden substance. The rest of her dishes were empty, and although they didn't represent the feast of yesterday, there was no doubt Rill had breakfasted well.

"Have they opened the doors yet?" I asked between bites.

"No, but Torren sent a confirmation of Ragul's last message." She raised another full fork to her lips, then paused, and the golden stuff began to droop. "He enclosed another bit of news. It seems Essoth tried to maneuver Amar into the Natog's clutches ... an accident of course," she added drily as she caught the drip and continued to eat.

"An accident! Like heck it was," I snapped. "He wants Lena, and if Amar was dead, and with her pregnant, he might well succeed! What happened?"

"Amar's escape maneuver left Essoth exposed to the very trap intended for Amar."

"The Natog got him?" This came from behind us, spoken in a voice that was soft with horror. We turned to see Lena staring at us white-faced and clutching Haoe's arm. Rill nodded.

"It was Essoth that got caught, Lena, not Amar," I explained quickly.

"I know, I heard you. Does that make everything all right? Have you no pity? Everyone was against him, no one gave him a chance! Even loving me was hopeless!" she wailed.

"Lena, he was trying to get Amar caught by the Natog, and he may well have been guilty of far more," I argued.

"Amar is alive, and what could be worse than being caught by the Natog?" she said.

"I can think of one or two things," I said, thinking of the dead women found at Gossot's place.

After a moment's pause, Lena agreed. "Yes, being left alive when your loved one has been taken ... that ... would have been worse." Suddenly, she smiled and held out her hands. "Forgive me, this has been a trying time for us all. We came over to ask if you would join us at Lady Garola's for a luncheon. It's a small celebration to announce Amar's claim, and I may invite whom I wish. Normally, his father would do the honors, but he's very busy, so the big event will be later, but I think I will like this one better ...

I don't really know many people yet, and they tend to stare down their nose so," she said, giving my hands a squeeze.

I bent forward and kissed her cheek, gently pressing her hands in return. "We'd love to come, my dear, but I don't know if we can. Ragul has plans for us, I believe … but if it's at all possible to get there, we will." I glanced at Rill, who nodded and started to gather up her tray.

She paused for a moment and grinned at Lena. "May you have many daughters, each with more eggs than Nerta!"

With squeals of delight from Haoe and blushes and laughter from Lena, they left us.

"Was there any more news?" I asked.

"Only that Gossot has found Essoth's death very convenient. Too convenient, in some people's opinion. Especially as Snard seems to have disappeared," she said, rising to take the tray back.

"Snard!" I echoed, staring after her retreating figure. To banish the memory of the soft, cruel man from the institute, I began to fold and pack yesterday's clothes. I was nearly out of fresh garments and made a mental note to ask Ragul about laundry facilities on this world.

It was past the seventh segment now, and the restless groups gathered around the sealed door swelled by the minute. Rill joined me and pulled her packed cloth bag from beneath the bed. Metal studs attached the leather bands to the soft green brocade fabric. So many of the things on Selene still seemed to be handmade by craftsmen, and then there were the high-tech things like the self-heating cans and holo screens … such a strange mix.

"We might as well join them." Rill's head indicated the groups by the door. "Torren will be waiting."

As it turned out, Torren was not the only one waiting for us. At the top of the narrow stairs, the small flood of women spread out across the large room, either heading straight for the exits or searching the waiting faces for a loved one. Torren was noticeable for his sullen, anxious expression, and Hagnot for his obvious enjoyment of Torren's discomfort.

Advancing, Hagnot took my reluctant hands and held them to his chest. "I have come to insist that you join our little celebration at my aunt's." He smiled derisively down at me. "I know it saddened you to leave her so abruptly last time. She was at pains to extract my promise to bring you to see her, if only for a very short time. It would have been unforgivable of me to refuse her … don't you think?" His eyes danced with wicked amusement.

"Lena gave us to understand that you would be much too busy for such things," I said, tugging at my hands, which he released slowly.

"Much, which is why I can stay less than a segment, but he is my only child after all, Lady Rowanna, and this will be the first official announcement."

I glanced at Torren, who shrugged helplessly. "I've explained that I'm to take you back to RADA, where Benot needs you urgently, he's waited overlong as it is," Torren said with an obvious look at his wrist band.

Satisfaction settled on Hagnot's face. "Ah. Well, there is a problem, is there not? Are you," he said, turning to face me, "on the personnel list at RADA? No?" He observed my bland face. "Nonpersonnel are restricted in RADA for forty segments after an emergency," he explained with false bonhomie. "It seems my aunt's invitation is especially opportune; it will give you time to decide what to do. You could, of course, go back to Lady Meranna, who is no doubt anxious about you …" He let his voice trail off.

During this exchange, I had noted several peripheral things. Rill had begun to drift away from our group toward an exit, only to be blocked by Lena taking her arm enthusiastically and saying how nice it was that we could come after all, with Haoe as the Greek chorus. Another was a waiting woman who began to glance as inquisitively at us as at the entrance. Lastly, I was aware there was no way of refusing such an invitation without arousing considerable suspicion and hostility.

I smiled as sweetly as I could. "Your invitation is too kind, First Councilor. Our only hesitation was due to a sense of duty … but since we are unable to fulfill these obligations at present, I cannot say how happy we are to accept your more than generous invitation." The sarcasm was not lost on him.

His smile warmed as he looked down at me. "My delight at your acceptance surpasses your own," he said formally, and his lips twitched. Taking my arm and leaving Torren to carry our two cloth bags, he guided us toward the exit.

As I glanced back at Rill, who was being escorted by Lena and Hagen, I saw the woman step forward as if to intercept Lena, hesitate, and then fall back. Her stare followed us out of the building.

Chapter Seventeen

Our arrival at Lady Garola's was widely noted, due to Hagnot's presence and the nature of the event. The security guard smiled us by without comment. The old lady herself seemed to derive considerable inner amusement from our presence, and she made no reference to our abrupt departure nearly two weeks ago.

I bowed and touched her fingers to my forehead as I murmured my gratification.

"Doing the pretty, are you girl? Well, that's good, that's good. You'll need to be able to hide your feelings in the rank you will hold." She cackled approvingly.

"That's true." I nodded. "Ragul will undoubtedly expect it of me. But I have nothing to hide from you, Lady Garola."

She chuckled delightedly and turned to Hagnot.

"Well, what do you have to say to that?" she quizzed him.

"If every plan that was made succeeded, we would have the heavens to ourselves and number more than the stars," he responded with a dry smile while Rill came forward to make her bow.

Lena had disappeared into a bedroom and soon reappeared wearing a wreath of flowers in her dark, shiny hair. Over her velvety pink underskirt and cream and rose tunic she had donned a white gauzy garment of medium length. It was reminiscent of a delicate poncho with a heavy fringe of threaded seeds. She was smiling shyly, but her eyes glowed with happiness at Amar's proud look when he strode into the room. He went to her and raised her hands to his forehead and then to his lips.

"Forgive me, my love, I couldn't get away sooner," he murmured before his lips found hers. Then turning, he approached his great aunt, who was trying to hide her delight.

"Greetings, dear lady, and my gratitude for this kind disposal of your time." He smiled with genuine affection as he raised her hands to his head.

Having bowed to his father, greeted me, and sent a gay salute to Torren, he turned to Rill. In response to a comment, his startled "Ragul holds you both?" drew a quick frown from his father, but before either could say more further guests arrived.

Having greeted Lady Garola, the three ladies fluttered toward Lena twittering ecstatically, the floating gown of one becoming briefly entangled with a small table. Their two male escorts bore down on Amar, who manfully accepted a well-intentioned pounding on the back and hearty congratulations. The ladies soon came over to him, and one coyly pointed out something about his attire. Amar looked startled and put his hand to his chest, and then glanced about as if missing something. Then he smiled and entered the bedroom Lena had used and emerged wearing a pendant on a long leather thong. The ladies chattered happily, and the men grinned. As equally symbolic as Lena's apparel, only of the pendant's extremely stylized form saved me from blushing.

As more well-wishers arrived and Lady Garola's serving girls began to circulate dispensing refreshment, I had time to ponder three questions. Why did Hagnot bring us here when he intended to leave very soon, and thus could not prevent our departure? I could think of several unpalatable reasons. Secondly, how soon could we leave, and where was Torren going to take us? I glanced in his direction, but Hagnot seemed to be talking to Torren. Rill's eyes met mine. The third thing that nagged at me was the absence of Lady Uronia. Amar wasn't a Councilor, but surely she would be here, at least to preen!

Rill moved to my side. Softly she spoke as we watched the swirl of guests. "I'm leaving," she said. I glanced at her quickly and away again.

"They'll see us. What explanation could we give?"

"They'd notice you, not me." She looked at me, and I swallowed the tightness in my throat as I recognized the obvious implication. I was endangering Rill's life. She could make it out on her own, but what then?

"You are right, of course, sort something out with Torren." I gave her a lopsided grin. Her smile was slow and lovely. I hoped I would see it again.

Just then, a serious gentleman in a long robe engaged Hagnot's attention, and Torren swiftly made his way to our side. "We've got to get out somehow," he hissed. "The place is filling up with people that know you or your mother—they just haven't realized it yet!"

"We guessed," I said somewhat tartly.

"With these all-day affairs, people are continually coming and going, so we should be able to slip out quite easily," he suggested.

"Not that easily. Hagnot is watching me like a hawk."

"Like a what?" he asked in surprise.

Ignoring him, I said, "You disappear with Rill and grab an air-car or something. If I'm not right behind you, or I'm followed, leave." Seeing Torren's look of doubt, I said, "How can you contact Ragul from here, for heaven's sake!"

Rill nodded, and taking Torren's arm in a deceptively light grip, began to drift away even as objections formed on his lips.

Forcing myself not to watch their progress, I took a brimming glass with a bright smile from a passing girl and moved across the room as if to join a group. A quick glance showed Hagnot's eyes marking my progress.

I positioned myself before a slender blue vase filled with delicate branches of silver grey wood. Without moving my head, I observed Rill and Torren melt into the background of a group standing very near the entrance.

Just as I was wondering if I should drop my glass or accidentally knock over the vase to create a mild disturbance to engage Hagnot's attention, the subject of one of my puzzles burst into the room, her momentum carrying her well into the middle before her eyes found Hagnot.

With an angry flush on her cheeks and her arm thrust angrily in my direction, she announced, "*You have been deceived,*

First Councilor! She is a despicable wretch, an eggless impostor masquerading as a *lady*!" Including Lady Garola in her tirade, she added in awful tones, "And your hospitality has been abused!"

I stared at her, the nausea of fear rising in my throat, my heart's echo pounding in my head. Like a mesmerized rabbit, I stood awaiting the inevitable. The happy hum of conversation died with barely suppressed gasps. In the moments of silence that followed, guests glanced at each other in horror and inquiry.

Lady Garola's angry words broke through the silence. "What in heaven's name are you babbling about? The only person who has abused my hospitality is yourself, with your tardy arrival and the manner of it!"

Lady Uronia's flush blotched, but she drew her portly figure even more erect. "Indeed! Well, I can tell you that only duty would keep me from my daughter's side at this time, my duty as a citizen!"

"Ha!" was Lady Garola's only rejoinder, but Hagnot approached Lena's mother and demanded to know who she referred to. I had the impression he knew.

While Hagnot's attention was focused on Lady Garola, I glanced toward the door. Relief eased the tightness in my throat. Rill and Torren were no longer there.

Venomously, Lady Uronia answered him. "The so-called Lady Rowanna! That's who I'm talking about, the cheating wench who bewitched you! You ignored a lady to follow the skirts of an eggless, deceiving, law-breaking scullion … no doubt you can visit her down the mines occasionally to satisfy your interest in her!"

A buzz of bewilderment and consternation broke out, and Hagnot turned to me. He looked long and hard. His face betrayed nothing. Ignoring Lady Uronia, he advanced on me. I lifted my chin and stared back.

Stopping in front of me, his eyes searched my face. "Is it true?" His voice was perfectly normal, but it was heard clearly in the silent room. His eyes glittered.

My mind had begun to fizz with alternative plans. I was also mindful of the delay Rill and Torren needed.

"I, an eggless wretch?" I forced a smile of derision onto my stiff lips. "I can easily prove myself, but I confess to a fascination to know the source of Lady Uronia's information, barring a jealous and vengeful disposition, of course." My casually spoken words gave Hagnot pause—he knew her thwarted ambitions as well as I.

Like spectators at a tennis match, all heads turned to Lady Uronia's indignant form with her theatrically out-flung arm.

"Would you indeed! I doubt that, you slut," she hissed. "But I shall tell you anyway! During the recent emergency you were in the lowest sealed chamber here in Jenna, masquerading as a pregnant lady." Hagnot's eyes narrowed; I couldn't guess what he was thinking. With a snatched breath, Lady Uronia continued. "Also, there was a Lady Pella, who many of you know." Her glance included the room full of guests, several of whom nodded. "You know her to be an upright lady. She didn't speak to you as she didn't know you, but while waiting at the upper level for her lord, she overheard your meeting with the First Councilor. She was stunned and thought there must be some mistake, but on arriving home, she went at once to her albums to check with some family and wedding holos. Then she visi-cast me." She paused, letting the moment hang there before making the final denouncement.

My laughter broke the tense circle of faces into glances of uncertainty. "Let me guess, I'm not the Lady Rowanna!" I strove to keep my voice light, and I avoided Hagnot's intense regard. "How excessively delicious for you! But, dear Lady Uronia, by what devious means did you come to the conclusion that I was eggless?" I asked with simulated interest. "I fail to see how a holo could lead you to such a conclusion … so enlighten us!"

That Lady Uronia was stunned by my reaction was obvious, but she hastened to recover. "Who but an eggless impostor would perpetrate such a hoax?" she asked in awful tones. There were nods, and the gazes returned to me.

"An errant wife?" I quizzed lightly, sipping my drink with a semblance of unconcern.

She gasped, then she shrilly declared, "I don't believe it! Not for one moment, you lying little hussy. Prove it, go on, prove it!

What's your name and number, your real name and number. Have it checked at once, Councilor!"

Another casual sip and I smiled at her. "And have a furious lord descend on me? Oh no."

Lady Uronia wheeled triumphantly toward Lady Garola. "There, what did I tell you! Call the guards at once. She must pay for this charade, though much of the damage is inalterable," she added bitterly.

"One moment." Hagnot's gesture halted Lady Garola's abrupt summons to a nearby girl. She had said nothing yet, but anger snapped in her eyes.

"If she were eggless, why the charade? Why would she not just join Ragul's household … or mine?" he added. "Why go to the dangerous lengths of removing the neck mark, of which I can see no sign, and live in the perpetual fear of inevitable discovery, for no more gain than is had by any beloved woman?" He asked the question of himself, but Lady Uronia answered.

"For the status, of course! To be a lady with money, power, and position!"

Hagnot looked at her with some contempt. "While eggless females are not alone in those ambitions, I would remind you that many achieve that status without such dangerous deceptions."

Two sharp claps caught our attention as Lady Garola gestured for a girl to help her rise from the seat into which she had collapsed. Then, standing with some difficulty, she glared in my direction. "This is my dwelling, and I have been grossly deceived. My hospitality has been abused. The guards will be called." Her voice was implacable.

"I think not, my dear aunt," Hagnot said, giving her look for look. "At least, not yet," he added, turning back to me. I said nothing as he looked me over. "You say you are pregnant?" I nodded. "Well, that at least is provable … or disprovable. Girl, get some PreVal tablets, would you? Thank you." She nodded and hurried away.

"Had any breakfast?" he asked me as he handed me a tumbler of juice and a tablet that had been brought to him. I was acutely aware of the room full of people watching me gulp it down, embarrassed by their intrusion into a personal matter. But better embarrassed than hauled away by the guards to who knows where! Besides, all this gave Rill and Torren more time. Torren would certainly contact Ragul, but when and how soon he could get here … and what could he do?

My mind twisted this way and that in search of a way out. I pushed aside one half-formed plan after another. Low conversations hummed back and forth, the reason for the celebration now forgotten. Newly arriving guests were pulled aside and regaled with the developments to date, with many muffled exclamations and furtive glances in my direction.

Lady Uronia, deprived at the moment of her prey, was busy among the guests favoring them with her premonitions of this event and tales of how she had tried to warn dear Lady Garola and the First Councilor. Her venomous remarks rose occasionally above the level of the surrounding conversations, only to be lowered to decant even worse theories into the ears of those gathered about her. She took no heed of the newly united couple, of Amar's protective arm around Lena's clinging form, or of his lowered head as he bent to catch her soft, anxious words. I felt a pang of remorse for their ruined delight in this day.

Lady Garola retired to her room, aided by her girl. The shock of Lady Uronia's announcement had betrayed her age. She seemed to have shrunk a bit and tottered slightly as she made her way from the room. I was sorry for that too.

At last, I reached some conclusions. I had no reason, other than embarrassment, for not wanting to prove my pregnancy. Indeed, I saw no possible way out of the mess without such evidence. I didn't know what would happen once I was cleared of Lady Uronia's charges of sterility, but I'd possibly just be kicked out, with some icy verbal abuse hurled after me for good measure. At least I hoped!

"Are you pregnant by Ragul or by your husband?" Hagnot broke into my thoughts.

I looked at him in surprise. "You have mentioned your condition to me before," he reminded me. A blush of remembrance heated my cheeks. "Do you think I'd let you take this test if I doubted you?" he continued in an undertone, his eyes boring down at me. "Will your lord release you to me, or must I challenge him? Do not think you are leaving here without me; I find you are becoming an obsession with me. Perhaps it's your unusual lack of ambition," he admitted with a twisted smile.

"Ragul isn't exactly a backward step for any girl," I said somewhat tartly. "And he is a Councilor. Being a First Councilor is a rotatory post!"

"True, but only if confirmed by vote. He is considered too young by many of the Councilors, and his involvement with that double-cursed experiment and its failure has done him only harm. Indeed, if it were not for his exceptional and proved abilities as a Warlord he would not be on the Supreme Council at all," he replied.

I could have turned a haughty shoulder to him and gazed elsewhere, but I had no desire to encounter the furtive and hostile glances of the guests that eddied on the edge of the large space that surrounded us. Instead, I bethought me of some news we'd heard while in the sealed chambers.

"Is it true that Gossot is suspected of having something to do with the missing experiments?" I asked with feigned indifference.

"Yes." His answer was short. Then relenting, he added, "He declared ignorance of the whole matter, but there is growing evidence that he lies." A shudder shook his frame. "I had believed his opinion of the experiment to be as mine, but it seems he felt something could be snatched from defeat, at least that would be my guess. I only hope he has managed to kill off the last four as well." After a pause, he continued, "He will have to pay fully for the deaths of the Selenese women. That was inexcusable. Unless, perhaps, if he has succeeded."

I stared at him in incredulous horror. My fears, which had foolishly been eased by his continued attention, returned with redoubled force. He must never, never discover my identity without Ragul by to protect me—and I doubted even he would be enough against this insane obsession of Hagnot's.

"Who is your lord?" he returned abruptly to his previous train of thought, "And what is your real name?"

I put my empty glass down carefully beside the slender vase with its silvery branches. "I think it's time I went and proved my condition," I said flatly and looked toward the washrooms near the entrance.

"Oh no, my lovely." His eyes glinted appreciatively at me. "The other ones." We made our way across the room toward the hall that led to the bedrooms and other apartments. While each bedroom had its own facilities, there was also a ladies room and a universal one opposite the entrance to the corridor. "Very convenient," I thought, excusing the pun.

Hagnot remained in the main room and stopped to speak to an elderly man, but he positioned himself so he had an uninterrupted view of the door of the powder room, for I checked as I turned to close the door. His eyes narrowed with amusement at my look, and lowering his head, he listened to his earnest companion.

Looking around the room, with its pink floor covering, gold framed mirrors, and cream seats and counters, I gave a little grin for the universality of women. The toilet shelf was at the end of the room, but I looked around first to see if there was another exit. As I expected, there was none, nothing to facilitate an escape. Taking a disposable beaker from the water dispenser, I turned again and made, to me, and incredible discovery.

Since leaving the institution, I had lived mostly underground, with two exceptions. The first was this apartment, and here I'd been on an inner wall, and the second was Belack's room, which also had no window. Knowing their fears of the Natog, I had unconsciously assumed that Selenese dwellings had no windows! I had quite forgotten the institute windows, with their heavy metal shutters pressed back against the ivy, and I had failed to register the many windows of the buildings I had flown past.

Here, with the sun pouring through it, was a rectangular window. It was not overly large, but adequate. It turned on a heavy central pivot, for easy cleaning I guessed. The massive top and bottom bolts were withdrawn, and it was partly open to allow a breeze.

Hurriedly, I secured the door to the room. The toilet was the usual thing, a wall-to-wall shelf about two feet in depth and about six inches thick with three central openings. It worked on a variation of the niche method, just horizontal. It would undoubtedly hold my weight. The window was above and behind it, so I climbed up and swung it fully open, and then looked out.

Automatically, I looked down and wished I hadn't. Hastily, I looked away from the narrow valley between the modestly high buildings and concentrated on the view to the each side. That was my next surprise. The buildings were obviously much older than I had supposed. They were very well kept up, but they probably predated the Natog invasions. Of course! With the drastic drop in the population, there had been no need or desire to build more housing. No one stayed in them during an invasion anyway! It had just looked modern to my unaccustomed eyes. The stones were weathered, and frequently the mortar had crumbled between them. Most of the windows had been considerably reduced in size, but between them were metal shutters that swung and locked over them. A diminutive ledge, some eleven inches wide, ran the length of the building, going past several tightly shut windows.

To the right, the situation looked much the same. The next window was about four feet away and closed. Barely nine feet beyond that, however, was another partially open window. Desperately, I tried to remember what was in that direction, but as our bedroom had been in the other, I had no idea.

I considered the distance again. The shutter to the right seemed securely clamped to the wall, although this meant the ridge was reduced by about three inches by its presence. Beyond the shutter, the mortar of the wall was uneven to the next window, but after that shutter, it was impossible to see the condition of the mortar for the last few feet of ledge before the open window.

The shadow of an air-car flitted slowly across the opposite wall; I looked up quickly. Damn! Three dimensional traffic! However, further scrutiny revealed that this was a narrow alley, with this side in the shade. The opposite wall was only a few feet away, and beyond each end of the alley, wider chasms streamed with layers of traffic.

I drew back to ponder the situation and nearly stepped on the forgotten beaker. No harm in filling it, I reflected. In fact, if my tentatively forming plan failed, it would be very good to have.

A few minutes later, leaving the beaker in a prominent place with its blue contents, I discovered that while climbing out of the window onto the ledge was not difficult, it was an action I never wished to repeat. I extended myself to a standing position beside the window, facing the wall and clutching the shutter with one hand and the window ledge with the other. With my heart pounding painfully, it seemed the next window had shuffled several more feet away.

With clenched teeth, I edged my way along the narrow ledge and reached for the edge of the shutter with my left hand. I felt that my bosom was going to topple me over the edge, and I clung tighter. A stiff breeze tugged fitfully at my long skirt and pressed the silky tunic to my clammy back.

Leaving the shutter, I found the handholds among the chinks in the mortar far less reassuring than those of the shutters, but the ledge was now a little wider. Where my fear of falling advocated clinging to the wall inch by inch, my fear of a passing air-car had me shuffling toward the next shutter. A quick peep in showed the room to be temporarily empty. A heart-stopping sidle past, and then a nightmare stretch along the section with newer mortar, made the past few feet seem a haven of security.

The next room was also empty, and my fear of an air-car had me slipping in through the window in desperate haste. A quick movement restored the window to its original position. I crouched by some stacked chairs as I made a quick survey of the room.

The door was shut, but beyond it I could hear eager chatter and the cheerful rattle of a trolley and further away the clatter of pots and chink of small plates. Within the narrow room were all the indications of it being a utility room. There were cleaning equipment and agents neatly arranged, a basket of clean rags, a press, a large work table and so on, but no laundry facilities.

I found inspiration in an unexpected guise. By one wall were several neatly folded linen bags. Printed on each bag were Lady Garola's name and variously, clothes, shoes, linens, etc. In the wall just above the bags was a large flap with a plastic handle. Of course, it could be another niche thing, but why put clothes into a bag to destroy them?

I slipped across the room and opened the flap. The chute was a wide one. It disappeared at a gentle angle into darkness. But what was beyond that gentle decent? An abrupt plunge down a huge shaft to the basement? Quite possibly.

My fear of the passing of time made me reckless. Suppose I hid in the chute, just beyond the shadow, until my disappearance was discovered and a search made it seem I had managed to leave the apartment? Then I could creep out later and slip away …

Footsteps outside the door had me crouching instantly, even though there was nowhere adequate to hide. They paused a moment, and then turned and went back the way they had come. But I had come to a decision. Bending down again, I slipped off my sandals and thrust them down the front of my tunic, trusting my belt to prevent their loss. I felt that with bare hands and feet I could wedge myself just beyond the light.

I quickly slid my lower half into the chute while holding the frame to prevent a rapid descent into the chute. As I wriggled my torso down further, feeling around with my feet, I found that my skirt bunched up to my hips, which enabled me to wedge my thighs securely against the sides too. Nevertheless, I felt very insecure as I let the flap spring back and I lay in darkness. How far should I wriggle down to be out of the light if someone should open the flap?

I cautiously edged further back, my feet indicating that the chute didn't end just yet. By stretching out my hand, I could still feel the flap, so I knew I hadn't gone far. My eyes became accustomed to the dark, and I could now discern a little in the refracted light from around the flap. I decided to go down just a bit further.

Abruptly, the door of the room opened and someone came in. There was a rattle of broken china into a container, muffled footsteps, and the door closed. My heart leaped erratically in my chest, and I wondered what to do if someone tried to dispose of soiled linens before I left? I must get further into the shadow, far enough for a bag and for me!

Deceived by the gentle slope so far, my feet were not wedged as firmly as I'd intended, and a sudden acceleration caught me unprepared. Suddenly, my feet kicked wildly at nothing and my forearms slid painfully along the sides. My skirt slid up further and prevented the tactile contact I'd relied on.

With a jerk, my feet slammed against something solid. There was empty nothingness beneath my thighs, but my hips and trunk were still in the chute. Cautiously, I felt around with one foot, the other firmly planted on the barrier. It seemed my legs were projecting across a shaft about three feet in diameter. Warm air stirred, carrying a faint smell of laundry products. I lay tense and trembling while I considered my situation. A three-foot diameter was no worse than some rock chimneys I'd climbed in the past, except I had no boots, ropes, proper clothing, and friends. "Skeered of going on and afeared of going back," an old-timer had once said about his freezing on a ledge. Now I knew what he meant.

In any event, going on proved very much easier than I had dared to hope. As I developed confidence in my ability to control my descent, my inching became a slow controlled slide, accompanied by the occasional drift of muffled conversation as I slid by the chutes of occupied rooms.

The increased cleaning smells, the hollow noises, and the diffused light from beneath me warned of the approach of the end of the shaft. I slowed my descent and stopped some six feet above its end. Peering down, I could see it ended abruptly over a pile of stuffed bags.

Voices sounded nearby, and a pair of hands grabbed a bag with practiced ease and bore it off. I waited for a lull in the noises and carefully slid the last few feet, dropped onto the bags and rolled to one side.

A huge pile of tabbed sheets lay waiting by a vast machine. Hiding behind the pile, I slipped on my sandals. "Now if anyone stops me, I'll pretend I'm lost or something!" I thought.

But I needn't have worried. No one marked my soft exit, nor my opening one large barred door, or my tentative and delighted steps out into the bright sunlight of the alley.

As suddenly as the fear and gloom had descended upon me at seeing Hagnot waiting for us this morning, now my spirits rose joyfully. It seemed hardly possible that it was not quite midday, after the lifetime I'd endured in the last hour or two!

"It's true," I reminded myself, "that I don't know where I am, nor where I'm going, not even what I'll do when I get there. But just at this moment, I don't care. I'm deliriously happy to be alive—and very hungry!"

Feeling the reassuring hardness of Ragul's tokens in the pocket of my sash, I promised myself something to eat as soon as I'd put some distance between myself and Lady Garola's apartment building. I stepped out briskly.

As I walked, I considered my options. I had no idea how to contact Ragul. If I took an air-car to any of the few places I knew the name of in the hopes he'd search them all, and heavens knew how one called up an air-car, Hagnot would probably have someone there too—the sealed chambers or RADA, for instance.

I had no idea where Belack's was and wouldn't be able to get in even if I did, and no one could find anyone at the Garage of the Seven Doves! Would a cab driver know where Ragul's mother lived? Even if he did, wouldn't it be an obvious place for Hagnot to look? He could use the experiments as an excuse. I shuddered at the memory of his expression when discussing them. I placed little hope in an abrupt change of heart!

I shook off the threatened return of despair and tried to concentrate on what I could do to find Ragul without being found by Hagnot or his men. Perhaps I could leave a message that only Ragul would understand, arranging a meeting or something. But how and where?

The congested pedestrian traffic, which seemed determined on catching up with three days of missed shopping and errands, made concentration difficult. At the first opportunity, I turned down a less frequented thoroughfare and continued to step out briskly as I pondered the possibilities. My feet found their own way as I tested and discarded several plans, but by the time I slowed and stopped, staring at nothing while a tentative "Eureka!" tugged a smile to my lips, I looked up to discover I was in an area of Jenna I had not even guessed existed.

Quiet in the heat of noonday, a barely rippling surface of a large river moved, its edges crowded with secured sea and river craft tugging gently at their moorings.

There was curiously little activity, although several craft seemed to be in various stages of loading or disembarking cargo. Not carrying people or animals, they would have been ignored by the Natog. Cranes hung motionless over gaping holds, and deserted gangways rose and fell with the movement of the river. Somewhere nearby, whistling was cut off by the closing of a cabin door. A swarthy fellow with a neatly patched tunic sauntered out of a nearby doorway, stretched, and made off down the stone dock toward one of short floating wooden docks.

A way out of Jenna! I grinned—but it would only work if everything could be worked out in time! Stepping out briskly again, I looked around to see if there were any small river boats that were almost loaded.

As I passed the boats, I glanced at large numbers written on each side of the boats' bridges, though that was a grandiose description for the squat little enclosures that held the steering and controls and sheltered men from the elements. I decided these numbers were the equivalent of the boat's name, which is what I would need to send Ragul.

I had already passed a small, flat-bottomed craft of thirty feet or so—it looked like the sort of thing a man and a lad could manage easily—with a nonperishable cargo already secured under heavy tarpaulins. From the order being restored to the decks, it appeared to be nearing departure. Turning back to her quickly, I watched the crates of machinery, bales, sacks, and baskets being covered by tarps. Crates of fowls were being tied down, and baskets of small trees were already secured, their roots bound in wet sacking. A few sagging bags of grain lay about.

"Yes," I decided, "this is as good as any, if it can be done." Her number was clear, if aged, and I hurried away to carry out my plan.

***

The heat beneath the heavy tarpaulin was suffocating. I had wriggled with my hastily purchased bundles as far into the middle of the main cargo as I could, but now I realized that my caution would have to be tempered with reality. Perhaps, in the cool of the night, I would be glad to return to these bales of cloth, but right now I would give anything to strip off and plunge into the cool river gurgling so tantalizingly close.

Squirming between a large crate and a lumpy sack of implements, I lay near the edge of the cover and gasped at the cool air. At last, eased somewhat, I considered again what I'd done. At a small outdoor market hard by the docks, I had bought such food and drink as I could, and then sitting beneath a bright awning of a drink seller's stall, I wrote out a message on a napkin.

It was to Benot, and I asked him to give it to Ragul. I told Ragul the message was in code, and he was to remove my identification number continuously from the numerical values of the alphabet to decode it. In code, I told Ragul the number of the boat. I would try to leave clues for him, but if I didn't hear from him in seven days, I would return to Jenna and the RADA complex. I sent my love. Folding this hastily, I scrawled Benot's name and addressed it to the RADA complex.

The drink seller looked an honest man, and with almost the last of my change in his hand, he assured me he would send the message. I could only pray that he would be as good as his word.

My hunger had vanished with the heat. There had been no time to eat before hurrying back to the boat and squirming my way out of sight. Indeed, I could only hope that the few people sauntering back to work as I returned were too concerned with their own affairs to be interested in anyone else's.

Certainly, I had been undisturbed so far, and we'd been underway for a couple of hours, with the engine making the soft chug-chug of steam power. I thought sleepily of how hot it must be stoking an engine on a day like this, and gradually the tensions of the day began leaking out of my weary limbs. My last conscious thought was mild surprise at how comfortable a wooden deck could be.

Chapter Eighteen

It was the quality of stillness that woke me. That moment when Nature holds her breath and pauses, timelessly, before letting the dawn flood the world.

Grey light heavy with dew seeped beneath the tarpaulin, carrying with it the chilly smells of river, boats, damp sacking, and ropes. Through the marginal reeds ran the first sighing whispers of morning. Moments later, the boat turned gently in the breeze to rub her fenders softly against a wooden dock. Water chuckled and swirled off with the news that day had come.

I lay there, in no hurry to move, watching the grey light become tinged with yellow, and cast long, inquisitive fingers under the cover. Nothing had marred my sleep through the long night, and I had no desire to move. Peace was my mattress and contentment my mantel ... activity would lose me both.

My mind wandered serenely. I had probably slept a twelve-hour stretch, and so had no idea when we had arrived here, wherever here was. This was no mere stop for the night; we lay beside a proper dock. Had the crew pushed on through the night to be ready for an early unloading? If so, was it for a quick turnaround, or were they going on further after unloading some cargo and taking on more? There must be more than one of them, for they couldn't go without sleep for long. For no particular reason other than the nonperishable nature of the cargo and a hunch, I opted for the latter.

Muted sounds from the cabin drifted forward. Someone came out, and from the river side of the boat came the long sound of a thin stream of water, followed by the clanking and splashing of a bucket on a rope, and then the brimming, slopping sounds of the pail being carried back to the cabin.

Delicious smells came faintly at first, and then lingered tantalizingly. With a sigh, I reached back into the darkness for my bundle, felt among its contents and withdrew an apple-fruit. I bit deeply into its crisp sweetness and then paused. Some foods should have a noise rating! Cautiously, I munched, grateful no one was on deck.

Disposing of the stem and stone with a careful aim into the rushes, I shrank further beneath the cover, for distant noises seemed suddenly louder as herd beasts pulling a wagon rumbled onto the heavy wooden timbers of the dock. Pushing my bundle behind me, I wriggled deeper into the cargo under the tarp.

A man hailed the boat gruffly but cheerfully, and someone emerged with a light step from the cabin. A woman's voice sounded with pleasure. "Father! Greetings! Teneb said you were laid up with that leg again, I hadn't looked to see you. Come on in, Folin's only started his feeding. I can cook you up something while you tell us your news."

I heard him climb down from the wagon, his good-humored murmurs of agreement tucked between her chatter. He seemed to be tending to the beasts, and then I could hear him swing himself stiffly over the railings. "Well, Getty, my dear, you haven't been changing over much. Still up with the birds and good tempered with it … not like your cousin's woman," he added somewhat grimly. "But she cooks like a dream … so let's be seeing what you can do, child!" They went to the cabin, and her happy laughter was muffled by the closing door.

Events proved me right. A while later, he took the tiny trees and the crates of fowl, his daughter's man helping to load them. From scraps of conversation, I gathered that he had a small patch of land and sent fruit and eggs to the city.

The boat was soon underway again, and above the chug of the engine and the busy noises of the river, I could hear the occasional snatch of conversation or cheerful banter, but the breeze whisked the words away so I soon gave up trying to hear what they said. As the sun rose higher, it became warmer under the tarp, and I crept back nearer to the edge and settled down. The sunlight no longer slanted under the covering but pored down happily and incuriously.

I began to feel bored and thought longingly of the books tucked away in my bag, which was presumably still at Lady Garola's. I spelled out Selenese words to myself and fell asleep thinking that I could make a fortune bringing Scrabble to Selene!

I passed the day with snoozing and eating, which explained why, with the coming of night and the retirement of the couple who owned the boat, I was nearly mad with restlessness and beset with a thousand doubts about what I had done, self-recriminations about what I should have done, and fears that the drink seller would fail me. My body screamed for activity, to leap up and run in the soft light of the double moons until I was too tired to think. My bladder agreed.

I slipped out from under the tarpaulin and crept across the deck. The boat was moored against a low bank of close-cropped vegetation that came to the water's edge. I eased myself up onto the railings and then down onto the bank; I had taken my sandals off to cross the deck, and the cool, damp leaves felt delicious against the warm soles of my feet.

Creeping behind a solitary bush, I paused. A few minutes later, I rose up and gazed around feeling much relieved. A mixture of pasture and woods were bathed in the gentle light. They were drained of color but with double shadows to every tussock, spreading tree, and rock.

It didn't take long to get beyond the view of the boat, and no lights disturbed the night. Staring around, I could see a slight rise near the edge of the wood, and inky patches resolved themselves into animals about the size of goats. They lay watching me, quietly chewing. The stillness was disturbed by occasional ripping of greenery as they ate, and its scent warmed the air.

Raising my arms to the moons, stretching and tiptoeing, I began running, leaping, and twirling in silent abandon around the meadow. The small flock got up with nervous disapproval as I whirled near, their long fleece trailing the grass as they moved away toward the trees, sometimes stopping to gaze after me.

I danced till the stillness was disturbed by my ragged breathing. I flopped down panting in the short-cropped meadow. Oh, to let my hair down, strip off my clothes, and dance into the arms of the dawn! I laughed softly to myself at the impossibility of doing my hair again and at the thought of a horrified flock of animals as disapproving as aging dowagers watching me. I laughed at the knowledge that if I possessed a brush I probably *would* have danced naked in the moonlight.

I was deliciously tired as I slipped back onto the boat, and no fears or doubts unsettled my sleep.

The next morning passed uneventfully, with only occasional fears that we were stopping and I would be discovered during unloading. However, as the sun rose overhead, I became more obsessed by this possibility, until by early afternoon, I had convinced myself that major unloading was imminent, and my discovery was a certainty. It was perhaps just as well that we entered a wide, shallow lake thick with whispering reeds around its shoreline.

The man had come forward and was swinging a weighted length of twine before the boat to gauge the depth. The craft moved very slowly, the engine giving an occasional hiss between chugs. It seemed there was a winding channel, but it was not well marked. He would put out one arm or the other for the girl to change course. It was late in the afternoon when we reached the far shore, and he called a temporary halt. She came forward as he wound up the twine.

"Glad we're out of that. Seems more poles missing than usual, and that's saying something." She held out a steaming mug to him. "No hope of getting to Kessel in time, I suppose?"

"Not a hope," he grunted as he reached for the mug. "They're supposed to keep that channel marked. That's what we pay our token for. Adds half a day to the trip having to check it as we do. And that means losing near the whole day tomorrow!"

I could see her nod sympathetically from my hiding place. "Aye, it do." They sipped in silence for a few minutes. "If there's cargo for further up the river, will you take it?"

"No. There wouldn't be a full load, and just after an emergency, they never have enough ready to bring back to make it worth it. 'Sides, there'll be nearly a full cargo for us to take back down from Kessel. I'm going to speak to Possen about the channel, I will, before we start back. A Natog disgrace, that is."

"Well," she said as she took his empty mug, "shall we tie up at the unloading bay or by the trees for the night?"

"By the trees, love, they'll never start on us tonight, but they'll finish whoever they're doing, be it never so late. That noisy it'd be, at the unloading bay."

They strolled off down the boat, and soon we were underway again, the soft chug chug filling the early evening air.

It was dark by the time we reached Kessel. It hadn't been a great distance, but we'd had to pass up through three massive locks, waiting at least twenty minutes for them to fill. Fortunately, there was little other river traffic, and so no queue.

They moored the boat with several others by a long stretch of trees with a light gravel path running smoothly between them. The thick trunks were covered with large red blossoms, and the air was heavy with their scent.

I expected a long wait for the couple to have their dinner and settle down for the night, but having checked the mooring ropes and so on, they cheerfully went over the side and strolled arm in arm down the path toward the lights of the town.

In a very few minutes, with my litter carefully rolled up in the bag, I slipped off the craft and followed their example. Quite soon, I passed a rather rusty and smelly container, and guessing its purpose, I thrust my garbage into it and passed on.

Kessel was not like Jenna. It was just a small town with maybe twenty thousand souls. I liked the charm of the place as I strolled into a small, prettily lit park and wandered along the walkways among the small families and couples taking their leisure in the outside cafes or in the picture galleries and craft stores that flowed onto the walkways. Also filling the pavement were artists, mummers and jugglers, fruit and drink sellers, and makers of individual hot berry pies. Potters worked in their open storefronts, and a mender of household wares sat on his stool mending a platter, with his wire, tools, and a knife sharpening wheel all to hand. A few boys with small barrows sold bright favors and cunning gifts: fans and straw hats, ribbons, and glitter-trimmed mirrors, and they happily demonstrated them to anyone disposed to stop and watch. They seemed clean and content, though often their trouser leggings and tunic cuffs lagged behind their growth. There seemed no closing time, and I became aware that no air-cars swooped above us, though I could see their lights somewhere away from the park.

Gradually, the conviviality made me feel alone, and delicious food smells made me more hungry, but my craving for water was the worst. Not a token had I left, nor did I see how I could earn some.

I wandered away from the more brightly lit streets, but not before I saw a child use a water fountain. I would have mistaken the fountain for a statue, but having seen him use it, I drank my fill and realized that I had passed others on my walk.

This incident highlighted one of my problems, I reflected as I wandered down the quieter ways. I had no idea what was available. I guessed there weren't dosshouses for fertile ladies, but what was there?

At this point, I entered a silent square on the edge of town. There were trees and fields beyond, some growing unfamiliar crops and others grazed short, all thrown into silhouette by the rising of the first small pale moon.

Directly in the center stood a very solid, squat building where I made out the words "Emergency Chambers," and in smaller symbols "Farm beasts and handlers." Somehow, that amused me, and as I wandered past, I thought that I wouldn't say no to a bale of hay and a mouthful of oats!

As I rounded the corner, I saw two very heavy, metal double doors, one of which was standing open and spilling light onto the flagstones. A cart and herd beast stood by, patiently waiting. As I passed the door, I looked in and saw that the walls were very thick, enclosing a huge room, and near the entrance, typical narrow stairs descended steeply into the ground. I couldn't hear anyone, but presumably whoever was around would be back soon. Then I remembered the food handed out during the emergency, the beds, the showers …

The narrow brick stair brushed both my arms and went down further than any stairway I had come across so far. Indeed, I seriously began to fear I'd meet someone coming up. After a series of sharp turns, I emerged abruptly into a honeycomb of passages. Hollow voices and a clunking of metal came from a passage on my left. I dived down one to my right. It wasn't carpeted, and fearing they would hear the slap of my sandals, I paused, pressing myself against the uneven limestone wall, the nausea of fear welling in my throat.

As the moments passed, their voices became more distinct, and it seemed evident from the panting voices that they carried something.

"It's no good saying everything must be cleaned and restocked by the third day after an emergency, I know that! But if I'm given old equipment that breaks down every few minutes, then I can't get it cleaned and that's that. The stock men have water to carry away the mess, the supply girls have nice strong young men to carry the stuff down, but what do me and my girls have? Equipment older than most of us!"

"Rules is rules," insisted a male voice. "You could have got more girls and done it by hand."

"Done it by hand!" screeched the woman as they stopped to catch their breath at the stairs. "I'd like to see you do it by *your* hand! You don't know what you're talking about, you don't, now get this lot up them stairs before I die of old age."

"That'll be the day. Reckon as if we left you out even the Natog wouldn't take you, and I don't see you carrying the heavy end."

"And you won't, my lad, so don't hold your breath waiting!" she informed him, and with much puffing and grunting, they continued their way up. Their voices became more muffled and faint.

I moved back to the bottom of the stairs as my heart slowed and looked around. Of the six narrow passages radiating from this point, two had rough carpeting. Choosing one of these, I moved down the sloping passage, wondering how a big man could pass this way as I felt the walls close on either side. Just as I saw a large cave ahead, the lights went off, and I was left in utter darkness.

The silence was total, and so was the impenetrable blackness. I remembered caving in the Cheddar Caves, how our leader had made us sit down and turn off our lights. To me, the warmth of the caves and the darkness had the loving quality of the womb, but few in the group agreed with me. Here, it was the same feeling, better even as there were no holes or crevasses to fall down, ladders to traverse, or other dangers lurking in the blackness!

I found the wall and followed it into the cave. Obviously, there would be a light source down here. After all, who would leave their lighting in the hands of the Natog?

Sure enough, in a few minutes I found the small panel and palmed the light to dim. I gazed around a large cave with its low ceiling. Above shoulder height, the cave was natural limestone and basically round with smooth dips and bumps suggesting that an ancient whirlpool had ground away the surfaces.

Below shoulder height, man had taken over. Across the expanse of coarse brown matting, scattered about with padded benches, I could see a long counter near the far wall. To the right were the cleansing rooms. I realized I must be in a general holding room, not a priority, extra-secure one. Wandering down the room to the counter, I saw that one end was for dispensing blankets and so on, while the other seemed to be for food. I adjusted my steps accordingly.

Going behind the counter, I avidly explored the deep shelving built in to the wall. There were no facilities for preparing fresh food, but far better, there were floor-to-ceiling stacks of singpaks! Scanning the legends on the containers, I selected four and made off to a comfortable and discrete corner with some eating utensils.

Few things have tasted as good to me as that rich vegetable soup did then. The next pack surprised me. It was a cross between a cheese soufflé and a Spanish omelet, but it wasn't bad. Regretfully, I admitted to myself that I had no room for the dessert, but I quaffed half a liter of some kind of juice.

Sated for the moment, I leaned back against the wall matting that gave five feet of warmth to the limestone walls, and I pondered my position.

Undoubtedly, someone would come tomorrow, but at what time I could only guess. Of course, there must be nothing to show that anyone had been here. Or was still here. I couldn't put used food containers into a bin, they would have been emptied, and there was no sign of a niche. However, I remembered that the stacks had been deep, so I could pull some out and put the empty ones back in, and then put the full ones at the front. I didn't like to do it, but I saw no choice. Perhaps Ragul could have them replaced?

I could mostly clean up after myself, but where could I hide during the next day? Tomorrow would be my tenth day of pregnancy … perhaps I should just give myself up? Then I remembered Hagnot and shivered. He would never wait to have the fertility of the embryo tested, and besides, suppose I was not carrying a potentially fertile child? No, without Ragul's protection, I had no desire to be discovered! So what could I do tomorrow and the next day and the days after that?

Having dealt with the empty containers, I wandered off to find a hiding place. The cleansing rooms contained a few showers. I wondered if the water was cold and decided I'd find out later. Sadly, the facilities, besides being very clean, were also very spartan and open. There was no place to hide.

Then I saw a discrete door near the entrance to the cavern. I hadn't noticed it in the dark. It wasn't locked, and as I entered, I saw my first Selenese map.

The room doubled as an office and medical room. In the office area near the door, a large-scale map was attached to the wall, from floor to ceiling. It wasn't of the whole planet, just the local area I guessed, as Jenna wasn't on it. A fascinating piece of work, it was three dimensional with an incredible amount of detail. Kessel was about three feet in diameter with the walkways shown and identifiable main buildings in tiny blocks. I saw that the river I had come up by in the boat must have been the one to cut out these caves in the long ago. It now came out higher and further to the west. I could see the three big locks required for the boats to travel between the upper river and lakes and the flatlands and the shallow lake below.

Each farm was shown among the rolling foothills and undulating low lands, with their buildings and even their fields! There were several small villages scattered about, and one lay near the edge of the map, close to a sandy wasteland and near to a circle containing two tiny symbols. I'd seen something like it on the part showing Kessel. Searching the town again, I found them and two more, rather smaller. One was on the building in town where I now stood; in it were three symbols that looked rather like a pill, a syringe, and a kind of surgical knife.

After much pondering, I decided that the symbols represented a pharmacy, a first-aid center, and perhaps the last was a small hospital with the ability to perform surgeries. The bigger the symbol, the larger the facility. I also felt justified in guessing that the circles represented sealed chambers where people hid for safety during the emergencies.

Time was passing, although I had no record of it as the bar clocks had not come on with the lights, and I needed to find a place to hide. This room had the slightly disordered look of a place half tidied. The medical end almost glowed with sterile cleanliness and order, while at this end the office area had the waiting air of work left unfinished.

It would be best if I hid where they had already cleaned, so I headed down to the only cupboards I could see. They were stuffed with files, papers, or boxes of medical supplies. Just then, I spotted two large wooden crates with slatted fronts against a wall. They looked more promising!

One proved to be half-filled with more boxes of medical supplies, but the second was much better. It was full to the brim with freshly cleaned sheets of the sturdy warm kind we'd had at the institution. There was no latch on the crate to lock me in, and I figured that if I hid some sheets behind the food packs in the other room, I could cover myself with a few and stay warm and hidden, and the slats would allow air to circulate. Perfect!

Suiting the thought to the deed, I swiftly arranged the sheets as I had planned, and the results were indistinguishable from the way things had looked before.

The water in the shower was divinely hot—perhaps it had been left on to help in the clean-up process. I stayed in the shower a good while, but I decided not to wash my clothing that night. Tomorrow perhaps, but just now I was tired and didn't want to wait up till they dried.

A couple more singpaks, but nothing more to drink, and I retired to my improvised bed, having palmed out the lights. Several warm sheets lined the crate, one was rolled up for a pillow, and some more covered me. A couple of wriggles and the lid fell into place. Safe, clean, full, and warm, I drifted to sleep on a tide of well-being.

My return to consciousness was as abrupt as it was unnerving! The sharp tap and hammer blows seemed to be aimed at my head, not at the crate's lid, which was where my quickly reorienting senses now placed them. The small, instinctive jerk I'd made upon waking had passed unnoticed as the lid was nailed securely shut.

I quickly came to the sensible decision that I'd rather risk a quick death with Hagnot than die slowly in this box, my horrid remains undiscovered until the next emergency!

I wouldn't have much time to get their attention either! My first muffled call coincided with a hammer blow, but even my second was muffled. I began to scrabble inadequately at the thick sheets.

Following another blow of the hammer, a man said, "This one's ready, so get it along to the air-car, there's a good lad, the other will be done by the time you get back."

"You haven't stenciled it," said a younger male voice.

"Don't need to," the older stated. "Any medical supplies with a limited shelf life, or things that are worn out a bit, go to the medical center in Vida. The hospital resupplies us at general alert. Vida can always use it, air-cars don't get out there much."

I had ceased struggling and lay curled in my darkness listening.

"Well," said a third voice, "we'd better get a move on. Vida's first on his list, and he said he had a sight more other places to get to today."

Vida was a long way from Hagnot … and I could tell whoever released me that I was running away from someone, which was true!

My crate was jerked from the wall and upended and heaved onto some kind of barrow, I was guessing. Soon we were bumping up the narrow stairs, and I was very glad my head was upward!

The air-shuttle must have been in the square, for after only a short trundle in the cool, damp morning air the crate was roughly hoisted into a confined space, judging by the hollow sounds. It was laid flat and pushed across a metal floor. It took a while for smells of the hold to penetrate the sheet crate: earthy tubers, faint traces of antiseptic, and tantalizing ones of fruit. I was left alone, and before ten minutes could have passed, the other crate joined me and the side hatch slammed shut. The air-car rose gently from the ground and curved up into a morning sky, I could only imagine.

During the hour or so that followed, all I heard was the steady hum of the craft. There was no cackle or hiss of air communication, no discernible movement, no whistling or eating. I never heard the pilot—perhaps he was partitioned off? If I hadn't been so apprehensive and thirsty, the flight would have been incredibly boring. I rather think it was anyway!

After the inevitable landing and unloading, I heard the air-car depart. I lay tensely waiting. Nothing. Sweat trickled down my body as the sun rose to its zenith and the crate became a padded oven. I scrambled again at the warm sheets and at last pulled away a small section by the slats near my face. There was no relieving breeze, and my thirst was becoming intolerable. The silence was unbroken, and tears of torment mixed with the sweat.

The silence was broken at last by a tantalizingly familiar, scolding female voice. "*You* thought! That'll be the day. We were sent these supplies because they are perishable. Leaving the medicines out like this! They will perish before we even get them to the center!" Her voice ended in a grunt as she tried to shift my crate.

"I reckoned it would be heavy," said an aging and satisfied voice. "That's why I wanted to wait till some of the field workers came by on their way home. These be too heavy for me."

She seemed irritated by his attitude. "Just get the dolly, Farley, we can do it easily between us."

He shuffled off muttering. I had been paralyzed with recognition of the voice, but with the memory came my certainty that she had cared deeply about me.

Through a gap between the sheets, I called softly to her.

"Mogan, for God's sake help me!" I heard a gasp of breath and hurried on. "It's me, Rowhan, but you didn't know my name. You looked after me at the institution, remember? The colored beads, the clay pictures, how you were so pleased the first time I took the lid off my own food? Mogan! Do you remember me? They are trying to kill me, *please help me*!" I began to babble desperately.

"Oh, by the Eggs of Nerta!" I heard her gasp softly.

"Please help me!" I writhed for breath in the tormenting heat.

"Hush," she hissed urgently. "He's coming back. Just hold on a little longer."

And I found I could. Her caution was my hope.

Chapter Nineteen

The dolly swayed and bumped somewhat wildly over the rough dirt surface. I was boiling to death in my own sweat, imprisoned in the sheet-filled crate. I clamped my teeth against the scream of anguish that was growing in my chest.

There was a larger bump, and the wheels ran smoothly across a floor.

"Into the storeroom, Farley," Mogan instructed.

"Why not the dispensary?" argued the ancient.

"Because after that heat I don't know if they are fit to be dispensed, so I don't want them getting muddled up with the good stuff." I felt the craft tipped and lowered to the floor. "Now go back and get the other one please."

His grumbles departed with him, and I couldn't prevent a whimper of agony. A cupboard banged, and Mogan spoke again. "I'll start undoing the lid, but I dare not open it until Farley's out of sight and sound. Please, for both our sakes, not a sound," she entreated.

I could hear the occasional screech of nails being withdrawn and Mogan's grunts of exertion. Every moment seemed the last I could endure; even madness would be a release.

The ancient returned with the other crate, and from a seemingly great distance, I heard his assertions that he shouldn't be doing this kind of work at his age, there was a pain in his chest and a buzzing in his ears and ... but Mogan silenced him firmly. There was no vestige of the timorous woman she had been with Snard, and she told him that if he was feeling so awful he was to go home for the rest of the day.

"But what about these crates? I always gets to help open them!" He sounded alarmed, as if he was missing an agreeable task, or possibly a profitable one, as there was no contents list that I could remember seeing. He sounded inclined to argue.

"With your chest and the buzzing in your ears? I wouldn't dream of it," stated Mogan with finality. I don't know what he may have said, for there was a buzzing in *my* head, and the darkness dissolved into a red mist.

I next realized that I lay face down on wet white tiles, in the recovery position. Although fully clothed, warm water was being sprayed over me. My head was pounding and my body throbbed and ached. I shuddered and tried to swallow a rising sob.

The water ceased, and I was gently turned over. Mogan's swarthy countenance hovered over me, her pale yellow eyes searching my face, her dark bobbed hair pushed hastily back behind her ears.

"How are you feeling?"

"Better." I tried to grin.

"Any headache?" I tried to nod, but thought better of it. She grunted. I shivered. "Are you cold?"

"Not really. I'm more hot and aching. My eyes are dry and gritty too," I said between clenched teeth. I shuddered again as if to disprove my words.

"Humph. As I feared." She looked concerned. She left the room and returned quickly with a syringe and a bottle. Inserting the needle through the stopper, she began to fill the syringe.

"Mogan, I'm pregnant, is that stuff safe?" I said through chattering teeth.

She looked at me for a long moment and then continued filling it. "Yes. It's not what I would normally recommend, but it's better than Sandhead."

"Sandhead?"

"A condition caused from drinking unprocessed river water. In this area anyway." I gloomily remembered refilling my bottle in the river at night, but then I hadn't much choice.

The prick was deftly done, and soon the contents of the syringe were in my arm. Mogan continued, "Most people quickly become immune, but the first bout or so can be nasty if you don't rest up and eat properly."

"Will I be able to rest up and eat properly?" Our eyes held for a long moment, until a smile stretched her thin lips.

"It won't be the first time I've taken care of you."

I smiled back as the shivers subsided. "But this is the first time I will be able to say thank you. For this time and for last time."

"I don't recollect that I was much help," she said sadly.

"Not much help!" I exclaimed weakly and tried to sit up. She pushed me gently back.

"Just lie there another minute or so." She turned on the warm water again and began to run the spray over my body. "This isn't as mad as it seems, it has three advantages. It's helping to lower your body temperature, it helps to rehydrate your body—I can't give you a drink just yet—and it washes off the sweat."

"I feel much better," I agreed. The pounding in my head was less, and although I still ached, the tormenting heat and throbbing of my body was growing less each moment.

"That's the effects of the injection." She turned off the spray. "By the time I have you in bed I'll be able to give you a drink without you vomiting." Gently, she removed my wet clothes as I began to shake with the effort of helping. Soon I was wrapped in a large towel, and I attempted to get up unaided, but I was glad when she shook her head and firmly pushed me back.

In moments, she brought from one side of the room a molded stretcher on an hydraulic base. It was the work of moments for Mogan and the machine to roll me onto the stretcher and wheel me into a room that was obviously her private quarters, where I was deposited onto the bed. All very efficient!

When Mogan returned from taking the stretcher back, she was carrying a shift over her arm and a beaker of pink liquid. When I was thoroughly dry, she helped me put on the shift, and when I was lying down, she pulled the inevitable warm sheet over me. It had always puzzled me that the Selenese had no blankets, but their sheets were actually warm!

"This may taste a little funny, but it's got lots of good things in it, so drink it all up." Mogan was returning to her motherly ways. I smiled at her weakly between sips. It was soon gone, and I felt so sleepy that all the questions I'd been aching to ask seemed to slip away. I didn't mind that she'd put something in the drink … it was probably compulsive after you have nursed for a long time.

A delicious smell woke me late the next day. My mouth watered appreciatively, and I struggled to sit up. The diffused light was dim. Glancing around, I saw heavy drapes across the window, and at my movement, Mogan rose from a stuffed, though slightly shabby, armchair and palmed the lights up a little.

"I rather hoped you would wake soon," she confessed. Helping me to sit upright, she inserted a couple more pillows behind me and placed a small, short-legged table across my lap. On it, she put a tray with several covered dishes.

"I expect you can manage these on your own," she said. "I expect you always could. I don't blame you," she added quickly, "how would you know who to trust? I trusted my superiors, and look where that got me!" She seemed more tired than bitter.

I caught her hand as she turned away. "It wasn't like that at all, Mogan. I don't know about the others, but I had only just returned to full awareness the day Snard ordered our termination." I saw her disbelief. "I'd been sort of half-aware for some time, like in a dream I couldn't make sense of. That nasty man in the morning, remember him? I didn't like him. I pretended I didn't understand anything he wanted me to do. But I liked you. I tried, I really tried, but everything was so strange! The language, the food, but especially me. That was the most confusing part."

I paused, looking back to my time in the institution. She nodded slowly. I said, "When everything did come into focus, it was abruptly, without any warning. I was lying in bed, you were just leaving, and someone in the hall spoke to you. I forget the exact words, but you said there were only three of us left, and you seemed to be pleading for us. He said you would never have to look after us any more." I fell silent. Mogan squeezed my hand quite hard. I glanced up at her—her eyes were tight shut and her lips compressed into a thin line.

"I remember." She spoke grimly. Releasing my hand, she turned and drew her chair near to the bed and sat down with her own tray.

I removed the lid from one of the dishes and picked up the smooth wooden spoon. The food tasted as delicious as it smelled, and the rich gravy was full of tender chunks of unknown plants and a kind of noodle. "I was terrified, Mogan, and I didn't think you had the power to help me … or us," I added.

"I didn't, events proved that. It's almost funny. In trying to help you, I must have nearly killed you."

I laughed. Looking back, it was rather ironic. "Yes, I just thanked God it wasn't an injection!"

"I thought someone had stolen you. Up until your arrival here, I thought just that, but they hadn't, had they?" Her eyes watched me quietly.

"No. We escaped. But the other three, from two quarters before, didn't. They were stolen, experimented upon, and died. Except one, perhaps, who may have gotten away."

"Ah, yes. They weren't my girls, but I remember them well. Even here, I've heard they found two of them." She looked older than I remembered, and sadder.

"What happened? I heard a rumor that it was you who raised the alarm." I asked more to take her mind off the others than anything else.

She sighed and settled back further in her chair. "I couldn't get you all out of my mind. Sleep was impossible. I began to worry that you would wake up and be frightened … The guard was a very lazy fellow. I had little fear of meeting him, so I went to check on you all." She gave a short laugh. "They could have heard my shriek in Dinni!"

"And you thought we had been stolen like the other three? But why did you raise the alarm? We were due to be terminated, wasn't it better to be stolen than dead?" I asked.

"Of course!" she replied bitterly. "If I'd stopped to think, I would have slipped back to my bed and let someone else find you missing in the morning. But old habits die hard. Someone had stolen my babies, and the instinct to find and protect you swamped everything else in my mind."

I nodded. "Yes, I can see how that would happen, but as it turned out, you did us a favor. Someone who helped us greatly would never have been where he was if it hadn't been for your alarm." I had finished every morsel of the first dish and now opened the second. It tasted rather like fruit in meringue with a sort of chocolate sauce, but not at all like real chocolate. Perhaps one day …

Mogan looked up in surprise. "You found someone to help you? Did they know who you were? I thought you must have stolen your clothes … how did you manage to avoid the search? Who helped you?" The questions tumbled from her lips like beads from a broken necklace. They scattered around me in hopeless disorder.

Laughing, I held up my hands in mock surrender. "Stop, stop! I can't answer them all. But I have to answer some because I need your help." I stopped and softly bit my lower lip as I thought. I didn't see how I could keep Ragul out of it. If I was going to get Mogan to contact him, or get a message to him, she would have to know who he was.

"Mogan, several people seem to want me dead, but top of the list is a man called Hagnot," I said.

She nodded. Of course, she would know the First Councilor's opinions about the experiment. "The danger has been all the greater because we met socially and he wants to hold me," I said.

She gasped. "By the city of the ancestors and all the Eggs of Nerta, what were you doing in society? I was amazed by the quality of your speech, but you would never, never get away with such a trick, you must be mad … or whoever helped you!" Then the last part of my speech seemed to hit her. "*He wants to hold you!*"

"Er, yes." I shifted with embarrassment at her open-mouthed stare.

"You are pregnant by *him*?" she whispered incredulously.

"Well, no. Actually, I'm held by Ragul. He's the father of my child." I felt myself blushing. It was made worse by the fact her astonishment had given away to disbelief.

"Ragul? Our Warlord?" she asked carefully.

"Yes, Ragul, *my* lord," I said stiffly, then I suddenly sat up with a jerk. "My letter! Oh no! My letter is in all those sopping wet clothes!" Thinking of my ruined letter from Ragul, that I'd cherished and kissed through these last fearful days, I burst into tears, covering my face with my hands.

I didn't hear her leave the room, but a few moments later, her hand touched my arm, and as I lowered my hands to speak, a dry, slightly grubby, and folded square of paper was pushed into my hands.

"There was nothing among your clothes so I looked in the crate. Is this the letter you wanted?" she asked quietly.

"Oh yes!" I said, clutching it with both hands and sniffing. I rubbed away my tears and gave her a watery smile. "Oh yes indeed."

She sat down. "Who's it from?"

"Ragul," I said firmly.

She nodded. "I rather thought it was. Association of thought, I suppose."

I hesitated. I didn't want to show her my letter, but I needed her belief. "Do you need to see it?" I asked.

She shook her head. "There's no need. It was just too incredible to believe at first, but somehow I do now. Though how you ever came to meet them I don't know! Do either of them know who you are?"

"Hagnot doesn't, but Ragul is the one who helped us. Mogan, I'm twelve days pregnant now. I don't know what Ragul wants me to do! Could you get a message to him. Please?" I watched her anxiously as she turned her cup in her hands.

"When he nailed you up in that crate, he must have had some plan, though personally I think it was an insane thing to do," she added.

"He didn't nail me in to it. That was an accident. He has no idea of where I am. I was running away from Hagnot. He had forced me to go to his aunt's apartments, and someone there accused me of not being who I was pretending to be. He doesn't know who I really am, of course." I felt confused by my own explanations! So I relented, and I gave a brief account of the events leading up to meeting Ragul and what had happened after leaving Jenna.

Mogan made no attempt to unravel it, she just seemed relieved it wasn't Ragul who had nailed me up in the crate, and having said so she continued, "Ten days is the very earliest it can be tested. It's not very wise to do so, but that you must decide between you. Now, where can he be reached, and what do we say?"

It didn't take many minutes to realize it wouldn't be that easy. I could leave a message with Benot or Foust, for example, but they might not be the only ones to read it if Hagnot was really determined to find me.

"What about contacting his mother and asking where he is so I could talk to him directly? Then I wouldn't have to leave a message or anything," I suggested after a few minutes.

"Hmm. That might be an idea. Especially if I use a visi-link and say I have information against Snard, that way her people would put me through to her, and if someone else is listening in … it would seem reasonable and unconnected with you," Mogan added.

"Well, let's get on with it!" I was eager to hear his voice, and I made a move to get out of bed.

"Not so fast!" Mogan stopped me. "Next you have to decide what to say to him when we do get hold of him, especially since we have no idea who else may be listening."

I sank back against the pillows. She was right. If anyone else was listening, it would be a race to see who would get here first.

"I sent him a message in code just before I hid on a boat and came up river," I said after a few moments. "He may not have got it, of course, but I could do the same code again."

Mogan looked surprised. "What kind of code?"

"Random numbers added to the numeric value of the symbols of the alphabet," I explained.

"What numbers?" she asked in bewilderment. Since Selene had been fighting for its life against a common enemy, it had little need for codes.

"My fake identification number, he made it up."

"But will he remember it? Was there anything special about it?" Mogan seemed anxious about this point, and I didn't blame her.

"I don't know, but what else do you suggest?" I argued, my own anxiety making me blunt.

I broke the thoughtful silence. "All right, what about this? First I will work on the code for this village and the medical center. Then when I speak to him, I'll ask him if he remembers the number, if he doesn't I'll say … the fourth sound of the packet he gave me at

RADA, that was the PreVal, the second letter of Lady Rilla's real name, the first sound of Lady Rilla's real home, and the last letter of the friend we came with. And when he gets here, he will be contacted." I felt a little relieved—he would at least have a head start over whoever was listening.

After I explained that these clues spelled out the name of this village, Vida, Mogan seemed quite content and went to get me writing materials to work out the more complicated code if we had to leave a message, but then I stopped her. "If I can't talk to him, I won't know if he remembers or not, so I guess we'll have to stick to the second one."

Such was my faith in the random code that it hadn't occurred to me that my first message might have been intercepted and decoded, and that even now Hagnot's men were reporting that, having searched the boat for traces of me, they were now centering their inquiries at the last up-river stop: Kessel.

I had forgotten that which Hagnot had not: on entry to RADA, everyone had to fill in a form …

Chapter Twenty

The medical center had a visi-console, and Mogan had no trouble finding the number of Ragul's mother, Lady Sinta, there being no ex-directory on Selene. Important people just had calls screened. When Mogan explained to the young woman who answered that she was trying to contact Ragul, she was put on hold. As the moments passed we became increasingly nervous. Presently, a rather thin and sad-looking woman appeared on the screen.

"I am Lady Sinta. You are asking after my son, I believe?" I stood at an angle to the screen so Lady Sinta would only see Mogan.

"Yes, Lady Sinta. I am sorry to disturb you, but I have information about a man called Snard that might be of interest to him. Could you tell me where he may be contacted?"

The pause lengthened. "You seem to be somewhat out of contact with developments in the city, Miss …?" Her face was still, but her eyes were alert.

"He wouldn't know me. I was an attendant at the research institute. My name is Mogan."

Lady Sinta nodded slowly. "Well, Mogan, my son has been detained in the city by the orders of the First Councilor. It is being said that, despite evidence to the contrary, Lord Ragul is the man behind the disappearance of the experiments from the institute."

She must have heard my gasp of horror, for her eyes left Mogan's frozen expression and flicked around the room, then returned to Mogan. She paused carefully and then said, "The First

Councilor discovered that the identities of the two young ladies held by my son were not only false, but they were actually two of the experiments. Some holos were made from the security guard's monitor records. One of these came into the hands of the man Snard you mentioned. The institute files had holos to support his accusations."

I leant back against the wall, my hands still pressed against my mouth, despair momentarily robbing me of the ability to think.

"Can I contact him?" Mogan asked quietly.

"It's most unlikely." Lady Sinta watched her intently.

Then Mogan did a very brave thing. Lifting her regard back to the face on the screen, she said, "Suppose it could be proved that he had nothing to do with it. That he met them accidentally after their escape and that they proved that some highly placed people were trying to kill them."

"It seems that would be impossible. They were vegetables, according to Snard and the reports. Though some people are asking how they could be in society if that were so." The words were spoken carefully.

"The reports were false. I was their attendant, and I know." She looked steadily into the eyes of the woman on the screen. "I could testify to this, if you can get me to the council alive. There may be others who met them after their escape who could also testify."

The woman's look showed her gratitude. "Where are you?"

"If I tell you, I could be telling anyone illegally listening to this call. Please give Lord Ragul this message ..." She proceeded to give the message we had decided upon. She continued, "Please tell him to give you the lady's real name as proof of who the contact is."

"The presence of even one of the ladies would be overwhelming evidence of what you say," Lady Sinta suggested hopefully.

Mogan was very firm. "There I can't help, I'm afraid. I know where one was, but not where she is. I thought it best not to know." She sounded utterly convincing.

"Ah well. I didn't think it would happen. Perhaps it's best. Hagnot seems almost insane in this matter. He would never let any of them reach the council alive ... though if they were sane enough to fool him they can't be vegetables I'd have thought!" She gave a wry smile. "The council gathers to hear this tomorrow. I'll contact Ragul at once. Some of the Councilors are still our friends, I think. Others are becoming increasingly disturbed by Hagnot's attitude too." On this oblique remark, she nodded to Mogan and the screen went blank.

For a long moment, we just stared at each other, then I came forward and took her hands. "I've got to get out, Mogan. Alive, I'm his vindication; dead, I'm more evidence to be used against him."

"I know, my dear." She gave my hands a quick squeeze. "And we must be very quick. It won't take them long to look up where I was sent in disgrace. At least I was sent so far away that Hagnot doesn't have any men on the spot!" she added with a smile at the irony.

We were quick. My clothes were creased but dry, and as I dressed, Mogan flew around gathering sundry things and stuffing them into a canvas hold-all. The monitor flashed busily, but she ignored it. She tossed a pair of boots over to me as she continued to stuff things into the bag. Maps, medicines, a torch, and other things went into the bag, along with water and food packs.

As I stomped my feet down into the boots, she swung a long cloak about my shoulders and hustled me out into a back hall. Pausing by the door, she thrust something into my hand. "There are only two vials in this. They kill instantly. Hold one end against your attacker's skin and push the button in the other. I pray you will not need to use it."

She turned off the light and opened the door. We stepped out into the night. Neither moon was up yet, and I followed her blindly, stumbling on the uneven ground. Out of the darkness loomed even darker bushes; we turned left and continued for some way and then stopped.

Mogan turned and whispered in my direction. "Walk in this shallow stream as long as you can, then go off to the right, into the scrub land. Hide in the bushes among the dunes. Don't move around in the daylight; it's very easy to spot things from the air."

"What about you? What if Hagnot gets here before Ragul's man?"

"I think I can hide well enough till morning, that should be long enough if he's coming. Besides, he wants you dead more. I just wish by all the Eggs that you could have had the rest you need. Take the pills I've put in the bag. Go along now." After a quick hug, she pushed me off in the direction of the stream and made her way back along the bushes.

I sat by the stream and pulled off the boots and stuffed them into the already crammed bag. Pulling my skirts up between my legs and tucking the ends into my belt, I pushed my arms through the bag's large handles, like a backpack, and hoisted it into a reasonably comfortable position. Then, twisting the cloak over one arm, I stepped down into the stream.

The water barely reached above my ankles and wasn't as cold as I feared. My feet encountered mostly sand, but my progress seemed very slow. I couldn't see the submerged rocks or the occasional root that tripped me nor the few branches that thrust out over the water. Falling and blundering along the twisting bed of the stream, I knew I could not do this till morning.

As time limped past, a small moon moved low into the sky, skimming along the horizon and sinking again after about an hour. However, during that time its pale light speeded my progress somewhat, and I could tell that I was entering an area of high dunes with spider-bushes and tussocks of inky spears etched against the sky.

The healing effects of the care lavished upon me by Mogan were beginning to unravel. Barely another hour of stumbling and splashing through this darkness and already there was a fine tremble in my body and a betraying weakness in my knees. Every step was torture for my feet. The coarse sand cut away at the tender flesh, the cold water was unable to numb the pain of stubbed toes and sharp pebbles.

Struggling through the darkness, I knew that with the rising of the next moon, I would have to look for a hiding place. I tripped over something and staggered forward awkwardly, trying to regain my balance. A branch whacked me across the face, and I clutched at it to steady myself. I stood there trembling in the darkness and panting with exertion. The branch felt smooth and hard to my hand, and it wouldn't push aside. I leaned on it, grateful for its support.

The light increased as the larger moon rose into the night sky, and I was able to see that I was among the few remaining branches of an ancient bole that had fallen next to the creek about two man lengths from the bank. Time had deposited an accumulation of sand and rubbish along one side, and from out of this grew knotted ropes of saget-berry vines and tall clumps of venta.

The branch I leaned on gleamed like bone in the pale light. I needed to get out of the water and lie down, if only for a while, and I realized that crawling along the branch would leave no tracks on the soft soil of the bank.

As the moon rose higher, casting sharp shadows, I reached the huge trunk. Suddenly, I caught the first distant hum. It didn't take many moments to realize it was the sound of an air-car. I listened intently, turning my head this way and that to catch the sound better. It was flying low. I couldn't see it, but it seemed to be zigzagging and moving in my general direction.

Frantically, I slithered down the trunk and wormed my way into some clumps of venta. Looking up through their thin branches and skimpy leaves, I realized their inadequacy as cover and scrambled back further, hoping they would be denser. The folds of my cloak hampered me. I tried to escape the cloak, but the bag secured it. I struggled harder as the hum grew louder. A final jerk and I overbalanced, falling backward. Flinging my arms across my face, I bounced off the tough stems and slid, coming to an abrupt halt half inside the bole.

The hollow inside of the ruined trunk almost covered me. I lay panting in the inky shadow. The hum was loud in the still air. Wriggling violently, I pulled my feet in. I curled, listening, the noise vibrating overhead.

I waited breathlessly as the sound decreased as it moved off to the left. Then it increased again as it swung overhead and searched off to the right. It grew softer as it progressed into the scrubland until its faint hum disappeared altogether into the distance.

At last I drew a normal breath and relaxed a bit. I was overwhelmed with weariness, and the shakiness returned in full force. Too tired to worry about what dangers might lurk in the black recess, I released the bag from my back and pushed it beneath my head. I pulled the long cloak around me and curled up in the darkness. Its folds were warm and comforting. I pushed my hand into the end of the bag and fumbled around until I felt the shape of a drink carton. In the dark, I pulled the tab on the bottom and felt it heating up. At last I peeled back the top and the appetizing smell of a rich, chunky soup filled the small space. Not a hot drink then, but it tasted as good as it smelled. The warmth eased my trembling limbs, and a feeling of well-being allowed the tiredness to consume me. My last thought was vague surprise that Hagnot's men had got here so soon.

I awoke to a gentle throbbing in my head. The gloom around me was only partially relieved by the mottled sunlight coming through the opening. Deciding this might be a good time to investigate, I hunted in the bag for the torch.

By its light I could see the trunk was hollow for quite a ways as it tapered to a narrow point. I had slid in nearest the wide end. When the plant had fallen, it had torn up roots and soil with it. The shifting sands of time had merely deposited more debris against this barrier. During the seasons, leaves, twigs, and hay like strands of vegetation had drifted in through the opening. The result was extremely dry and comfortable.

Indeed, as I looked around by the flitting beam of the light, I was astonished at the amount of dry debris. Had I felt better, I would have made a more extensive examination, but my head throbbed more vindictively by the moment, so instead I searched the contents of the bag for the pills Mogan said I was to keep taking. Only after upending the bag and searching among its scattered contents did I find them. The instructions on the small pot of pills advised taking them one every five segments, which I guessed meant three times a day in Selenese, but by this time I wasn't very fussy. Opening a carton of juice, I gulped one down and lay back waiting for relief.

I emerged from a light doze feeling rather better. While my first desire was for a wash, I decided it would be much wiser to find out what my resources were. There might even be soap among my scattered possessions! Due to the desperate haste of our departure, the contents were very haphazardly organized. I was delighted to discover that more than half of it was food packs. There was also a jumble of other things that included a knife, a serrated wire, a map, a bowl and spoon, and a box of medicated bandages. There was also soap! I grinned in the gloom.

The things had been scattered when I emptied the bag searching for the pills, and as I collected them up I discovered a further length of neatly coiled fine wire and a plastic flask half full of something that looked like water. In fact, I was almost sure it was water. But why only half full? I could understand grabbing an empty flask or completely filling one, but why half full? It was a silly point, but for some reason it troubled me.

Making a neat pile of my treasures, I restored them to the bag and busied myself with selecting a meal and waiting for it to warm. Until this moment, I had been able to push Mogan's possible whereabouts resolutely from mind. But now, with the pack warming in my hand, my fears suddenly overwhelmed me. Had she managed to elude Hagnot's men? Had she been able to make contact with Ragul's people when they arrived? *Had* they arrived? Was she at this moment convincing the Council of our sanity and Ragul's innocence … or was she being "persuaded" to help Hagnot with his search?

I opened the container and ate the three hot pastry rolls stuffed with vegetables and ammoch, their version of cheese, while barely tasting them. My thoughts were abruptly brought back to my own situation by the soft hum of an air-car to the north. Thank heavens I had heeded Mogan's advice and decided to wash at twilight! I became still, my head turned toward the sound, listening.

I heard the slight rustle of the venta bushes almost overhead and an imperceptible slither among the soil and leaves by the entrance. A figure erupted into the confined space. I flinched back, too surprised to snatch up my lethal vials.

It curled into a ball, soundless and tense for long moments before releasing its breath in a long, shuddering gasp of agony.

She had almost slumped into an attitude of exhaustion when gradually she seemed to tense again, and the head swiveled around. She looked straight at me, her irises large with pain but the eyes fearless, even calculating. I guessed I didn't look particularly dangerous, even to a badly injured Dejan, and I felt sure she was both.

The sound of the air-car was much louder, almost overhead. My eyes jerked involuntarily up as I listened. We both listened. It passed over and headed on south.

As the sound grew fainter, I lowered my regard to the young woman again. She was less tense, having come to the conclusion that I was hiding too. But she was still shrewdly surveying me from her crumpled position.

Uneasily, I remembered Rill. Even injured, this woman could be extremely dangerous, so I decided it would be wise to clarify my position before this Dejan chose to decide my future for me. Carefully, I chose my words.

"I have a friend, Rill. She comes from a planet called Dejan," I said. I saw her slowly tensing and hurried on. "She and I and another girl escaped from the institute." I felt her disbelief, but not from her expression, which was now completely blank. "Do you remember those colored beads and the plastic strings and bags we were made to use? She made a really good weapon with those. Two bags of beads at each end of a long thong. I saw her use them twice, very effective!"

She seemed to be listening, and I had no intention of telling her that on one occasion I was the intended victim! "She was the head of her family on Dejan. It doesn't sound the sort of place I would like to visit." I felt I was starting to babble. "Her opinions about men are not like here! She says that when this is all over and we are proved capable of producing fertile children, she will not be held. She will have children but won't be attached to any one man." There was no doubt now—despite her evident pain, she was listening intently. I waited. I had no idea how much she could understand.

"Who are you?" she asked at last.

"Rowhan. I come from the planet Earth, like one of the two found dead in Gossot's buildings. The rumor was that there were three women smuggled out, and that one escaped. You are very like Rill, you know. Not so much in looks you understand, more in feel."

"How did you escape?" Then she hissed through her teeth, and after a moment said, "Don't bother, it doesn't matter at present."

She looked to be in bad shape. I ached to help her, but I knew instinctively she wouldn't let me yet. She closed her eyes a moment and opened them again quickly, still uncertain of me.

"Show me your neck," she said around clenched teeth. I took the torch and shone it on my neck, both sides.

"You are quite right," I said, "they'd never let a fertile lady come out here looking for you. And if I were just an ordinary woman running away from an irate husband or father, I wouldn't know about you or Rill or anything. So if we are finished with the preliminaries, shall we get on with dealing with your injuries? I don't promise to be much good, but I'm all you've got."

"True," she whispered, and she rested for a moment before slowly uncurling. For a long moment, I rather wished she hadn't. The front of her dark shift was stiff with dried blood and filth. A pad was bound clumsily to the lower left side of her neck and shoulder. Then I saw that her right hand held her left arm tightly against her swelling belly. A bone gleamed whitely through the tattered remnants of her sleeve. There was comparatively little blood.

Slowly, I emptied the bag again and offered her some food. She devoured the warm vegetable stew straight from the container and then eased back against the trunk. I showed her the bandages and she nodded permission. To keep her mind off what I had to do I asked her how it had happened. Silly really, but that's what they do in the movies.

It seemed that the same air-car I had hidden from had sent her racing down the slope of a dune to lie in its inky shadow. The sand had hidden an abandoned dwelling, and she had come down through the weakened skylight. She had lain unconscious among the broken fragments and a slow cascade of sand. Getting out had taken hours. Exhausted from my ministrations, she became silent and seemed to doze off.

The wound in her neck was reasonably clean and not as deep as I'd feared, but as far as I could tell, at least one of the bones in her forearm had been broken, and the jagged edge of one end protruded through her flesh. This wound was the one I feared. I cleaned it as best as I could and bound it across her front, above the gentle swelling of her stomach. I checked it every quarter hour or so to make sure the bandages didn't become too tight as the arm continued to swell. It was badly bruised of course, but at least it didn't smell bad—that sweet, rotting smell that bodes no good.

I leaned my head wearily on my knees and wished I could just topple over and sleep like the Dejan. There wasn't time, I knew that.

It was already mid-day, and I would need some light to see my way. I was beyond tired.

My supplies wouldn't last long. I had used nearly all the bandages, and she would need fresh dressings. There were only seven food packs left, and one drink, though I now guessed the other half container of water was hers.

She had probably survived by hunting, but she was in no condition to hunt now, and I didn't know the way of it. It was also obvious she was pregnant, though neither of us had mentioned it, and I was worried about the effects of a bad fall. Pregnancy was probably our only chance of staying alive.

I just couldn't see a way out of this mess. I checked the map. Not only was Mogan's medical unit the only one around, it seemed to be the only *anything* around! The farms were all beyond the unit, and they were widely spaced. Why the unit was where it was I couldn't guess, but one thing I was reasonably certain of was that unless Mogan had managed to get to the Council and persuaded them of our sanity, or to at least allow us the chance to prove it, then the unit was about the most dangerous place I could go. But what choice had I? Even by myself, how long could I hold out? With Sandhead, not for long. Two days at the most, I guessed. That reminded me to take my pill, with as little water as I could manage.

I was not really aware of the approach of the air-car until it was almost overhead. The sound increased, and it was passing northward when the hum changed. It seemed to stutter and then caught again … and then dead silence. I raised my head and listened intently. The hum of an air-car changes as it lands—this had just cut off. I didn't think they'd glide very far. Would they explode on crashing? I hadn't heard anything!

Damn. I passed a hand wearily across my aching head. How would this effect my plans? I tried to think. If the pilot was healthy, I didn't want to meet him. Injured, there was nothing I could do to help him—and even less if he were dead. Besides, his pals would soon be by. Then I raised my head slightly. Supposing I got there first … surely a search craft would have medical supplies and emergency rations? How soon would they get here? It had happened so suddenly. Would he have had time to get a message off? I thought not, but I decided not to waste any more time.

Careful not to wake the sleeping woman, I eased my way out of the narrow opening and wiggled through the tough clumps of the venta and climbed out on to the huge bole. On one side was the stream and wasteland beyond that, but on this side scrub-covered dunes of varying sizes lay in the baking sun. Careful to leave no foot marks to betray our hideout, I eased my way down.

Walking between the dunes, I made my way north for several minutes before crawling to the top of a dune to peer over the crest. There was nothing. I started to slither back down when I saw two crushed bushes on the brow of a dune some ways ahead. One had been recently upended, its pale purple roots pointing to the sun. Squinting hard, I was able to make out score marks on the ridge too. There was nothing else to see.

I slid down the hot sand. Resting at the bottom, I longed equally for a head covering and a refreshing drink. I had neither. After a moment. I got to my feet and moved off in the direction of the damaged dune … the only sound was silence.

Chapter Twenty-One

The silence was broken by muffled cursing. I halted my advance around the dune and crouched listening. A groan, then silence again. I wanted to turn back, but perhaps not all was lost. Creeping on, I rounded the end of the dune and edged forward using the bushes for cover.

A thin, sagging man in uniform had his head leaned against the side of the craft while his arm was inside a hole made by the removal of a panel. Unfortunately, although battered, he was too unharmed for me to risk anything.

I was about to begin my reverse journey when he turned and I saw his profile. His eyes were shut, and he struggled to reach something within the craft's side. I saw the blood across his forehead and the whiteness of his face.

I gasped in shock. I recognized the face, the tall, thin form … My God, it was Matul! But he was Hagnot's cousin, I reasoned, I couldn't help him!

As I was about to move backward, Matul's form slowly buckled, and he slithered to the ground. Without thinking, I rushed over to the craft and the youth on the ground.

"Matul, Matul! Can you hear me?" I gently shook his shoulder.

He raised his head slightly toward me. "Lady Rowhan?" he whispered. "Is that you? I've been looking for you."

"I'll bet you have, Matul, but don't expect me to come quietly to be murdered by your grand-uncle. I'll just help you, and then I'm leaving. How long before your call is answered?"

His eyes opened for a moment and squeezed shut again. "No call. Daren't. Not supposed to be here." The young face was pinched with pain. "Help me fix the air-car."

"I don't know anything about air-cars, Matul, hadn't they told you that?" But I was beginning to wonder what was going on.

"Ragul thinks you can do anything." He gave a weak grin. "But all you have to do is reattach the cable to the voltrolizer. I can't do it by touch and only one arm."

Looking down at him, I realized that one arm was at a funny angle ... or was it the shoulder? Rolling him over a bit to see better, he gave a yelp and fainted. Well, I thought, it wasn't a move they had taught in first-aid, but since he was unconscious it seemed a good time to put his shoulder back.

Grabbing his outstretched arm with both hands and wedging my feet just under his arm, I gave an almighty heave and the errant shoulder popped back into place. He groaned, but I brought his arm down and stuffed the hand into the front of his tunic.

Clambering into the craft, I rummaged for a medical kit and, finding one, brought it out to my patient. I bound the arm in place so the shoulder wouldn't move. Covering his face from the sun, I went back into the air-car and found the emergency supplies in the back nets. I glugged down fortified water and gobbled a dehydrated food bar.

The heat shimmered off the sand as I checked Matul's head wound. I was bandaging it when his eyes fluttered for a moment, and he gradually focused on me. "I guess he was right," he whispered, but I didn't understand what he meant.

"Matul, I need an honest answer. Are you here to take me to Hagnot or someone in his hire?"

"No!" He looked shocked and struggled to sit up. "I've met you, I know you are not mad! Ragul said no one would suspect me of trying to save you, but all his people would be watched, really Lady Rowhan!"

"All right, all right, just rest." I thought for a moment. "Where were you going to take me?"

"Straight to the Supreme Council session. Ragul's hearing started this morning, and it isn't thought to last long." He lay back, but he turned his head restlessly. "We have to repair this and get going!"

"Very well. What do I do?" I wasn't going to tell him about the other woman yet. I'd wait and see if anyone turned up while I was helping him fix the air-car, just to be sure.

"Look in that hole."

I got up and did so, it looked like a maze to me.

"On the right is a blue box behind some wires."

"Yup, I can see it."

"Now, halfway down to the left, on that box, is a snerger."

"A what?"

"A metal bit sticking out that looks like something can and should be attached to it," Matul bit out painfully.

"Yes, I can see that.'

"Now, hanging down on the right should be a black cable with a shiny end that looks like a cup. *Don't touch the end!*" he added hastily.

I looked about the dark interior for some moments before I saw what he meant. "I see it. Now what?"

"Look around on the ground out here and find a plastic-handled tool, then use that to push the head onto the metal bit."

"It's safe to touch the wire?" I asked.

"Yes."

Minutes later, I turned to him. He was looking pretty sick, but he was now trying to get to his feet. No one had come yet.

"Matul, I've done that, now what's to stop it falling off again?"

He had me rummaging through the tool kit and applying some kind of special tape that would hold for the moment. And suddenly, it was decision time.

"Matul, I'm not the only one here. There's another woman. She's very pregnant, but she's been injured. She will die here, and if you are telling the truth, not only could she help Ragul's cause, but she may get the help she needs too."

"Another!" He had got himself into the pilot's seat and was doing the preflight checks, but he stopped and looked up startled. "There can't be! And we don't have time!"

"You stay here. I'm off to see if she will even risk coming. She has no reason to trust the people of Selene."

And with that, I sped off, leaving him with his mouth hanging open.

I was a lot faster returning to our hiding place, but I had the presence of mind to call a warning before I slid into the depths. I was wise to have done so as she had woken and was armed.

I looked into her intense eyes and knew there was too much to explain in too little time. "Listen, I don't know your name, and we don't have much time. I am Rowhan. There are two types of people searching for us, the good guys and the bad guys. The bad guys have put one of the main good guys, Ragul, on trial, and it started about an hour ago. One of the good guys broke down near here and is injured, but he can take us to the trial, and if we get Ragul off, we get to live. If not, we die. Want to come?" I felt that got it all in, if somewhat simplistically. "I can explain more as we go."

She grinned. "And if I don't like what I hear, I can hijack the craft?"

"If you drop me by the place of the trial, you can take the aircraft where you like. Ragul saved my life, and I'm not seeing him go down for it."

"Well, we're dead if we stay here, so why are you delaying?" she asked as she moved carefully toward the entrance.

I grabbed up my bag and followed her out. I offered her my arm, but she had phenomenal resilience, and though obviously in pain and fatigued, she made as good time on her own as I did.

She hung back as we approached the air-car, but she seemed reassured by Matul's youth and injuries. But she took no chances and took the seat directly behind him once we had scrambled up into the craft. Matul told me to get behind him too and for both of us to get down and hide as best we could. He had looked hard at the Dejan, but he was too worried about time to do more than nod at her.

"How long will it take to get there, Matul?" I asked, rummaging through the emergency supplies as I felt we should all eat something before we got there—and I was dying of thirst.

"Just under an hour if all goes well, but I may literally need another hand to get her up. Lady Rowhan, could you come back here and do what I tell you, when I tell you … unless you know how to fly one of these?" he added hopefully.

"No such luck, Matul, but I will do what I can." I passed opened drink and food containers to the Dejan and clambered with more into the front.

"What are those for? We don't have time for that!"

"We will when we are in the air, and we *all* need to eat if we are to be any use when we get there," I snapped back. "Now what do you want me to do?"

Minutes later, somewhat bumpily, we rose into the air and were soon flying low but straight, below sensor range, according to Matul. While he flew with his one good hand I fed him and helped him wash it down with a hot drink and the Selene version of an aspirin, which he admitted, after a few minutes, was a great help.

Sliding into the back I checked out the medi-kit and called to Matul the names and uses until I found one I felt would help the Dejan. She had been very quiet, and I knew from my experiences with Rill that she was probably gathering her strength and biding her time, but at least I got her to tell me her name was Vaal.

"I think this is what you will need for that arm," I said, nodding toward her midriff, "till we get real treatment. And just in case things don't work out as planned."

"Yes," she smiled. "Let us not assume the best."

Checking the instructions with Matul, I injected the Dejan in the suggested area and at last turned to my own needs. Searching in the bag, I found the last few Sandhead pills and took one with some fruit juice, and then I relaxed with a hot stew.

I had finished and was cleaning up when the air-car changed course and elevation. The Dejan tensed, and I called to Matul.

"Are you alright, Matul? If you are, please keep us informed! Sudden changes could be bad for all our health!"

"Sorry. I am resuming normal flying height, and now we are coming in from another direction. I thought it would be less suspicious." He sounded very tired. I went to climb back beside him, but he stopped me.

"No. Stay back and hide, we will be in traffic very soon."

And we were. Soon Matul was having to answer various hails. The fact he was Hagnot's cousin came in handy, and I expected we would never have made it as far as the city with all the extra security the hearing had generated.

"Matul? That you?" came a youthful voice from the speakers. Not waiting for a reply, the voice went on, "Hey, you're looking a bit scraped up! Jossand will want that report in triplicate!"

"The snerger came off its boyle. Bad maintenance. If I'd been over water, we wouldn't be having this conversation. Heard anything on the holos?"

"Wow. Yes, Hagnot's got the upper hand at the moment. He's trying to discredit some little drab from the institute. She says they were all bright as buttons, the ones she looked after anyway. He's pulling the reports to show that's not true. They have some guy called Snard there from the institute who's saying she's being paid to lie."

"Nockie," said Matul after a pause. "Would you do a friend a favor? Could you fly with me and tell everyone that my radio's out and that I have something Hagnot told me to bring and his orders are to see I get there?"

"Crap, Matul, what are you up to?" came his friend's startled voice.

"I'm just asking you to tell people truthfully what you have been told. Yes or no?" Matul sounded desperately weary.

The Dejan had shifted position.

"Of course yes!" answered Nockie.

"Then radio silence starts now," responded Matul, and he snapped his speakers off without waiting for a reply.

"Wait!" I yelled at the Dejan, who was crawling toward Matul. "Give him a chance to explain!"

She halted and just looked at me.

"Matul, you had better talk quickly, she thinks you have duped us."

"Too many for me." He sounded terrible. "Use their strength to get us there. Then it's up to you."

I realized what he meant, and I was very glad to see the Dejan also guessed he was using the enemy to get us in to the trial.

In the next few minutes, several air-cars flew right beside us and inspected us, but we knew not what they and Nockie said to each other. I did see we were getting an escort, one on each side.

The city was beneath us now, and any chance the Dejan had of hijacking the air-car was long gone. Suddenly, Matul spoke again.

"There is a landing place in front of the Great Hall, but firstly they would never let you get from the air-car to the Great Hall, and secondly, I don't think I can land her." His voice wobbled slightly with fatigue and youth.

My eyes flew to the Dejan's and back to the front.

"So this is what I'm going to do," Matul said, ignoring my squeak of dismay, "I will try to fly into the Great Hall at lowest speed, then do a quick reverse rev and aim for the curtains. Wedge yourselves."

"Matul, for God's sake. What curtains?" I screamed as I crammed myself into a position that also held the Dejan in.

But Matul used the last of his strength to drop the craft as if to land, and then rolled her sideways and flew between the columns while the other air-cars went nuts.

We were squashed into a corner with the roll of the air-car. We saw the colonnade flicking past dangerously close outside the cabin window, and then the sudden shadow as we entered a great room through a huge open doorway. I saw vast tapestries forming a fabric wall from ceiling to floor about halfway down the room. We clipped something as we passed and began a spin. I glimpsed the tiers of marble galleries and benches crowded with men and a grand dais before we slammed into the curtain, and then we, and they, fell slowly to the ground.

Chapter Twenty-Two

In the muffled silence, I heard nothing from Matul, but the Dejan was cursing softly and trying to get me off her.

I could see by the interior lights that the air-car was swathed in the tapestries. "It will take them time to get to us," I hissed at the Dejan. "I'm not going to wait for them to make a plan. I'm going to the trial and testify … or at least try!"

While the Dejan struggled to rise, I grabbed my bag that now lay on the ceiling of the air-car and emptied it out and grabbed the vials Mogan had given me. I opened one, and it was easy to see how they worked.

I was about to pocket them both when the Dejan held out her hand for one. "They are a one-dose, instant and deadly," I cautioned after a momentary pause. Then I added, "I can't wait for you. There is no time left to lose."

And with that I crawled into the cabin across the interior roof, and pausing only to confirm that Matul had a pulse, I tried to open the door. The tapestries were heavy against them. Moaning in frustration, I tried kicking at it, but my foot slipped to one side and hit a red button. Instantly, the door exploded off the craft. It moved only a foot or so, but it was enough for me to squeeze out.

The dusty blackness was frightening, and the heavy folds of cloth could easily suffocate me with their weight. Reaching back into the craft, I felt for the light stick that was still in its clip by the door.

Focusing its beam into the stuffy darkness, I saw two opposing folds going in the right direction that seemed to be keeping each other from collapsing further. Keeping the light ahead of me, I wriggled between them. For the first time, I had a real understanding of claustrophobia. There was so little room to maneuver, and the material seemed to have no give at all.

I quickly realized two things: there was no going back, and there was no flow of air in the heap of wall hangings. To shut us up, all they had to do is wait. I wondered if they had guessed that.

The dust coated my nostrils, and my mouth was getting dry. At one point, the folds came to a tangled halt, and I thought bitterly that my life had ended in a dirty, useless, shabby sort of way, but in the next moment I felt a slight movement of dusty air on my cheek and, peering down, saw a little cave formed by the crumples. If air could get in, perhaps I could get out!

Wriggling into the cave, I saw a spot of light revealing the finely stitched face of a bored lady holding a naked baby in a most improbable way. I turned my light off and squeezed closer to the light source. Sounds increased as I drew closer. Then I could make out some voices, some raised in anger.

As I squirmed toward the entrance, I realized that I was close to the floor and that the folds formed an overhang where the light came in, which was why they must have missed it as an access point.

I peered out from beneath the ledge and saw the Great Hall in its grandeur. It was a rectangle of marble and stone. Along the lengthy right hand wall were tiers of seats and balconies and galleries with fretted stonework railings in shades of rose and cream. The long wall to the left had the dais, or rather three of them, each smaller one resting on the larger one beneath it, like a squat pyramid. The huge open doorway was at the far end, and to the left, one of the several large statues lacked an arm, which lay several feet away in small heaps of rubble.

The room must have been crowded when we had flown in, for now it was packed as guards strove to keep the masses of male Selenese from getting to the pile made by the curtain and the air-car.

"Who's in it? We have a right to know!" several robed members of the Council, to judge by their clothes, demanded.

"You have to keep back, sirs, they could be dangerous. Insane they are," bawled a noncommissioned officer as his men looked confused. Ragul was their Warlord, but he was the one on trial. Hagnot seemed to have taken over.

"They are not insane, I keep telling you that," wailed the only female voice I could hear.

"How could she be insane? The First Councilor wants to hold her!" shouted another.

"I don't know anything about that, sirs, stand back if you please, gentlemen," intoned the noncommissioned officer as he rallied his men and firmed up the cordon around the curtain.

Then I heard approaching footsteps and heard Hagnot's dreaded voice. "Take Ragul back to his cell. We'll reconvene when this interruption has been dealt with."

Screams of outrage came from the crowd, and no soldier was able to exit the small ring they had formed around the massive pile of fabric.

I knew I had to act fast, or it would be too late. I remembered the vial, and as I searched frantically for an idea, Hagnot strode along the edge of the pile.

It had been one of my sister's tricks—to lie under the bed and grab my ankle as I passed. I always fell down as she grabbed the one I was putting my weight onto.

As I yanked at Hagnot's ankle in its laced-up boot, he fell just as I had all those years ago. I lunged out and slammed the end of the vial against his bare leg with my thumb over the button and screamed, "*Back off!* If you don't, I'll kill him. Don't forget, I have *nothing* to loose."

Hagnot slowly turned his head and stared at me. The crowd and the soldiers gaped in amazement at the sudden change in the situation.

I couldn't give them a moment to think. "You men, put your weapons down *now*." They hesitated, and I made as if to press the button.

"Put them down, men. Do as the lady asks," said the noncom in his calm voice.

"Put one on stun and kick it over here," I ordered.

It didn't reach, and I made no attempt to get it. "You have one more chance to get it right," I said harshly. "If you want him dead, just keep making mistakes."

The next gun slid right up to me, and in one fluid movement, I grabbed it up and shot Hagnot—and not a moment too soon as he made an abrupt roll away from me.

I was on him again as the line of men swayed toward me, and again I slammed the vial against his skin. But now it was his neck I held, and he was unconscious. They moved back again and stared at me. By now more were coming around the pile to see what was happening.

"You," I screamed at the noncom. "Secure his feet." I edged around to keep Hagnot's head beneath me, keeping the man in my sights at all times. Oddly enough, I wasn't bluffing. I had every intention of killing Hagnot if I could see my own death was inevitable.

Still holding the vial steady, I kicked one of his arms behind him and then the other and told the man to secure his hands. As he was on his stomach, this pretty much would incapacitate him even if he awoke.

With my free hand, I waved the man back. "Now. You lot start getting the air-car passengers out of this pile alive. We took Matul prisoner, and he's pretty badly hurt." That got them moving pretty quick. Matul was of a very powerful family, and someone would be asking questions if he didn't survive. I had also given him an excuse for being there if we didn't make it.

"Where's Ragul?" I yelled over the increasing babble.

"Locked to his keeper," someone called out.

"Then get him unlocked and down here," I called back.

I could hear a rumpus and raised voices, and then a rather battered Ragul plunged out of the crowd toward me. "Stop right there," I said, indicating the vial. He stopped, puzzled and panting for breath. Evidently not everyone had wanted him released.

"I've had enough of you bastards. You steal us, torture us, hunt us, experiment on us, and kill us. You and the Natog ... not much to chose between you from where I stand." I meant every word of it.

"You will drag this lump of crap up to that dais with me holding this to his neck. Then we will have a *real* hearing, and we will do it *my way*," I screamed.

Ragul was looking at me intently, and I knew I must look like a crazy woman, but I was beyond caring.

***

A few minutes later, as the crowd was reseating itself at my command, I sat on the steps of the top dais. Hagnot's head lay in my lap, and the vial pressed hard into his neck. I had no idea if he was conscious or not. I had made Ragul retreat down to the lower dais.

"So, who have you heard from so far?" No one responded, though many whispered. Then Mogan called out.

"Everything against. I was the first *for* you, but they didn't believe me."

"Oh. So they proved we were so dumb that we couldn't take in the elite of Selene in social gatherings? We are so like vegetables that we couldn't gate-crash a hearing and take hostages? Is that what they said?" I spoke to the silent crowd.

"Certainly that you were incapable of doing so," Mogan answered calmly.

"Well, Councilmen? Does their evidence hold up under scrutiny? Are we bright enough to do that or not? *I can't hear you!*" I shouted harshly out of a dry and dusty throat.

One old man rose to his feet. "We have all seen that their supposition of your intelligence doesn't hold up. But lady," he hesitated, "are you *sane*?"

I smiled what Ragul described later as an evil smile and said, "Well, we shall have to look at that, shan't we?"

Then I called out, "Are Benot, Foust, and Sendal here?"

"I am!" called out Foust. "And the others can be sent for!"

"Do it," I ordered, and then I beckoned Foust with my free hand. "Come up to the first dais and tell these people what you know of me."

As he made his way through the crowd, I added, "But first tell us if you had been called to give evidence at this hearing."

As Foust stepped up to the first dais, he looked up at me and bowed, raising his hands in formal salute. I heard the ripple of whispers.

"Actually, Lady Rowhan, I had been refused a hearing. I was told there was no evidence that the woman in RADA was you, and therefore my testimony was irrelevant."

"Do you recognize me?" I asked Foust while I watched the crowd tensely.

"Of course, Lady Rowhan. We spent several days in close company. Your ideas were so original and brilliant that *everyone* knew who you were and recognized you!"

"Are you *sure*?" I stressed.

"Perhaps, Lady Rowhan, you could tell us who were the first people you met on arrival on the lowest level. As I was there, I would know if It were true or not."

"I asked a girl where Benot was, because I hadn't the foggiest who he was and didn't want to anyone to realize I couldn't recognize him as I'm not from this world. Then I approached the table you, Sendal, and Benot were at, with one or two others I can't remember."

"And you and Benot hit it off at once?"

I looked at him in surprise. "Hit it off? It was instant mutual dislike! We got over it later on, but he was insufferable!"

Foust smiled. "Indeed, Lady Rowhan, the lower levels had never seen anything like it, and they gossip of your row still!"

"So, Foust, please tell these people what your experience with me was, and considering your calling, your opinion on my sanity."

Over the next few minutes, Foust gave a very calm and rational account of his time with me, the reports and pictures he had been sent, and his beliefs about why the reports and facts were so far apart.

His final comment was, "I had maintained that the shock of their time with the Natog would be very deep, and we would need more than the usual resources and time to aid the aliens' recovery. It seems that time is very important in the process. From what I gather, all the aliens that recovered needed in excess of eight months to do so. However, once recovered, they are not only sane, but of very high intelligence!"

Amid the rustle of murmurs that followed this, there came a louder commotion from the far end of the hall. Benot and Sendal emerged from the crowd and hurried forward. A swift glance around appraised them of the situation, though I guessed they had been brought up to date on the way over.

Benot bowed to me formally and said, "Lady Rowhan, greetings. After your services to this world, I am ashamed to see you brought to this desperate state. May I give my testimony to the Council and the people at this time? I had been restrained by Hagnot's men and prevented from attending."

A babble arose, and the elderly Councilor again stood up. "You and Foust were *prevented* from giving testimony?" He seemed incredulous and worried.

"Not just us, Lord Ingulot, many wanted to testify as to the aid Lady Rowhan has given this planet, as well as to her sanity, though," and he smiled slightly, "her courage in the face of great odds was never realized at the time."

"Oh dear, oh dear!" said the old man. Then he waved at Benot. "Get on with it, man, tell us more." He sat down again.

Benot told them how I had invented a new math that had been invaluable in the defense of the planet and would extend the range of Selenese space travel, and that my other ideas had struck the first blow at the Natog on their home planet.

People were on their feet shouting for explanations, and Sendal mounted the steps to tell of the infected animals sent on the Natog ships. He had to stop as yells and screams of joy reverberated around the Great Hall. He shrugged at Benot and waited till some calm was restored, though many had run out into the square to spread the news, even though the holos were still running.

Sendal held up his hands for silence, and when he had it he continued, "More, my friends. She has done more than this. She showed us the way to use our enemies' technology, the very technology we feared, to actually reverse our infertility. Wait!" he shouted into the storm of voices, and they fell silent again. "She gave us the ideas, but it is up to us to put them into practice. It will take time, but we will do it."

People were standing and shouting and hugging each other. Some were even crying. In their long robes, it looked slightly like something out of a Roman frieze. I picked up the gun at my side and fired it on stun into the air. The crack reverberated around the room in the sudden silence.

"So, Councilors. Do you find me sane? What does one have to do on this world to be allowed to live? What other miracles must we perform?" I sounded bitter, and I was. I was very, very angry. It takes a great deal to rile me, but when I am, the flames aren't easily doused.

The councilors murmured to each other and then to the old fellow, who rose to his feet again.

"Lady Rowhan. If you are insane, it is an insanity Selene sorely needs! We declare you sane, and you have earned it indeed!"

I rose to my feet shaking with rage. "Earned! No one should have to *earn* the right to live! You have condoned despicable behavior. You perverted your own laws to prevent people from having just hearings. *You* allowed Ragul to be held by Hagnot, *you* allowed Hagnot and his ilk to prevent these men, and others, from giving their testimony! Shame on you! All it takes for evil to triumph is for enough good men to *do nothing*!" I had no hesitation in using other men's wise words.

I ripped the cords from Hagnot's body and kicked him so that he rolled down a few steps. "Here's your First Councilor back, he seems to represent more of you than I thought."

As the crowed stood dumbfounded in shock, Torren ran into the hall.

"Stop the proceedings! She's pregnant, and it's fertile!" He gasped as he stumbled up to the triple dais.

"What's he talking about?" called out a white-robed Councilor who could have posed for Nero.

"The alien, the Lady Loona, has been tested and found to be carrying a fertile female child!" he shouted. Then turning to look up the dais, he began to realize something was different. He looked wildly around and saw Ragul, bruised and bleeding slightly, standing on the lower dais, and in bewilderment, he looked up at me.

"Is she sane?" shouted another voice and murmurs of agreement rose to follow his words.

"Of course she's tarding sane!" yelled Torren. "By the Eggs of Nerta, why wouldn't she be? She's not Selenese! It doesn't effect them like it does us!"

Ragul strode forward and raised his hands. "People of Selene, before we go further with this, there are people stuck in that pile of hangings. They need our help. Some of you relieve those working, and others arrange pulleys to carefully raise the fabric. If nothing else, they need air!" He moved off with a group of men toward the trapped air-car.

I felt a stab of guilt at having forgotten Matul and the Dejan, and suddenly I sank to my knees and began to weep uncontrollably. I felt rather than saw the presence of someone near me, and I looked up through my tears to see Hagnot standing and looking down at me. His face was inscrutable.

A hated voice spoke behind him, and I heard Snard talking as he came up the steps. "Don't worry, Hagnot. I will prove they were insane, and dead aliens have nothing to say in their defense."

As Hagnot turned, Snard raised a weapon and aimed it at me. His face was contorted with his venomous words.

I heard a shout from across the room and Ragul's pounding feet, but Snard's finger was tightening on the lever, and I knew Ragul would never make it.

Hagnot stepped between Snard and I. The weapon fired. Snard's shriek as hands grabbed him and bore him to the ground echoed faintly in my head as Hagnot fell, his face turned toward me. He was still looking at me, rather puzzled, as the light left his eyes.

As the unsteady room faded from my view, I too slipped into oblivion.

Chapter Twenty-Three

The sunlight filling my room roused me from my nap. I stretched luxuriously in the large bed and gazed through a window set in a thick stone wall to a wide sweep of green that I now think of as a lawn. It's made up of durable plants reminiscent of chamomile that are lovely to smell when we walk there. I love the vast and stately woomina trees growing on each side. They are over a thousand passes old, Ragul told me, and at this season the leaves shine almost pure gold and the creamy blossoms perfume the air with an exquisite scent.

I heard Jenni's soft tap on the door, and I happily bid her enter. Jenni's my personal maid, and I was glad that as the wife of the First Councilor I would be able to help her become one of the first to receive the fertile eggs when they became available. She and Mogan and Lady Sinta were and are my mainstays, as I had no idea of what a First Councilor's wife should do and should not do! Ragul had no time to help me, as there was so much to do before he could go on the journey that is so near to our hearts.

"Lady Rowhan, Lady Sinta called." Jenni put the tray by the bedside and reached to puff up my pillows behind me as I sat up. "She said that if you need help with the seating arrangements of the dinner tonight, she would be glad to do it for you."

I leaned back gratefully and accepted the glass of water. A bowl of chopped fruits lay on the tray alongside soft rolls of fresh bread that I had taught the cook to make. They sat in a folded napkin near golden curls of simini, like butter, from the female longabeast, a very hairy, six-legged cow.

"Thank you, Jenni. How kind of her! I have no idea if I shall ever learn all that I need to know. In fact, I'm not sure I even want to! Isn't that terrible?" I confessed. I had no interest in palace life, as we would have called it on Earth, nor the intrigues that seemed part of it. Ragul really needed someone to watch his back, and I had told him so. He had just laughed and said he was well hedged with good friends and family.

"Not really, Lady Rowhan," Jenni said comfortingly. "No one really expects you to, being one of Them, which is nice."

It was interesting how much backlash there had been as the people of Selene discovered what Igan, Snard, and Gossot had been doing to the women recovered from the Natog ships. They were equally furious about Hagnot's obsessive hunting of us, the injustices he had perpetrated upon Ragul, and the perversion of their laws for his own ends. Their deep rage had its basis in every injustice or betrayal that people have had to endure. Only Hagnot's death while saving me had prevented his family being stripped of all his holdings. Not so for Gossot, Igan, and Snard. Not only were they stripped of all their possessions, Gossot and Igan were sent down the Ogat Mines to work for the rest of their lives. Snard was in solitary captivity till the Natog came back ...

When the people discovered we were all pregnant, and all the fetuses were fertile, there was rejoicing all over the world. They knew they would have to wait, but it was hope where there had been hopelessness.

"The doctor is due soon. Shall I show him up when he comes, or would you rather he examine you elsewhere?" Jenni asked.

"Up here thanks, Jenni, and please stay as usual."

She smiled and began tidying my clothes. I always took them off for a nap, and I was napping a lot these days with my daughter due very soon. The eyes of the world had been on Vaal, the Dejan I'd helped, when she had given birth six months ago to a fine, fertile daughter; Loona had surprised everyone by having twins, a fertile girl child and a sturdy little fellow for Degal a few days ago. He offered to continue to hold her, but she wanted someone younger.

She happily handed their children over to him as she wanted to be unencumbered, and as he had lost his only son in the attacks to acquire the aliens, this had seemed fitting. Degal was inarticulate with joy.

Much to the surprise of Selene society, Vaal and Rill refused to be held, so the Council had presented them with lands and holdings—in fact, the same ones they had removed from Igan, Snard, and Gossot!

The women of Selene seemed to admire the two Dejans very much, which was rather unsettling to the men of Selene, who tried to hold Loona up as a better example, without much success. We were all referred to as Them, but I seemed to fall into neither Loona's nor Rill's group. I had asked Rill why that was. She had just laughed and suggested I ask Ragul. Even though she was due any day, she was still very active and had been over all her holdings and taken the reins of command firmly into her own hands.

The Council had granted Loona a dowry when she accepted a young Councilor as her lord holder. She intended giving him a daughter as quickly as she could!

I rose and wandered over to the open window. I munched on the tender roll as my eyes wandered from the walled garden to the closest wing, where I could see Mogan ordering the arrangements of the nursery.

I had had several children in my life on Earth, and lots of grandchildren, but now I found I was glad of the help. Perhaps though my body was young, my spirit was worn a little thin by the events of two lifetimes. Sometimes this worried me, but Foust had been reassuring. He said it was my way of protecting myself, and that it would pass.

All those who had been aiding Ragul had come out the better for their risks. Degal was now a Council member; Torren and Matul both got promotions and more land. Foust became the head of Selenese and Alien Psychology—even Benot and Sendal got recognition! Dear Mogan had been given a pension for life, but instead of retiring she chose to come with me to look after the children.

I leaned on the cool frame of the open window and sniffed appreciatively. Glorious weather! I wish I could be out in it, but

I had never seemed to recover my strength after the Sandhead. I sighed.

"Is everything alright?" Jenni asked, looking up from laying out clothes on the bed.

"Yes, I'm just being silly," I replied and turned to prepare for the doctor.

***

The dinner was a large function, with the crème de la crème of Selenese society and politics. I was surprised to find that holo-corders were being erected, but I was assured that they were just for some speeches at the end. Thankfully, I had not been expected to arrange any of it. Ragul had just told me airily that all I needed do was turn up! Of course he had been mistaken, as men usually are about domestic matters, as my opinion had been sought on several trifles that came up, but with Lady Sinta's help I got through them pretty well.

The dress my mother-in-law had insisted I get made was lovely, in spite of my shape. Ragul said it made my eyes even more blue, and I felt I looked quite graceful in its soft folds, low-cut over-bodice, and modest neckline. As I turned around slowly for Ragul's approval, he halted me and said I needed something. He pulled from his sash pocket a small case that he opened to reveal a necklace like a river of fire that must have cost a queen's ransom.

As I looked in the long mirror, he secured the clasp, and I was aware of how lucky I was to be married to someone I loved and who loved me. He even thought I looked beautiful pregnant!

The dinner was as long and tedious as I had suspected, but the food was good, and everyone seemed cheerful and enjoying themselves. I was delighted to see Rill, Vaal, and Loona among the guests, which I hadn't expected as I had not seen them on the list. As the meal drew to a close, I knew the speeches would begin, but I was unprepared for Degal to raise his goblet and start. I was thinking about how I liked Degal and what a decent sort of person he was when I caught my own name in his discourse.

"And so it is my great privilege to present Lady Rowhan, on behalf of the Council, with this covenant of the lands and holdings and all their proceeds." He bowed to me and came around to where

I sat and, bowing again, presented me with a golden tube holding several scrolls.

I rose hastily and thanked him very much, as well as the Council for their kindness, though in truth I had no idea what it was about.

I turned to Ragul for guidance, but he had risen and was setting his goblet down.

"Dearest Lady Rowhan, I have been asked as First Councilor to represent all the peoples of Selene in granting you this next token of our love and respect for you, and for all you have done for this planet and the peoples thereof."

Matul had come to his side with a big grin and a silver tray on which lay a crimson cloth. On it was a simple but heavy gold ring.

"This is our highest honor, rarely given, and you are only the second woman ever to have received it and the privileges that come with it." He turned to Matul, and taking the ring from the cloth, he turned back to me.

Taking my left hand, he put the ring on my finger saying, "To all Selene you are now Lady Rowhan Lessand. No door is locked to you, no information can be kept from you, no law binds you, nothing costs you."

I gaped at him as I tried to understand what he was saying. "What does this *mean*, really?" I asked.

"That we trust you completely," he replied, and he saluted me on both cheeks. And I began to weep. The gentle tears washed away the memories of pain, fear, and loss. A tightness started to uncurl in my chest. Ragul took me into his arms whispering, "Dearest lady mine," and the whole table rose to drink to me, smiles and happy calls coming down the table, and silently the holo-corders passed it on ...

Selene:
Weal's People

Wendy C Giffen

wendycgiffen@gmail.com
www.wendycgiffen.com
@wendycgiffen

Published by
SANDYS · HEATH & BALCHIN
PUBLISHING HOUSE LIMITED
Salt Spring Island, BC, Canada

In loving memory of Anne McCaffrey

who gave me the world of Pern,

and inspired me to write.

Prologue:

Abruptly, Rowhan woke. An unknown terror catapulted her from the large raised bed.

Moments before she had been deeply asleep, snuggled alone beneath the soft wool filled comforter. Now, running to the large carved door she threw it open and raced from the room. Her pale, slight figure hardly visible in the dark as she ran, her long night gown and unbound hair flowing behind her.

Fear constricted her throat as she fled down the shadowy stone corridors, avoiding the heavy furniture by instinct, her bare feet smacking the warm marble floors. The prescience of danger was so strong that she could taste the metallic tang of fear.

Yanking open the solid nursery door the lingering smells of bathed children, damp hair and their supper of grilled ammoch on toast assailed her nostrils. Her glance flashed around the moonlit room, taking in the sleeping children, the nursery furniture, the short curtains moving gently in the breeze, and the half-open door to the nurse's room.

Everything was quiet. Everything seemed just as it should be, but something was very wrong.

She moved toward her little daughter's bed, low and beautifully carved. The four-year-old lay on her back, lips parted and a halo of curls spread over the pillow, her covers and soft toys drained of colour by the moonlight. Rowhan jerked away, the danger wasn't there. The little boy was on his front in his cot, with his bottom humped up and his thumb near his mouth, all the softness of an infant clear in the brilliant moonlight. A beam of light lancing through a snow globe bathed his head. The heavy open window tapped gently back and forth with the night breeze.

The danger was here! Urgently, she grabbed her son out of the cot and hugged him. He stirred sleepily, smelling sweetly of bath soap. Turning to stare around the panelled room she felt the danger diminish but she could see no cause for it.

Just then, a gust of wind caught the open casement window and jerked it wide, causing the latch bar to strike the heavy glass globe. Briefly it teetered, and then it fell heavily into the cot where moments before Jaden's small head had rested.

She stared as a damp stain slowly spread across the sheets.

Nine years.

It had been nine years since the last event. She had thought they were over.

Rowhan shuddered, whether with the aftermath of terror or the fading premonition she didn't know.

Wendy is an unrepentant lover of life, author, certified hypnotist, erstwhile potter and teacher at present living in Canada.
She loves dawns and riding a bike.
Amongst other adventures she trained as a teacher at Cambridge, designed and built a house, owned and ran a hypnotherapy clinic, farmed, potted and had several children.
Her children groan at her puns, whilst her husband sighs at the housekeeping, when he notices, which is rare.
When not in a kayak or sailing around the islands, or driving a horse and buggy, she can be found tucked away with her dogs; writing, writing, writing...

wendycgiffen@gmail.com
www.wendycgiffen.com